WALK THE DOG

ISABEL JOLIE

ONE

Delilah

The singalongs from last night coalesce in freeze-frame mental snapshots. Once again, I'm co-cooned in my bed, hoping with all my might there's no photographic evidence. It's another Saturday morning.

A retching sound drifts through my bedroom. Nausea curls in my belly. It's the most revolting sound. What *is* that sound?

I peer down at the floor. A mound of brown hair wheezes. *Fuuuuck. I'm dog sitting.*

The dog continues to heave, and I sling my

legs off the bed, searching the ground. Where's the vomit?

She stands still on all fours, tousled hair partially covering her eyes. Something's wrong. She's not looking so good.

I stumble into the kitchen, almost face-planting when I trip over my black stilettos from last night. My head pounds. That dog's sounds are not helping my nausea.

I pop a Starbucks thingie into the Keurig. While I wait for my mug to fill, ripped paper all over the floor catches my attention. *What the...?*

Remnants of dry food lie around my kitchen floor mixed in with frayed edges of the dog food bag. The colossal bag that I set down in front of my dishwasher yesterday no longer blocks the stainless-steel door.

Oh, Mylanta. That dog ate the whole blooming bag. That can't be good.

I frantically hunt for my phone to call Olivia. I finally locate it underneath my jeans on my bedroom floor.

There's a text from an unknown number saying he's glad he met me. I vaguely recall a guy with brown hair. For the love of nuts and berries, I need to stop this shit. I block the number. Nothing good can come from that. Drunk Delilah doesn't meet good guys. Not even halfway decent guys. Sober Delilah needs to lock drunk Delilah up in a vault and throw away the key.

I press Olivia's name. She'll know what to do. Voicemail answers, and I hang up then text her to call me.

I pace the room. *Think, Delilah. Think.*

I snap my fingers and grab my laptop. Google.

I search "what to do if my dog eats a whole bag of food." And nothing is coming up when she vomits. But I don't type the extra stuff. That's too long of a search.

I scan the search results. Canine bloat. Can die within hours. Gastric torsion. Panting, drooling, acting like wanting to vomit. Retching.

Yup. That's the sound.

I'm the worst dog sitter on the planet. My friend's dog, dead. RIP, Chewbacca.

Okay. Vet. I search my kitchen counter for the piece of paper with dog information on it. Two bills, one credit card solicitation that claims they have great news for me. I close the Cheetos bag. Thank goodness it's not empty. At least I went to bed before polishing off the family size bag. *See, Chewie? That's how you do it. You don't finish the whole darn bag.*

Where is that paper? Is it in my pocketbook?

Coffee in hand, I empty the contents of my tote bag. A crumpled piece of paper catches my eye. That's it.

Anna's handwriting is a scribbled mess. I can make out the words Chelsea and Veterinary. I Google, and yes, there is a Chelsea Veterinary Center.

The cab drops me and my brown, furry, unwell overeater on 26th Street. A chalkboard sign hangs on a glass door with stainless steel trim.

The chalkboard sign reads *50 Shades of Spay. No Litters, Baby.*

I double-check the address on my phone. 248 West 26th Street, but it's feeling a lot like Fuck Me Lane. Chewie, the enormous, sixty-five-pound labradoodle I'm dog sitting, curls in on herself as she dry heaves. When I tug on the leash, she extends her neck but refuses to follow. *Stubborn. Animal.*

I bend down and hoist her up in a half fireman hold. Tufts of brown fur tickle my face as I manage to catch the door handle and stumble inside the clinic.

The musty smelling fluorescent-lit room holds three rows of hard black plastic chairs with shiny silver legs. Framed posters of dogs and cats line the wall on one side. Bags of dog food and treats fill shelves on the other side. It's similar to clinics I've been to in the past, but this one is in Manhattan, and the waiting room is narrow and noticeably smaller than what one would typically find in Louisiana. On the opposite end of the room, a slim shelf and a bank teller style window beckons.

A woman with bright magenta hair in a loose poodle perm sits behind the glass. She's on the phone, chatting away. There's a small black sign with white plastic letters beside her window that reads *Dinosaurs never went to the vet. Look What Happened.*

Cute. I make a mental note to ask Anna how she went about picking her vet, then I send off a quick plea to the spirits that this is indeed her vet.

The receptionist greets me with a warm smile the moment her call ends. She confirms yes, Chewbacca is a patient, and as luck would have it, I am listed as an emergency contact.

As I'm midway through explaining the emergency at hand, the tiny woman thrusts an extremely long violet fingernail into the air and says she'll get someone and disappears behind a door. Within minutes, a woman in plum scrubs enters the room. She pauses in front of me, and before I can repeat my story, she bends over Chewie, hands roaming all along her mangled, unkempt brown fur. "What's going on?"

"I couldn't get through on the phone, and I had to carry her in here, literally carry her, and—" My hands fly in the air, as bottled-up freak-out emotions rise.

"With the dog?" The woman is calm and stern.

"Oh. She ate a whole bag of dog food. She's dry heaving, but nothing is coming out."

As if on cue, Chewie emits a wheezing, cough-like sound. I jump back in case something finally emerges.

Plum's face contorts, and, if I didn't know better, I'd say a bit of animosity spews my way. She mutters to herself, "Wouldn't want to get anything on those shoes of yours."

"What?" I'm wearing beat-up tennis shoes, a pair of Golden Goose I found at Barney's. I like the extra inch they give me in height and the casual vibe.

The woman's hands cover Chewie's belly on both sides, as if she's hearing through her palms. "How much did she eat?"

I fidget on my overpriced but coveted, beat-up shoes. When I don't answer, she stops and stares at me. This woman lacks a positive bedside manner. Her aura is all kinds of negative.

She seethes the words as she repeats her question. "How much did she eat?"

"I don't know. I'm dog sitting. The bag was about like this big." I hold out my arms to show her how big the bag was. "I wouldn't have left it out if my ESP was functioning last night." And, you know, if I had limited myself to one or two bars as opposed to turning the night into more of a pub crawl.

The woman huffs and barges off toward the door. She mutters something that sounds like, "I'll be back."

Her statement comes across like a threat. Or maybe a villainy kind of promise. For the tenth time, I call Olivia.

Olivia is in Canada and should have cell reception but is not answering. I type out yet another frantic text to her. She's the one who told me I could do this. Me. Delilah. The blonde. I'm, like, two mental steps out of college. Yes, chronologically, college was a while ago, but it *feels* like yesterday.

. . .

Me: Help me! Chewie is sick. Super sick. Call me!

Finally, finally, three bubbles appear then a text comes through. A lifeline. Someone to help me calm the fuck down.

Olivia: Take her to the vet.

    Me: Help me!

    Olivia: Didn't Anna give you the info before she left?

Jesus, Mother, Mary, and Angels. I press her name to call her. Before I can say anything, Olivia answers the phone with, "I can't do anything. I'm in Canada. Call the vet."

I screech, "Anna loves this dog and I think I killed it. For the love of nuts and berries, why did she ask me to watch her blessed dog! I can't keep plants alive! I hire someone to water my plants. Why'd she ask me?"

There's a pause while I'm panting. My insides roil and I pace back and forth in the empty waiting room. "You hire someone to water your plants?"

"Oh, Mylanta! Pay attention! Her dog is dying. And it's my fault!"

"What did you do?"

"I left the food open. The dog ate the whole freaking bag. Like, all of it. Even some of the bag."

"But Anna keeps the food in a canister. The lid snaps shut. How—"

"The dog is at my place! I didn't carry that enormous canister home. Now the dog won't stop dry heaving."

"Calm down. You need the vet."

This phone call, my lifeline, is no help. My heart pounds. I can't possibly tell Anna I killed her dog. Olivia's speaking to Sam, the new guy in her life. I focus on my breathing to calm down. I hear Sam say something about taking Chewie to the vet. And walking her. As if she's up for a jaunt down Fifth Avenue. Fabulous advice. *Thank you, friends.*

Eventually, Olivia asks, "Did you hear that?"

"I'm already at the vet! This place is a small hole in the wall. The vet here is treating me like I'm a criminal. I'm half expecting animal protective services to come and arrest me any minute now. So, if I call you again, you pick up the bloody phone because it means I need you to bail me out of jail."

"You aren't going to jail." Olivia's calm voice rings through the line. "These things happen."

No. I've never heard of this happening to anyone. "They should have asked Chase. He's a better human than me."

"Oh, please. Hush. Chewie is going to be okay. Besides, Chase would probably come home drunk and throw up on the dog."

Chewie's lethargic, her sides expanding and contracting. A big, heaving, brown mass of hair. Everything about her, from her jerking body to her sad eyes, says she's in pain. Tears blur my vision. *What have I done?*

An incognito door opens to the side of the reception desk. Bitch on wheels pushes a low cart past the line of chairs. I set the phone down and grab Chewie's front while mean girl helps with her behind. She doesn't say a single word to me, treating me as if I forced open the dog's jaw and poured food into it.

She's charging out of reception, pushing the cart away, leaving me dumbstruck, when the cheerful magenta-haired woman slides the glass window open and says, "You don't have to stay out there. You can come on back here with your doggie."

I pick the phone up off the chair and whisper-shout, "I'm being allowed back with the dog. I swear this woman hates me. If I call, answer!"

I slip the phone into my jeans pocket. The magenta-haired woman stands by the door, holding it wide open with a warm smile. I clutch her hand and squeeze, grateful to be the recipient of kindness, as she says, "Hi, sweetie. I'm gonna get some information from you, and then you can head on back to be with your baby."

"Oh, she's not mine, remember? Her name is Chewbacca Hendricks. I'm dog sitting. You know, I'm the one on the emergency contact list." I add the last part to remind her of the conversation we had three minutes ago.

"Well, that explains why I don't recognize you, sweetie. I'm so good with faces. You had my brain whirring trying to place you. I'm Elisabetta, but most people call me Bet for short."

I bounce from foot to foot and tap a pen on the counter. *Tap, tap, tap, click, thud, thud, tap, tap, tap.*

"Sweetie, what's your name?"

"Oh. I'm Delilah. Chewbacca's mom's name is Anna. Anna Hendricks."

"Oh, yes. Sweet Anna. How is she?"

"Good. She's in the mountains. No cell service." I tap the pen frantically on the counter, hyping up my heartrate as I do. A gentle hand falls on mine. Her long nails are rounded and thick. I glance up, and Bet pats my hand then takes my pen away. "Honey, you've got a case of the nerves. Let's get you on back so you can be with your baby."

Not my baby, but that's fine. I inhale and exhale and long for my yoga mat.

She points me to a small room. Chewie's been placed on a long stainless-steel table.

"Dr. Herriot will be in soon. Wait here and make yourself comfortable."

After Bet leaves, I watch Chewie's still form. She is standing, head hanging low. I rub her ears and scratch underneath her neck. Kind, golden-brown, soulful eyes peer up at me. She swallows and strains. Her rib cage expands and contracts, filling the room with barely audible wheezing sounds.

Minutes go by. My heartrate calms. Chewie has all the markings of a sick patient, but she's not vomiting. She's still dry heaving, but they left her here with me. They must not see her case as mission critical. I bury my face against her neck and rub the brown, mangled mass of fur. *Please be okay.*

The door opens, and I slowly straighten. A deep male voice rumbles, "Hi, I'm Dr. Herriot."

I'd expected bitch in scrubs, but I much prefer this vet. He extends his hand as I admire his dark hair, faded navy scrubs, and white lab coat. A tuft of curly black hair surfaces near the V in his scrub top. He has a rugged doctor image befitting a poster for any TV hospital drama. His warm hand engulfs mine, and the muscles on his forearm flex slightly as we shake. His energy flow passes through, and a tingling sensation follows. Ms. Zelda from home would say he has a vibrant aura.

A stethoscope hangs out of one of the long, rectangular pockets. The man's eyes are enigmatic, an unusual green, infused with hues of saffron and honey. The extraordinary color has me leaning forward to analyze the shade. Dark stubble creates definition along the lines of his jaw. This man should be on one of the sexiest veterinary calendars. I'm not positive there is such a thing, but if not, there should be. I'd buy twelve photos of him in calendar form without pause. I wouldn't even care where the charity money went.

Sexy man slips his hand into his coat pocket, a scrumptious smile on his face.

I follow his gaze downward and notice my boobs. You can almost see the darker color of my areolas through the cotton. I curve my shoulders forward, as if by hunching my back my braless boobs will disappear. The white top I threw on in a panic features a support shelf. In my rush out the door, I didn't remember a bra or check for see-through cotton, but with my boobs, I should know better. These puppies need full support and coverage. I didn't think. About much of anything, really, other than Anna's dog. That's the moment I realize I didn't put on makeup, and my hair is one wild, crazy rat's nest on top of my head.

His thick, dark eyebrows lift with expectation, and it's apparent he's waiting for me to introduce myself. Because that's what normal people do in situations like this. "Delilah."

A low, barely audible rendition of *Hey There Delilah* comes out, hummed in a deep timbre as he flips through Chewie's file. Guys sing this song to me all the time. On a normal day, in a bar, it's my signal to head the other way. I like originality. In his case, though, right now, he may not even realize he's humming the song. Even if he does, I don't mind. He's going to work magic on Anna's dog. And he's being a bit of a goof. Goofiness is good. The weight of my worry lightens, and without thinking, I sway to the overplayed song.

Chewie wheezes and emits one of her stomach-churning vomit sounds. Poor, sick doggie. I stroke her ears and scratch her throat, below her collar. His attention shifts from the file to the patient. "What have we got going on here?"

"She ate a whole bag of dog food." I cringe, anticipating judgment. It's my fault. There's no sugarcoating it.

"When?" He feels her sides and stops at her belly, groping all around.

"Sometime this morning."

For a fleeting moment, he observes me before the dog consumes all his attention. Concern flashes across his face as he listens through his stethoscope. When he finishes, he washes his hands, dries them on a paper towel, then leans against the counter and addresses me in a calm, instructional, doctor voice. "Chewie is experiencing canine bloat. Overeating causes pain receptors in her stomach to stretch, which in turn causes discomfort. Did she eat dry food?"

I answer affirmatively, and he nods like somehow he already knew this.

"The dry food absorbs moisture from the body and causes dehydration. We have two things to worry about. One, the hydration, is easily solved. We can give her fluids through an IV. Our other concern is GDV, which stands for gastric dilatation volvulus. The fear is that her stomach will twist. If her stomach or intestines start to twist, she may require surgery. I'd like to take an x-ray, see more of what we are dealing with. Then we'll complete a baseline radiograph now and possibly another one in twelve hours. Does that sound okay to you?"

I suck on my bottom lip and nod. I'll do whatever he says.

"I'm going to get her off to x-ray. I'll be back in a moment."

With grace and ease, he lifts her off the stainless-steel table and onto a wheeled contraption. He hurries as he moves, and my first thought is she's in danger.

"Is she going to be okay?" I squeak out before the interior door closes behind him.

Through the door, I hear a muffled question asked in a quick, commanding tone. "Ashley, can you please go talk with 2B?"

She answers with a loud, "No." Other indecipherable words follow.

Moments pass. The door opens, and Dr. Herriot's head peeks in. Compassion and tenderness flow. This man has a good bedside manner. "She's going to be okay. In a worst-case scenario, she'll need surgery. But I'm hopeful it won't come to that. I'll be back when I know more." In a flash, he's gone again.

How on Earth will I tell Anna about this? She loves that dog. Before Jackson returned, she referred to her dog as her soul mate. *Soul. Mate.* And I had to go out and drink too much and stumble home and leave the dog food out. There are over seven billion people on this planet, and praying for a dog doesn't sit right, but it might be time to do more than tent my hands. It might be time to send healing chants out into the universe.

TWO

Delilah

A slight tap, tap, tap sounds before the door opens and Dr. Herriot hurries through. In a flurry, he arrives at the black plastic scoop seat, and as he sits, the rushing that ushered him through the door transitions to a calm, kind, compassionate manner. Beads of sweat line his brow.

Those emerald eyes find mine, he inhales, his chest rises, then he speaks in a methodical, practiced rhythm. "She's looking good. We're going to monitor her heartrate and pulse through the night and walk her every hour. The best thing we can do is to have this food start passing through her natu-rally. She's a larger-sized dog, so I'm optimistic. A smaller dog would most likely require surgery. I'll call you if anything changes, but I expect by to-morrow this time, she'll be a much happier dog. I can send Ashley in to go over the related charges for the visit. If you don't want to do another radiog—"

"Do whatever you need to do. I'll cover the charges." I almost killed my friend's child. The least I can do is pay the medical expenses. "I want to stay with her. She doesn't feel good, and she doesn't know anyone here."

A warm smile breaks out and extends across his face, exposing a line of symmetrical white teeth. "I appreciate the sentiment, but we can't allow you in the back."

"Why not?" I might not be the most mature individual, and I might not be able to keep another living being alive, but I have seen my father work his magic and transform a no into a yes. "How much will it cost?" I glance around the small room. This isn't a well-endowed hospital. I can't expect a VIP suite, but there have to be options. "How much would it cost for you to set me up in a private room? This room will do. Or it doesn't have to be private. I can sit with her in whatever situation you have her in the back. I'll pay extra. Whatever it costs."

He rubs his chin as he considers his answer, and his lips turn up in a way that says he's amused by me. But amusing him is not my goal. My gaze falls to a poster hanging on the wall. *Four little paws can change coming back to an empty house into coming home.* I read those words and envision my close friend Anna with her big smile and kind heart. I am not leaving without Anna's four paws.

"It's a Saturday. All of you seem rushed and busy. Let me stay. You said she needs to walk. I can watch the time and walk her. And she won't get frantic or worried because she'll be near someone she knows."

As I'm talking, he glances at his watch. I suspect he has at least two other clients in similar little rooms to the one I'm sitting in. Places like this take people out of the waiting room and into these private rooms. He and bitch on wheels are the only vets I've seen. She's not wearing a lab coat, so it's possible she's some kind of assistant.

His phone vibrates, and he pulls it out of his coat pocket. The way he holds it, I can't help but see *Amber* flash on the screen before he hits decline and drops it back into his pocket. He exhales and returns his attention to me. "We shouldn't need this room for the rest of the day. If you want to stay here, you can. But you don't need to. We will take good care of her."

"Please. I'd prefer she's not alone." I have this vision of them locking her in a crate in the back room. At least here, I can comfort her. Leaving Anna's baby in an understaffed, small veterinary clinic on a random street in Manhattan does not jive.

He barely nods as he pulls his phone out of his pocket and the door closes behind him. I rest my head back against the wall. *Come on, healing vibes.*

The windowless room offers little distraction. I take out my phone, and the five percent battery life makes me realize I forgot to charge it last night. Fabulous. There's a new text from Mom. Checking in. She's been checking in with greater frequency lately. I am not pleasing her. Choosing a friend's Thanksgiving over going home did not go over well. Today is not the day to think about any of that.

I drop down onto the bench and doze off. At some point, the door opens. Chewie is sprawled out on a stainless-steel table with wheels. She looks a little out of it, and my forehead wrinkles as I try to grasp why she seems doped up. It's my way of asking without verbalizing my questions to this angry, unhappy woman with an abundance of negative energy.

"We gave her a mild sedative to keep her lying down and relaxed. The IV has rehydrated her. I'll be back to take her for walks. Don't let her roll around on her back." Her dark ponytail twists in the air as she spins and speeds away.

I rub Chewie's head, scratching below her furry ears. I bring the chair over and sit, so if she opens her eyes, she'll see a familiar face. With one hand on Chewie, I check my phone again. 3% battery life. The countdown is on. I toss it onto the bench and sit, rubbing Chewie to bring her comfort.

Every hour, Ashley stops by and checks on Chewie. She opens the door and motions for me to follow her. We walk down a narrow hall and turn right, then she opens a door into a courtyard behind the clinic. Chewie follows obediently but doesn't go to the bathroom. When we return, Ashley guides Chewie back onto her dog bed then scurries away.

Bet checks in around lunch time. She drops off a deli sandwich, chips, and a large bottle of water. "Dr. Herriot thought you might be hungry." She winks at me and loves on Chewie before returning to the reception desk. I then spend the afternoon alternating between daydreaming about a sexy, heroic vet with muscular arms and freaking out every time Chewie attempts to vomit.

Around five p.m., my stomach growls, letting me know the sandwich I inhaled is long gone. Chewie's doing better. The IV fluids do seem to have helped. She has urinated. The dry heaving has spaced out. Five more hours before her radiograph. When I rub her ears, she tilts her head and stares at me with sad, dark orbs. Her version of a hangover makes mine look like a walk in the park.

Ashley opens the door, and her sudden appearance scares the crap out of me. "We're closing now." Some of the hate and annoyance from our first meeting has dissipated. She rubs her shoulder and stretches her neck to the side. "You need to leave."

Ashley's ponytail is now wrapped into a low bun. Something about her is familiar to me. "Have we met before?" I ask.

Ashley's nose wrinkles as if she whiffed an unappealing odor. She grunts, "No." Her black Dr. Scholl's shoes are splattered with gunk, and her plum scrubs are now littered with stains and animal hair. I could swear something is familiar, but

I can't place her. I tend to go to so many of the same bars and nightclubs, frequent the same small shops in Soho and Chelsea, there's really no telling where I might have seen her. She stares at me, tracking my every move, but I've got nothing.

"We're closing up. If you've got everything you need, I'll walk you out."

I throw my shoulders back. "I don't want to leave her here. She needs to be walked every hour." I scramble to my feet, ready to duke this one out. Dr. Herriot enters, and the tension breaks. He says something to Ashley about a cat in room C that needs one more vaccination. Once she leaves, he pets Chewie on the head and strokes her sides. There's a gentleness to his manner.

With his hands still buried in her fur, he addresses me. "I still need to do another radiograph. I'd like to keep her overnight for observation."

"Can I stay here with her?"

His gaze falls on me with a sympathetic, warm smile, and not to sound cheesy, but it's the first sunny moment of my extraordinarily crappy, hungover day. "No."

Wait. What? "Why not?"

"Our insurance policy wouldn't allow it. And trust me when I say staying overnight here is undesirable. It's probably the least comfortable accommodation you can imagine."

The magenta-haired receptionist, Bet, pops her head in and waves. "Goodnight, sweetie. I'll pray for your baby." Then she points at Dr. Herriot. "I left zinc tablets on your desk. You be sure to take those. We can't have you getting the flu too." He bows his head and assures her he'll take her proffered pills like an obedient boy.

After the door closes, he leans back on the counter. Exhaustion paints his frame. "Man, what a day. We normally have two vets and three vet techs."

"Flu?"

"Yeah. Saturdays are always busy, but today was..." He pauses and scratches his chin as if he's undecided about how to finish his sentence.

I wave and smile to assure him. "Thanks for letting me camp out here. I appreciate it."

"You can stay a little longer while I finish up the reports, if you wish, but you'll need to leave when I do."

"Doesn't she need to walk each hour?"

He rubs his neck while he watches her. "Yes. We can do that for you, or you can take her home." He flicks his wrist to check the time. His phone vibrates again, and a distinct humming fills the quiet room. He pulls it out, and this time I see the name Cindy. He holds the phone close and says, "I'll be right back," as he steps out of the room.

My stomach rumbles as I scratch Chewie. She rolls over and spreads her legs wide for a tummy rub. I check the time and realize it's time for our hourly walk.

When Chewie and I return from the small, dingy, outdoor courtyard behind the building, I see Dr. Herriot and shout, "She peed again! That's a good sign, right?"

He nods and studies her thoughtfully. Strong hands with manicured, lithe fingers rub her belly and chest, then he presses his stethoscope to listen, moving it around her rib cage. I remain still, watching his face, searching for any facial expression that indicates if he's hearing good or bad noises. After several minutes, he exhales and stands. "She's doing good. Do you want to take her home, or would you like to leave her here with us for observation?"

I do not like these options. I don't particularly trust myself and would prefer to make sure she pulls through this under professional care. But I don't treasure the idea of leaving her here by herself. She's sad and in a strange place. My phone battery has been dead for hours. There is no lifeline to call for advice or to double-check my decision. "I want to stay here with her." I might be whining.

He scratches Chewie's ears. "I'm sorry, but that's not an option."

"Why?"

He closes his eyes, and his chest lifts as he inhales. It's quite possible he's praying for strength. When his eyelids reopen, he props himself against the counter and faces me.

I don't give him a chance to speak before uttering, "Please."

"Ms..."

"Delilah," I answer for him.

"Delilah. I don't mean to be short with you, but I can't let you stay here overnight. I can assure you if she stays with us, she'll be under good care." He frowns. "Let's see what the radiograph says. I'll do it in thirty minutes. Earlier than planned, but...I can tell you sleeping overnight in this clinic isn't what you want to do."

I grin. "What? Sleep on the floor? I can do it. Won't be the first floor I've slept on."

He opens his mouth to say something then closes it. Then grins. "I have a hard time believing that's true."

"Nope! Scout's honor. Camping out for tickets. Music festivals. All the time, we'd sleep on the ground at festivals. You know, when we couldn't quite find our way back to our tent. One time, we forgot sleeping bags."

"Music festivals, huh? What's your favorite kind of music?"

I kick my legs out a bit and stretch. My muscles are sore from alternating between the hard bench and sitting on the floor. "Jazz." I wave my hands, shaking the fingers, aiming for flamboyant jazz hands. "I love everything. All kinds of music. But I've got deep love for jazz. What's your favorite?"

He pauses before answering. "If I had to pick a favorite, I'd say Tom Petty. But I like pretty much anything too." He places heavier emphasis on the words "pretty much" and the corners of his lips lift as he says it.

"Favorite music festival?" One thing I'm good at is getting to know people and keeping conversations going. My goal is to wear him down. I always get my way.

He chuckles, and his gaze roams over me as I stretch. I suck in my stomach as heat rises through my neck and face. Then he blows me away when he answers, "Never been to a festival."

Blown. Away. So much so my eyes almost pop

out of my head. "What?" I half scream. "How old are you?"

He laughs again, a soft laugh, but enough to be heard. "Thirty-two."

Not too old, then. And sans wedding band. "So, thirty-two. What about in college?"

He scratches his chin. "Vet school's competitive to get into. Had to focus on grades." He shrugs. "Didn't have the option, the time or the money."

"What about after vet school? No time then?"

He exhales loudly. "After vet school, life. Life happened." He checks his watch again and sighs. "Let's get this radiograph done and see what we're dealing with."

He bends and picks up the dog bed, complete with the dog, and lifts it onto the cart. His biceps flex from the weight.

The squeaky wheels screech, and Chewie lifts her head, questioning. A good sign. Interest in anything has to be a good sign. "Dr. Herriot?"

He doesn't stop, nor does he turn around, but he does say, "Call me Mason."

"Okay. Mason. That's a good sign? It's good she lifted her head, right?"

He mumbles something along the lines of "yeah" and technical jargon before the door closes.

My muscles ache. The hard floor of the vet clinic is unforgiving. Minutes go by, and I'm going out of my mind with boredom in this small, cramped, fluorescent-lit room. I stretch into downward dog pose, then alternatively bend each knee. I stretch my ass higher into the air to deepen the full body stretch. My shoulders and the backs of my thighs burn as the tension escapes. A muffled cough sounds behind me. I shift to standing and finish out with a sun salutation out of habit.

"What pose were you doing?" Mason's hands slide into his pockets as he relaxes against the doorjamb.

"Walk the dog. It's one of my favorite full body stretches. Works everything."

He grins. "I like the name. I'm always telling people to walk their dogs. It's not good for them to be cooped up in an apartment without exercise. I guess it's not a full body exercise, but it's such a good thing to do, for the dog and the owner. I guess it's a symbiotic relationship, beneficial for each participant."

I pull my arms behind me, stretching the tight muscles across my chest. "I get it. Kind of like a full body stretch. Good for all involved. I get you."

"Where are you from? I detect a bit of a southern accent."

"It comes out sometimes. New Orleans."

He grins, rocks back and forth on his feet, then remembers his purpose. "Chewie's doing good. She's not showing signs of abdominal duress. You can take her home. You'll need to walk her every hour until the food is passing, though."

I glance around the tiny room as if a great white light with instructions will appear before me. If she was mine, I'd take her home, but it seems safer to be here. I don't want to take any more risks with Anna's dog. I've proven I'm a full-fledged nincompoop. I chew at the corner of my lip, unsure what I should do. "It will be easier from here. You have the door that goes right out-side. I have to take an elevator and go through a lobby, and she doesn't like to go on concrete, so it's an even longer trip to dirt or grass. And if some-thing does go wrong, what would I do? Is there an emergency number?"

He rubs the base of his neck while staring at Chewie.

I interrupt his thoughts. "You can lock me in here. I'll be fine. And I can text you if something seems wrong."

"She doesn't have to stay here tonight. You should take her home." He sounds firm and in-sistent.

I leap over to him, landing so close I have to tilt my head up and give him my persuasive, big-eyed plea, a trick that has always worked with my dad. Fittingly, Dad calls them my puppy dog eyes. "Please? If Chewie isn't okay, I couldn't live with myself. I don't live in a good place to take her out every hour. If she doesn't survive this, I couldn't face Anna. Please. Please let me stay here. It's better if I'm here. Safer. Please." I'm begging like a pre-teen girl, and in the words of my mother's longtime crush, Rhett Butler, I don't give a damn.

His emerald eyes widen in surprise. Something tells me I might be his first client to beg. He backs up, creating space between us. "I'm sorry, but your choices are to either leave her here or take her home."

No one says no to me. For a moment, I have no words. "How much will it cost for me to stay here overnight with her?"

His phone vibrates. When he checks it, I can't see the name on the screen. But this time, there's a seriousness to his expression that wasn't there before. He answers the call. "Amber? Yes. I'm finishing up with a client, and then I'll call you back." When he drops his phone back in his pocket, he's all business and ready to usher me out.

"If I leave her overnight, does she have to stay until Monday? Or can I pick her up in the morning?"

"We're closed on Sunday. But if you tell me what time, I'll be here so you can pick her up."

This is not ideal, and I resist the urge to stomp my foot because this is not what I want. But if there's any chance of Chewie having issues during the night, it's safer to leave her here. I chew on my thumbnail as I mull over this predicament, and the sound of his exhale rushes my answer. "Okay. I'll leave her here."

I walk over to her. She's back on the dog bed on the floor, and I bend to place kisses on her head. He offers me a business card with a hand-written number on the back. "We'll take good care of her. That's my personal cell. If you want to check on her during the night, feel free to call or text."

I stand and shove his card into my pocketbook, and it hits me he needs my number. "Let me give you mine. In case anything goes wrong." I hold out my hand for his phone. He looks a bit confused, and I stretch my arm toward his lab coat pocket for his cell. "I'll enter it. Or I can write it down." I glance around the sparse room for a piece of paper.

The corners of his lips curve up a tad as he hesitates then exhales, punches his code, and passes me his phone. As I'm entering my information, a text comes through from Ashley. I hand the phone back to him. Women reach out to him non-stop, it seems. I envision meeting him in a bar, and, yeah, I can see it. If I met him out and about, he'd be the kind of guy I'd try to meet. He has a seriousness to him that's a huge turn-on. And those eyes. It's a rare color reminiscent of a forest, green tinged with golden brown.

"What time can I pick her up in the morning?"

"You tell me. I'll be here."

"Are you staying overnight?"

"No. We have an on-call vet tech who will be with her overnight. But I'll back here early in the morning."

"Eight a.m. good? I'll treat you to breakfast."

He offers a polite smile and steps to open the door for me to leave. "That won't be necessary. I'll be here by eight. If anything changes during the night, I'll text you. But don't worry. She's going to be fine."

He guides me out of the now empty clinic, and as he opens the door to the street, his hand comes to rest on my back. He's probably fighting the urge to push me out the door, but the warmth of his touch has me pausing and glancing back into those iridescent orbs.

"Thank you." When I say it, I mean it more than I have in a long time. He didn't let me have my way, but he did put up with my crazy all day by letting me occupy one of his patient rooms. He's a good guy. Kind. Thoughtful. He bought me lunch. He saved the dog. And he happens to be sexy as all get-out.

As I head home, weaving through the pedestrians crowding the sidewalk, an idea forms in my head. An idea that has me humming a tune and perking up as I pop into my favorite pizzeria for a slice.

THREE

Mason

Sunday morning, an empty, dark waiting room greets me. I flip the lights out of habit before heading to the back. It's not even seven, so I'm not surprised at all when I find Eric, our on-call vet tech, stretched out, snoring on the cot in our back room. We pull it out when someone needs to stay overnight. We have two cats that are staying with us until Monday, recovering from surgeries. They are each curled up on their fleece beds. One watches me as I walk by. There's an extra-large crate on the floor, and I bend to check on the patient whose wellbeing Eric has been in charge of all night.

The large, brown labradoodle stands, and her tail thumps the side of the crate. As I'm opening the crate door, Eric speaks from behind me. "She's doing good. She's passed some big piles of poop."

"Great," I tell him as she looks at me with her soulful orbs then licks my face from chin to brow. I stand, reach over, and grab the extra Starbucks coffee I picked up on the way in and pass it to Eric. Now free, the dog sniffs around the edges of the room, checking out the space. She looks like an entirely different dog from the one who arrived yesterday in distress. "Thanks for coming in last night."

Eric stretches his arms. "That's what I'm here for." Eric prefers the night shift, as he's pursuing acting by day. I've always suspected he could earn more as a bartender than a vet tech. Asked him about it once, and he concurred, but said he'd rather spend his moonlighting time with animals than people.

I flip my light on in the closet I call an office and take my place in front of my laptop. The brown dog follows me in and sits by my side. I reach out and scratch her ears, then lean down to lift her tag to read the inscription. *Chewbacca.*

Cute, but long. No wonder they shorten it and call her Chewie.

When I shift my attention to my laptop, she lies on the floor by my feet. An email from Rob, one of my partners in the clinic, catches my attention. He's found an ideal spot for a second location in Connecticut. My shoulder muscles tighten as I read through his email, attempting to ignore the mild burning sensation. Fuck. Rob's right. Opening additional locations will be important to our overall income growth. But I bought into this practice five years ago, and the debt from that, as well my debt from vet school, is sizeable. And now, as soon as we've gotten a handle on business debt, he wants to take on more.

There's a tap on the doorframe. "I'm heading out, okay?"

"Thanks again, Eric."

"Anytime. I've fed the cats and set out food on the shelf for this dog. You can decide if you want to feed her. Don't work all day on your day off."

When he leaves, Chewbacca and I stare at each other. Then it occurs to me that she's not supposed to spend the whole day here. I grab my phone and scroll through my contacts to locate her owner's name. Well, not her owner, her dog sitter.

I grin as I read what she's typed into the notes section on the contact field.

Thx for saving Chu. Namaste

Yesterday was a shit storm. Saturdays are always busy, and as the only vet not stricken with flu, the day pushed manic. But I do remember her. For some reason, Ashley couldn't stand her. Said something about her type being all about money. I didn't get that vibe, but what do I know?

She definitely cared about this dog. And the dog cared about her. In my book, that is about the best character check around. Chewbacca raises her paw to my leg, requesting more scratching. She twists her body against me as I scratch, hitting a good spot. The blonde's warm smile comes to mind. Then I remember her shocked expression when I stood firm and didn't allow her to stay overnight with the dog. Hell, maybe Ashley is right. She definitely acted like she'd never heard the word "no" before. And she did ask me how much it would cost, as if throwing money around would change my answer.

I tap out a quick text to tell her the dog is well, and she can pick her up as planned.

Then I click open the spreadsheet to study the financials Dave prepared for converting to a twenty-four-seven vet clinic. I've been worried about the space, but he has this idea that we can buy a van to drive boarders to the Connecticut location, thus expanding to provide boarding. His ideas sound good, but every one of his ideas increases expenses. I'm knee deep in his explanations for each line item when my phone vibrates with an incoming text.

Delilah: I'm at the door.

I close my laptop and stand to stretch. A mild tension headache is forming across my forehead.

When I open the door, Chewbacca bounds past me and almost knocks her over. The movement takes us both by surprise. She has a tray full of coffees she's holding up in the air as she laughs. The dog's paws have landed directly on her breasts. I rescue the coffees and stand back, holding the door for her to enter. Her hair is down, and in the morning light, it looks like spun gold.

She's wearing a form fitting long sleeve gray t-shirt, faded, ripped jeans, and brown boots. Yesterday, I did notice her, but it was too manic to take in much. Today, I have time, and I mindlessly linger on those soft, healthy curves.

"She's feeling better, huh?" Delilah's long blonde hair falls almost to her waist. Her slim gold nose ring glimmers in the light, as do the diamonds lining the edge of her left ear. She's wearing a pale pink gloss that glistens on her full lips. The day before, she'd had messy hair piled up on her head and looked exhausted and frazzled. Today, she looks fresh and young. Energetic. A stark contrast to yesterday.

"Yeah, she's doing better. We'll mail the bill to you, and you can be on your way home." In the back of my head, I hear Dave bitching that we charge at the time of service, but I don't really want to have to figure out how to run a credit card. The receptionist normally handles payments. I do know how to do it, but it's been a long time.

"Billing is fine, but I need to get the bill. Not Anna. Or, if you tell me how much it is, I can pay now."

I take slow steps to the reception desk, trying to remember what I need to do. I sit at Bet's desk and am lost among the smattering of Post-It notes lining the monitor and all over her desk. I was hoping her username and password would be on one of the sticky notes, but all she's written down are ridiculous animal jokes.

"I did pick up some coffees. I wasn't sure what you drank, so I have one black, one with skim, one with cream, and one with soy. All Pike's Place." She's holding the tray out to me like a happy waitress offering nirvana.

"You really covered your bases, huh?"

She smiles, showing off brilliant white teeth offset with candy pink lip gloss. "What do you drink?"

"Any and all caffeine. I'll be fine with whatever you don't drink."

"What? No. What's your normal order?"

I resume reading the Post-Its. "Anything, really. I'm not picky. You take what you like, and I'll have what's left over."

"Okay. I took the soy. Which one of these do you want?"

I glance up at her. She does have a soy girl persona. I wouldn't be surprised if she's also vegan. "I'll take the one with cream?"

"Cream? Really?" She sets the tray down on the ground and pulls out the requested coffee for me.

I puff out my chest in mock bravado. "Is cream not manly enough for you?"

She giggles and squirms a bit. "You're my hero. Even with cream in your coffee, you're still manly."

"I didn't do anything, really, but thank you." I didn't do anything. Now, had she needed surgery, then I'd feel like I did something. But I always prefer to avoid putting an animal under anesthesia, so I'm relieved she didn't need surgical intervention.

Delilah bends to Chewbacca's height, and the dog licks her, the same kind of thank you lick she gave me this morning. Dogs have an inherent wisdom and kindness. These two might be simply dog sitter and dog, but a visible bond has formed.

Yesterday, Delilah struck me as a carefree spirit, her hair bouncing around on top of her head and her fingers fluttering in active affirmation while she spoke. In another life, her carefree spirit alone would have had me asking for her number.

No matter what Ashley thinks, Delilah's concern for the dog yesterday was genuine and real. She can't be all bad. "When are Chewie's owners back?" I ask.

"Oh, today. Do you think she's out of the woods now?"

"Yes, I do." Then I accept that I'm not going to find Bet's username and password and push the roller chair away from the desk. "Can I write down your home address so we can mail you a bill?" I should know how to work this system, but it's been years since my training day.

"Oh, I can pay in cash if you don't know how to do the credit card."

Damn. We were slammed yesterday. I don't even want to ask, but I do. "Did anyone provide an estimate for services?"

"Oh, yes." She bounces on her heels, sending her hair and those full breasts, which happen to be at eye level, bouncing. She pulls out a folded piece of paper and holds it out for me. I open it, and sure enough, estimated charges are on here. Ashley completed a nonsurgical and a surgical estimate. The nonsurgical estimate is for $1,800.

Business is not my strong suit. I became a veterinarian due to my love of science and animals, not because of some entrepreneurial drive. While I'm staring at the paper, a stack of cash is thrust into my face. Then she leans across me and scribbles on a piece of paper. The curves of her waist are inches from my face, and I peruse her svelte lines down to her tight ass defined by the stitching on the jeans pockets. *In another life.*

A familiar smell wafts from her—camelia. We had potted camelia bushes growing up. It's been ages since I smelled that scent, or even thought about Minnesota.

When she's done writing, she passes me the paper. "Here's my name and address. That's two thousand, but if the estimate was off and I owe more, just bill me. Does that work?"

I stare down at the stack of money. *Why is she carrying so much cash?*

"Now, do you have to work here today? Or can I take you to breakfast? There's this great little place around the corner, and they have sidewalk seating so Chewie can sit with us."

I stare at her breasts for a minute then realize what I'm doing and have the good sense to lift my head. I focus on her sky-blue irises, not the curve of her breasts rising above her bra cup. She's trying to be kind, and I recognize that, but I really do have work I need to get through this morning. We are meeting with bankers next week, and I'll be damned if I'm applying for a loan without full confidence we can pay it back. "That's not necessary. But thank you."

Her shoulders sag, and guilt for turning her down nips at me. When I stand, I pull open Bet's drawer and stuff the cash inside. As I close the drawer, my gut tells me that's not a smart place to put it. My phone buzzes, and when I see the caller ID, I forget all about the money. I've got to take this call. I hold up an index finger to Delilah to let her know I'll be a moment and take a few steps back.

"Amber. Hey. You're up early."

"Or late. Depends on how you look at it." Background noise carries through the phone, and I cringe.

I raise my voice so she hears me in whatever nightclub she's calling from. "I'm sorry I called you back so late last night. So, you're in town next week?"

"Yes. One more show tonight, then we'll be driving back. Should be back around Tuesday or Wednesday."

"Great." I blink as a whirlwind of emotions catch me off guard. I haven't seen her in years. "Text me, and we'll figure out where to meet up."

Amber agrees, and then she's gone. I'm not entirely sure if she hung up or we got disconnected, and as I stare at the phone, Delilah's movement by my side reminds me she's here.

"Sorry about that. Um, here, let's go back and get Chewbacca's leash. That should be everything you need."

Delilah follows me into the back room. She walks straight up to the orange tabby's cage and sticks her finger through, but she's looking all around. "So, this is the room I wasn't allowed in yesterday."

I hold up a leash for Delilah to confirm it's hers and smile a bit at my blunder and her calling me out on it. "Yeah, I'm not exactly batting a thousand this morning. So, here you are. Behind the curtain."

She grins up at me, quizzically. "Curtain?"

"Like *The Wizard of Oz*. Seeing the inner workings." She turns on her heels.

"What do you think?"

"Groovy." She beams her smile at me. This girl is all sunshine. She steps closer in a flirty way. I'm out of practice on this front, but with her hip out to the side and the way she runs her tongue over her lower lip, drawing my attention to her pale pink lip gloss, it's possible. When she runs her fingers across my wrist, I can't hold back my smile because, yes, she's flirting with me. "Are you sure you can't have breakfast with me?" She tilts her head as she asks and bats her eyelashes. She's cute. And tempting. Fun.

It's Sunday. I don't feel up for going out, but at the same time, my empty apartment has no appeal. It strikes me as the opposite of fun. "Actually, I'm on my own tonight. Any chance, and don't feel pressured at all," I hold my palm out to emphasize this point, "but any chance you'd like to come over, and I'll cook for you?"

She smiles and pops up onto her toes and bounces a few times. Excitement, maybe? Then she halts and stands flat on her feet, tilting her head as she swirls a strand of long golden hair around a finger. "Sure. I'd love to."

She grabs her phone then smacks her palm against her chest. "I was about to suggest we swap contact info, but that's already done. Text me your address. If it's okay, we can confirm a time a little later today, once I know for sure what time Anna and Jackson will be home to receive their baby. They're aiming to be back this afternoon, but with traffic, you never know."

I grin. After four years of being a vet, you'd think I'd stop noticing when people refer to their pets as their children, but I still love it. Dogs, in particular, are some of my favorite people.

"Oh, wait. Hold this." She shoves her phone in my palm and digs through her massive pocket-book, then pulls out a wrinkled paper bag.

While I'm holding her phone, a jingle announcing a text sounds. I barely glance at the name before she waves. "It's my mom. I'll text her back later." Then she swaps her phone for the bag. I peer inside and see a couple of doughnuts and muffins. "I figured you might not agree to go to breakfast with me, so I brought some for you in case."

She's sweet. A sugary breakfast isn't my first choice, but my rumbling stomach reminds me all food is welcome. Bringing me breakfast is thoughtful.

I lead her out of the clinic, rethinking this. What am I doing inviting her to my place? Should I tell her before she comes over? I don't have experience with this. Then again, why say anything now? She's gonna get the whole picture laid out for her in a vibrant technicolor explosion this evening. Worst-case scenario? We have dinner and agree to be friends.

FOUR

Delilah

"Welcome home!" I burst through Anna's apartment door, arms held high to wrap her in an I-am-so-fecking-glad-to-see-you-hug. Chewie leaps in front of me, ecstatic to be home with her mommy. My heart echoes the dog's sentiment, and I can't help but laugh. Oh, sugar, what a freaking relief to be delivering a healthy dog.

Anna crouches to love on her furry beast. Jackson shouts out a hello from the kitchen and asks if I want anything to drink. "Nah, I'm good. I'm not gonna stay long."

From her bending position, Anna checks out my outfit. She grins. "You look good, girl. Have you got a date?"

I grin right back and pretty much bounce over to one of the kitchen stools. Being free of dog responsibilities feels damn good. One long nap, shower, and a blow out on my hair, and it's a new day. So much brighter than yesterday. "Yep, I do. Your vet asked me out!" I almost squeal.

"Dr. Herriot!" Anna exclaims. "Wait, why did you go to the vet?"

I twist a little on the stool as I flutter my fingers around to indicate she can calm down. "Everything's fine, but we did have an incident. A small incident. It's all okay."

Big brown eyes stare back at me. She's not exactly mad, but she's definitely waiting for the explanation. She continues to comb over the mangy mutt's curly hair as if she's hunting for the injury.

"Yeah, so, Chewie ate an entire bag of dog food."

Jackson chuckles behind me. I continue, "You told me you'd be out of cell range. Thank the gods you had me on your caretaker list. And she's fine now. He did give her an IV because I guess the dry food dehydrated her, but she's good. Been pooping like a champ today." I grin, proud. The dog's alive. I'll probably never dog sit again, but she survived. Alive is good. "Once I knew she'd be okay, I figured telling you all about it in person was preferable to me sending an email or text."

Anna crosses her legs on the floor, and the brown mass of fur attempts to crawl into her lap and curl up. She's too big to actually fit, but her tail wags back and forth, oblivious. "She's such a good dog. A healthy, hungry girl, aren't you?" Anna tilts her head to me, a big smile across her face, the happiest of dog moms. "So, Dr. Herriot? He's hot as fuck."

Jackson's voice sounds from behind me, a mixture of curious and wary. "Who is this?"

"Oh, my vet. You haven't met him," Anna answers as she scratches Chew's ears.

Jackson steps out of the kitchen, gives me a quick hug, then pops Anna on the head. "Sounds like maybe I should. Hot as fuck. Really?"

"Not as hot as you, babe." She blows him a kiss, and he smirks, shaking his head as he walks to the back of the apartment.

My phone vibrates, and I pull it out. Mom's calling. I decline the call and slip it back into my clutch. There's no way I'm answering her call on the same day I have a date. She's got, like, crazy black magic powers and she'll sense through the phone line what I'm up to. Definite decline.

"So, yeah." I lower my voice in case Jackson's listening in. I reach out with my leg and toe Anna to get her attention. "You never told me your vet is so freaking hot! And he's super nice. Like, such a good guy."

Anna smiles. "Yeah. He's a nice guy. But, Dee, you don't normally go out with a guy more than once or twice. You're gonna be good to him, right?" She angles her eyebrows seriously. "You aren't going to force me to change vets, are you?"

"No. Not at all. He's not even that into me. I was prepared to ask him out, but then he asked me out!" I squeal that last bit because it's exciting. Even Anna described him as sexy, and he has women calling him right and left. What girl doesn't get jazzed when a hottie asks her out? Anna's wearing her skeptic face, so I reassure her.

"It's not a definite date. He didn't use the word *date*. This is almost more like friends getting together. Besides, I'll be moving back to New Orleans."

"When?" Anna's quick with the question. I often talk about moving back to New Orleans, but since we work together, she's always questioning my plans.

"There's no date set. It's gonna eventually happen, though. These are my fun years." I jump off the stool, arms wide open, attempting to mimic the dramatic *Titanic* moment on the bow of the ship.

Anna returns her attention to Chew while shaking her head. I'm not sure she gets my impersonation.

"Be good to him. He seems like a nice guy. I'd hate to see him added to the long line of heartbroken men in your wake."

"Oh, sugar! Heartbroken men, my ass," I snap.

She rolls her eyes, and I brace for her to spout off names, but she drops it. "So, tell me more about what he said about Chew. Anything I need to watch out for?"

"Not really. Make sure she continues to drink lots of water and has regular bowel movements. She had diarrhea, but her poo seems to be hardening up. I'm so sorry. I'm the worst at taking care of things."

"No, you are not! She's doing great. And she's overeaten with me before too. That's why I keep her food in a locked container. She's a greedy little minx. Don't be hard on yourself." For effect, she points, scolding me. "Don't ever say that again, girl. You are great at taking care of those you love. No self-degradation in this room. Got it?"

Well, I survived this test. I'll give myself that much. The dog is alive.

FIVE

Delilah

I pay the cab driver and step out onto Pierrepont Street. Two scrolled black iron doors with matching fall-themed teardrop wreaths greet me. The Beaux-Arts style entrance compliments the traditional brick apartment building smack dab in the center of Brooklyn Heights. I step up and ring apartment 8D. A buzzer sounds, and I push the heavy door open. The nondescript lobby has marble floors and several brass door elevators. No doorman. Interesting. I recommend to anyone who asks that they live in a doorman building.

The convenience is worth the extra expense. Not to mention the added safety.

When the elevator opens, I glance down the hall. Mason stands with his apartment door propped open with his foot, a smile on his face. He's wearing faded jeans and a tucked-in button-down flannel shirt with a well-worn brown leather belt. His sleeves are rolled up on his forearms, and he has several plastic bracelets on one arm. I didn't notice those yesterday. They're the kind of bracelets that support various causes.

He bends to give me a polite welcoming hug then pushes the door wide. We enter a narrow hall. Immediately to my right is another door. The door is open, and through a small window at the end of the bathroom, I can see a skyline view of Manhattan. The short entrance hall opens into an expansive loft-like space with a dining and living room combination. I don't see a kitchen, but I assume it's on the other side of the wall near the dining area. The high ceilings and oversized windows make me think the room must be quite sunny during the day.

Less than two steps into the great room, I halt. On every single wall, pieces of paper are taped. For a minute, I'm unsure, but no, it's most definitely children's art. Some of the paper bears the marks of age, faded colors, and dust. Those are mostly comprised of lines and scribbles. Some of the fresher papers include torn-out pages from coloring books, carefully drawn in the lines. A few are colorful paintings in the abstract. Handprints and footprints. Others landscape and animal drawings. Many cat and dog line sketches. I point at the paintings and grin. "Do your kid owners send you artwork?"

He slips both hands into his front pockets and closes one eye, as if he's thinking about my question. "Kid owners? You mean my patients' owners?"

"Yeah." There's a ton of art here. He must have been collecting these for years.

"No. My daughter is a budding artist. These are all hers."

Jesus, Mother, Mary, and Angels. I did not expect that. A single dad. I've never done that before. Dated a parent. People with kids usually seem so different.

His shoe taps mine. "You can close your mouth."

"Oh, no, I ah—"

"I should've said something yesterday, but I didn't really know how to bring it up. I haven't dated, or tried to date, since she was born. If it's an issue for you, we can just be friends. Really. I've got a great vegetarian lasagna in the oven and a huge kale salad, so I hope you'll still stay for dinner. An adult dinner without a child at the table is a rarity for me."

As he's talking, I twist around, studying all the art, wishing my brain would catch up. This is fine. What does it matter if he has a daughter? I'll probably never meet her. I mean, isn't that kind of a rule among single parents? You don't introduce dates until you're serious? And I'm gonna be moving. I don't do serious. But wait...

"Are you single?"

He exhales, and it sounds like a mixture of a laugh and relief. "Yes. Never been married, actually. Kara lives with me. Her mom's in a band and isn't around. Or...she hasn't been." He calls as he heads to a hall at the end of the room, "Can I get you something to drink? Wine? Water?"

"Wine, please." Yes, this situation calls for alcoholic reinforcement.

He disappears around the corner, and I meander along the wall, perusing the art. One piece proudly proclaims, "I LOVE DADDY." I reach out to touch it, the thick, dried paint uneven beneath my fingertip. I can't help but smile. As the kid of a painter, the abundance of art reminds me of my afternoons spent drawing and painting away beneath mom's expert tutelage. Some of the favorite days of my life.

Mason joins me at the wall and hands me a glass of red. With a slight smile on his face, he sits down on the oversized worn brown leather sofa and motions for me to join him.

"I probably should have asked you out to dinner. It's been so long." He sets his glass down on the table. "This whole dating thing. My life." He shakes his head and stares out the window. It's dark, and other than the random lights from an apartment building across the street, there's not much to see. "Kara was born less than a year after I started working, right out of vet school. Exhausting days. And nights. Kara came home with me from the hospital. She's four now, and the clinic's getting a bit easier." He lifts his shoulders, inhaling deeply. "As you saw, it can still be manic and nonstop, but at least now I don't have to refer to books to double-check every single diagnosis. And four is easier. Each month it gets easier with Kara. But those first few years were not easy. At all. Dating wasn't remotely on my radar. I haven't done the online app thing. The idea of creating a dating profile? No, thanks. Do you have kids?"

I giggle-snort at the ridiculousness of the question then immediately sit straighter and compose myself. He's got a serious face going on. The man's not joking. Right. "No. I don't even babysit." Oh, Mylanta. He's going to usher me out the door before dinner. "So, um, Kara came home with you from the hospital. Is that normal? Or were you guys living together then broke up? For the love of nuts and berries, I should stop talking." I slap my palm over my forehead, and he grins in response. At least I'm entertaining.

He kicks his feet out on the coffee table and crosses one foot over the other. "It's fine. Kara's mom wasn't ready for motherhood. We hooked up a few times when I was right out of vet school. Pregnancy wasn't in her plans. She told me she was going to put the baby up for adoption, but the adoption agency wanted her to get the father to agree." He stares toward the back of the room, as if lost in the memory replaying before him. On an exhale, he lifts his gaze. "Here we are."

It all makes sense. "So, where is Kara now?"

"She's at Rockaway Beach with my mom. They get back tomorrow. My mom's been a godsend. I don't know what in the world I would've done without her. She cares for Kara during the day and when I work late, like last night. Kara will be starting kindergarten next year. Which is insane to think about. You wait. When you have kids, you'll see. It's like they take everything out of you. You have to be on every single minute they're awake. Then it gets easier, especially when they eat on a more regular daytime schedule. Then they start moving around, and it's like you have to have eagle eyes, watching for danger. Then they start to get smarter and don't pose such a risk to themselves. Then you blink, and you have this wunderkind who's learning her letters and numbers and talking to you like a little adult, and you can say something like 'pick up your toys' and she does it!"

He's full of disbelief, and I suppress my laugh. He's so animated when he talks about his daughter, it's like he comes alive and loses some of the serious man vibe.

I don't have any personal experience with what he's talking about, but I love listening to him. So full of life. His forearm muscles flex when he shifts his wine glass. Dark, curly hair covers his wrists and a touch of the back of his hand. Everything about him says he's relaxed and at home, from his socked feet crossed on the coffee table to the way he rambles. The laidback vibe works for me. So much better than the bar scene I frequent.

I kick off my boots and pull my legs up onto the sofa.

He scratches his head, ruffling his hair a bit. "What am I doing? You don't want to hear about kids. I mean, do you want kids? One day?" He asks the question as if the thought just crossed his mind.

"Yeah, I do. They're part of the plan." One day, when I'm older. Have grown up more. Can take care of a dog without an emergency visit to the vet.

A buzzer sounds in the kitchen, and he stands. "Lasagna's ready."

I follow him into a kitchen with a lovely window over the sink and Silestone counters and white appliances. The tiny kitchen offers limited counter space but has a cozy vibe. I stand on the edge, searching for a way I can help. He bypasses me with the lasagna, and I refill our wine glasses then follow him to the dining table.

He's already set the table for two. A couple of candles are set out, and while he lights them, I duck back into the kitchen and grab the salad I saw sitting on the counter. When I round the corner, I collide with Mason, and his arm wraps around my waist, and some part of his anatomy brushes my ass. A flurry of sensations shoots through me, and I instinctively press my body closer to his and breathe in his fresh herbal soap smell.

He holds on to my hips and steps back with a sexy smile. "Sorry."

"It's okay." This man can rub against me all he wants.

The lasagna is loaded with cheese, finely chopped vegetables, and spicy marinara sauce. I moan with my first bite because it is that good. It's so much better than anything I could cook. I tell him so.

"Single dads kind of need to cook." He gives this modest shrug, as if it's no big deal. "What do you do, Delilah? When you're not saving dogs that eat too much?"

I laugh, maybe a little louder than the situation warrants. I'm typically not one to get nervous, but he's more mature than a lot of the guys I meet. Better looking too. That must be why the nerves are shooting off a fireworks extravaganza deep in my belly. "You mean, what do I do when I'm not out attempting to kill my friends' pets?"

He flexes his socked feet as he stretches out his legs. "Don't be too hard on yourself. So, you know I'm a vet. You're one up on me. What do you do?"

"I'm an art director at an ad agency."

His thick dark eyebrows angle inward towards his nose. "What's an art director do?"

"I'm the one who works on the layouts for ads. The photographs or illustrations." I splay out my hands in the air and shift them around to kind of give him a visual aid. "I decide where the headline goes, font for the body copy, where to put it on the page, that kind of thing."

"That kind of thing. Hmmm. So, why an art director?"

I twirl my glass, swishing the wine around, trying to remember exactly why I went into advertising. "Well, I always wanted to do something with art. My mom, she's a painter. She doesn't make any real money, but she loves it. I love painting too, but I also love graphic design, photography, illustrations. She's an introvert, so spending time alone works well for her, you know? But I'm more of an extrovert. I'd go crazy if I didn't interact with people during the day. In an ad agency, I get to work with art, but I work with people all day too. It fits my personality best. And it was a middle ground for me and my parents." I sip more of my wine as I consider how to change the subject. "Why'd you become a vet?"

He grins. "Love of animals. Probably what

drives most vets. And science. I've been into science for as long as I can remember."

"Life motto?"

He sort of chuckles. "Excuse me?"

"We're asking questions. Getting to know each other. What's your life motto? The words you live by?"

Within seconds, he answers. "Be kind to all living things."

I nod a bit, appreciating the depth of his motto and the appropriateness, given his career.

"Your turn. Life motto?" he asks.

"Love is all around." Somehow my life motto, stolen straight from one of my all-time favorite flicks, *Love Actually*, doesn't seem quite so impressive when compared to Mason's.

"Cute. Life goal?"

Did he shade my life motto? "Um. I don't know. Let's see. Life goal." I've never been a goal-oriented kind of person. "Be near family. Be happy." Don't rock the boat. "What's yours?"

"Give back." That could also be a life motto, but it's not like I'm gonna shade his life goal. "Favorite city?" I ask.

Seconds lapse before he answers. "Minneapolis." Wow. Unexpected. "Yours?"

My response is instantaneous. "Barcelona. Favorite airline?"

He smiles a warm smile. "I don't get to travel much. No favorite airline. Or I guess it'd be the one with the lowest fare. What's your favorite?"

I chew on a bite of lasagna, reflecting a bit. "I'd say it's a tie between British Air and Virgin. First class in both blows any of the domestic airlines out of the water."

He mutters so low it's almost as if he's speaking to himself, "I'll keep that in mind."

There's a lull in the conversation as we each finish the first helping of lasagna on our plates. Every now and again, our eyes meet. The silence feels awkward, so I pull out the king cake of conversation starters. "How old were you when you lost your virginity?"

He almost spits out his wine but manages to hold it in, a big grin on his face. He half chuckles as if he can't believe I asked the question. Come on, now, big handsome guy. Once you know me, you'll accept this as par for the course.

He licks his lips. "I'll answer, but after I do, it's your turn." He raises his eyebrows in an unspoken request for agreement, and I nod my consent. "Sixteen. High school girlfriend. Dated her until we left for college."

"Oh, wow. High school love. Still speak to her?"

"Sure. She's in LA."

"Do you still love her?"

"No. We had an amicable split. A long time ago. No drama. We're friends. You?"

"Me?"

"Yeah, you."

"Seventeen. High school boyfriend. Quarterback for the football team. I was head cheerleader. A tale as old as time. He went and told the whole football team. Pissed me off. I dumped his ass and created a voodoo doll of him. Which might have been a bit over the top because he broke his leg one week later. He wasn't on his way to college ball, anyway, but still. Kind of harsh. But, to be clear, it's not like I asked for his leg to break. I wasn't specific with the..." I trail off and don't finish the sentence. There's no good way to finish the story. "Anyway, it was one and done for me. He wasn't too skilled. Not a great first."

Mason sets his wine glass down and rests his elbows on the table. "I'm not sure where to go with that one. Voodoo doll? Where are you from, again?"

"New Orleans. Home of black magic, jazz music, and Bourbon Street. You?"

"Minnesota, originally. Then New York. Tell me about jazz music. Specific artists or bands you love?"

Now, music—music, I can talk about. "Let's see, where to start? Isaac Hayes, Nina Simone, Ella Fitzgerald, Armstrong, Sinatra. I could go on and on. There's a new jazz artist I'm starting to love. Sasha Masakowski. I also love bands like The Shins and Vampire Weekend and Jack Johnson. Any songs with a happy beat or vibe. What about you?"

"Alternative rock. Rock. The kind of stuff you hear on the radio. If I'm in the apartment and I want music to play, I'll often ask Alexa to play Tom Petty or Bob Dylan."

"Solid choices." I consider diving into my list of favorite Tom Petty songs, but he doesn't seem like he's so into music. I flip through my mental conversation cue cards and whip out, "What childhood memory stands out the strongest in your mind?"

He takes his time answering. "You first."

I answer with confidence. "Hands down, my 'doll' Christmas. The year I got a Barbie Dream House, the Julie Albright American Girl Doll— she's from 1974—and I also got her egg chair and bed and her pet bunny. Stuffed bunny, not real."

He squints. I sense the judgement. "That's what you remember? Stuff?"

"Well, no. There's more. I remember walking down the stairs and passing a video camera set up on a tripod. Then another camera. Then another camera. I turned into our living room, and flashes went off as both Mom and Dad stood there snapping pictures. It was insane. My parents went over the top every Christmas, but that year, it was especially insane. I felt like a celebrity."

"Only child?"

"Oh, sugar, you know it. What about you?"

He stares across the room as he answers, his voice solemn. "Me too." He sips his wine, focusing his gaze on a spot somewhere over my shoulder. "My clearest memory is of us moving. Mom and I moved from Minneapolis to New York to be closer to her family after she and Dad divorced. I remember Dad standing by the front door. I sat in the back seat, watching him through the rear window as he got smaller and smaller."

In my mind's eye, I see a young boy with longish hair waving goodbye to his father. My heart aches for the precious little boy. "Bless your heart. How old were you?"

"Six, maybe seven years old."

We both finished our dinner a while ago, so I

help him clean up the dishes, and we return to the table. He sits down in his chair and refills our wine glasses. We talk more. He opens another bottle. Our conversation roams around everything and anything, and I get the sense he's going to be a gentleman. The trouble is, after a couple of glasses of wine, brave and bold Delilah comes out to play.

"So, you say you don't date much?"

He nods his answer.

I remember the women calling him and find it hard to believe, but if that's the way he wants to play it, I'll roll with it. "You know, I don't want to be too forward. Well, who am I kidding? I always tend to be a tad forward, but not this kind of forward." The wine in my glass sloshes around as I talk. "It sounds like you have a lot going on in your life." He opens his mouth, and I can tell from his expression he has no idea where I'm going with this, and I continue before he can speak. "And that's okay. So do I. I mean, my life..." I flutter my hands, my best explanation of my life at this point in time. "Anyway, I so rarely meet a guy who I spend time with and am attracted to. My friends say I'm overly picky and... they could be right. But the side effect of pickiness is it's been a long time for me." It might all be in my head, but his eyes seem to widen. "Would you be at all open to us having sex? Tonight? No strings?"

He catches his lower lip with his teeth as he grins at me. After what feels like a small eternity, he asks, "Are you for real?"

Oddly enough, he's not the first person to ask me that. "Totally, one hundred percent real." For extra effect, I add, "Mostly organic."

His lips twist into a sexy smirk as he shifts back onto the sofa. "I'm open to sex. Very open. But applying the word 'complicated' to my life is a bit of an understatement. Are you okay with that?"

"Very." I lift my wine glass and sip it as we eye each other. The current in the room feels almost electric as awareness of what we're considering doing filters through. We've been making small talk all night, but sometimes a girl's gotta take it up a notch.

Holding my wine glass, I saunter around the table to his side. I stand in front of him, and he shifts his chair, so it's facing me more than the table. I straddle his legs, wine glass in one hand, and rest my arm around his shoulder. Sitting like this, we're almost equals, but his lips are still a little higher than mine. He leans down and presses his lips to mine, tentative at first, then we dive deeper, exploring. His hands roam my back, quickly making their way down to my ass. I rock my hips against him, and he groans. He breaks our kiss for a moment, takes my glass from me, and sets it on the table. He caresses the side of my face, and his thumb rests near my lip.

I tilt my head and playfully nip his finger, and he rolls his lower lip beneath his teeth. "You are a breath of fresh air. Has anyone ever told you that?"

My heart thunders, and I shift my hips, searching for friction, desire building. I swallow. "Believe it or not, yes." I reach up and pull his mouth to mine. Enough small talk.

He holds on to my hips, stopping the kisses once again. Dark, hungry eyes probe mine. "You're sure? If you change your mind...we can go slow. We don't have to rush."

I understand. It's our first date. I could regret this. But I'm not going to be around long. And, damn, slow is not what I want. It's been too long. And right now, I want to experience a night with this gorgeous guy. Seize the day, live in the moment, and all that good stuff. I grasp his shirt and pull, as he lowers his lips to mine. Our tongues collide, and his hands shift to my ass, gripping and kneading.

He stands, lifting me with him and bumping the table, almost toppling the wine glasses. He grunts and carries me down the hall. I wrap my legs around his waist. He kisses my throat and growls, "You sure?"

I respond by shoving my tongue into his mouth and practically climbing him.

He drops me onto a bed, and I sink into the comforter. I register this is his bedroom and not much else. I sit up and grab the edges of my sweater and lift it off and toss it across the room, exposing a white lace semi-cup bra. His eyes darken, and within seconds his shirt is off and tossed to the side. He's muscular and ripped in a lean, athletic sort of way. Dark, curly hair lightly covers the firm lines of his pecs and tapers down. I reach out and pull at his belt buckle, wanting to see more.

"You know, I had a hunch you'd be fun, Delilah." He trails kisses from my neck, down to my chest. "But I really had no idea how much fun."

Before I can unbutton his jeans, a firm hand pushes me back and grasps the waistband of my long, loose cotton skirt and slips it off, taking my moist panties with them. I didn't plan on anything happening tonight but send a silent thank you to the gods of the universe my waxing appointment was last Friday, and another that my practical self always carries condoms in my purse. A girl's gotta be prepared.

"Damn. You are gorgeous." At one point in my life, my D sized breasts embarrassed the hell out of me. Not tonight. I push my shoulders back, displaying the ladies at their best angle while tossing my hair over my shoulder. He kicks off his jeans and boxers. Naked, he crawls over me, his firm erection aiming outward.

His mouth reclaims mine, and as his weight falls over me, I wrap my legs around him, and his cock presses against my belly. He shifts to my side and lavishes attention to each of my breasts as he slips a finger inside me.

I gasp as his thumb presses and circles my clit. "Oh...My...lanta that feels good." I tilt my head back as pleasure overwhelms me. A little nagging voice tells me it's our first date, and I'm gonna regret this in the morning—but, damn, this feels good.

He lies on his side, removes his finger, and places it in his mouth and sucks. It's as if I can feel the suction on his finger, and I push him on his back and straddle him.

He removes his finger with a popping sound,

and with a slight smirk, teases, "Hhmm...so good." He grabs my hips, and with one quick movement, flips me over so he's back on top, and I squeal out loud in surprise. He slides his long finger into me while using his thumb to work my clit.

"Ah, fuck. Right there. Just like that."

"Hmm. I like this bare pussy. So wet. For me?"

I sound out a wispy "yes" or something like that. Whatever I say, he understands. His lips curl up, and he shifts, his hand still pleasing my lady bits to the point golden spots dot my vision.

He bites the edge of my bra and pulls it down, releasing my breast, then circles my nipple with his tongue and sucks, working the sensitive skin to the point I'm writhing below him from pleasure overload. He releases my nipple and kisses it then moves farther down and dips his head.

I sit up on my elbows and watch as his tongue enters me and licks up my center, straight to the bundle of nerves awaiting attention at the top. I run my fingers through his thick hair as his tongue spins magic and plays me like a fiddle. My muscles quiver, and I let out an uninhibited scream as I climax, a happy, exalted sprite dancing on the edge of fire.

I'm shaking and shuddering, my muscles quaking from his ministrations. As he places soft kisses along my throat and the sensitive skin below my ear, I reach between us and wrap my fingers around his hard shaft, the skin soft, smooth.

He groans. "Shit. Condom." I continue to work him over, toying with the precum dripping on the end. He lies on his back and stares at the ceiling, clearly enjoying what I'm doing but distressed. "I don't have a condom."

"No problem." I drop a quick kiss on his jaw and hop off the bed, naked as a jaybird, and sprint into his den to locate my bag. Within seconds, I'm running back into his bedroom and jumping onto the bed, throwing two condoms his way. He picks one up as his lips curve up into a smile then rips the condom packet open with his teeth.

I take the condom from him. "Let me."

He shifts onto his back and watches me with raw hunger. I grip him with my hand, moving up and down, then wrap my lips around him.

When my tongue flicks over his precum, he grunts. "I'm...God I want your mouth, but I don't—"

I don't let him finish. I take him into my mouth as far as I can. He grabs a fistful of my hair. "That's. Oh. Amazing. But, stop. It's been too long. I won't last." I place a small kiss on the top of his shaft then slip the condom on, taking care to ensure room at the top, because one thing's for sure, he will come.

I push him back onto the bed and run my fingers down his chest as I straddle him, his cock between my legs. I slide against him, wetting him with my juices. He kneads my breasts, and I lift my head back, loving the gentle caresses and firm pressure from his long, strong fingers. I shift my hips over his tip, then shift again, stretching around him, taking all of him.

We both moan as we join, eyes locked on each other. Holy fuck, the sensations rip through my body, forcing me to still. He lifts me up, then drives into me. I lean forward and angle myself so I can ride him hard. And I do. As I rock back and forth, the pressure works my clit, and I'm on the verge of oblivion when he flips me over and he's on his knees, ramming into me.

My toes curl as I scream out, "Yes, yes. Mase, right. There. Harder. Mase. Mase." I sputter out fractions of words and complete nonsense as my muscles contract and golden flecks scatter behind my closed eyelids. He tenses and grunts as he releases deep inside me, his contractions coaxing and mingling with mine. He collapses onto me, and I circle my arms around his sweaty back, out of breath.

"Holy shit. That was…"

"Amazing," he grunts.

"Unbelievable," I gasp. As my breathing slows and my brain function resumes, I place light kisses on the base of his neck, tasting his sweat. "Needed. Oh, so needed. How have I gone so long without sex?"

He grimaces slightly as he pulls out and rolls off me. He places a kiss on my neck, then nipple, pulls the condom off, checks it, knots it, and tosses it into a garbage can on the floor next to a tall wooden dresser. He pulls me against his chest, and I drape one of my legs over his, my heart still slowing to a resting beat.

He squeezes me. "If I never have sex again, I swear, as long as I can remember you, tits bouncing as you ride me, holy shit. And your noises. That memory. It's all I need for the rest of my life." He shifts to give me a long, slow, deep kiss. "You're staying here tonight, right?"

I smile a lazy, happy smile. "Yeah, I'm staying here." I settle myself onto his chest, listening to the rhythm of his heart and loving the way our naked bodies fit. I could easily fall asleep, content and peaceful, but I force myself out of the bed and to the restroom before sleep claims me. I stumble over to the door across the room and open it to find a closet filled to the brim with clothes. I circle around the room as I ask, "Bathroom?"

"Down the hall. Near the door where you came in." Naked, I tiptoe through the apartment in the dark, the only light from the glow of outdoor streetlamps. What a strange apartment layout. I don't think I've ever been in a bedroom where the bathroom wasn't attached or at least across the hall. I'd hate this. Next time, he'll need to stay at my place.

When I return to the bedroom and crawl under the covers, he kisses me quickly then jumps out of bed to pad through the apartment to the bathroom. When he returns, he slides beneath the comforter and pulls me close. His fingers trace my side, skirting the curves of my breast, the rough pads of his fingertips caressing my skin. My fingers play with his dark, curly chest hair, until I relax and rest my head against his shoulder as we hold each other. I slip into sleep while trying to come up with something to say.

SIX

MASON

The sunlight cuts through the bedroom window. As I shift to shield my face, I become aware of a warm body against mine and the beautiful, soft breast I'm cupping. I inhale. A floral aroma invades my senses. Delilah. A rush of memories hit me as I shift my quickly growing hard-on between the supple globes of her ass. I place a soft kiss on her shoulder and squint at the intruding morning light.

Her lips lift into a smile, but her eyes remain closed. "Well, good morning to you." She squeezes her ass, and the sensation feels incredible. My erection hardens to an almost painful apex. I reluctantly release her breast and glide down her curves to her smooth, bare pussy. I slip one finger then another inside. She's drenched. Within minutes, she's writhing against me, and all I can think about is slipping into her tight warmth. So tempting.

I force her hips to still then reach behind me to my nightstand where I tossed her extra condom. Within seconds, I'm ready and inside her. Holy fuck. Heaven. She's so tight, so wet. We are side by side in bed, her hair flowing over the top of our pillows, and the sheets are pushed down, giving me a perfect view of the sexiest woman I've ever laid eyes on. The view of her breast and her lush, round nipple is almost as memorable as the one of her bouncing on top of me last night. My palm presses against her clit, the precious bundle of nerves that provide a portal to this gorgeous woman's pleasure, once, twice, three times, and she detonates, quivering and milking my cock. I release into her and wrap my arms around her. This might be the best morning of my life.

I have zero desire to get out of this bed—ever. But I need to dispose of this condom and hit the toilet, so I grab a pair of pajama pants and head down the hall. The bathroom being at the other end of the apartment has never really bothered me before. In New York, there are all kinds of apartment configurations. This one has the added benefit of huge windows and loads of natural light and a big, open living space. But I've never had a girlfriend while living here. I can see how making this journey with Kara's bedroom door opposite mine might be fraught with potential issues. *Girlfriend.*

I duck into the kitchen and grind coffee beans. Kara. What the fuck am I doing? Delilah's twenty-six. She's not a kid, but so much of her carefree persona reminds me of an undergrad. She bounces and radiates giddy energy as if she exudes her own inner light. Kara would love her. She'd be a moth to the flame.

I run through my options while waiting for the coffee to brew. I want to see Delilah again, but Kara is my priority. My little girl is my life. My everything. The reason I haven't thought about dating. Or *fun.* I need to ask Delilah what she wants. I'm not just a single guy. I'm a single *dad.*

I'm staring at the coffee pot, waiting for it to fill, when an arm circles my waist and soft lips touch the base of my neck. I twist in her arms and wrap mine around her. As I hold her, a sense of peace fills me. I wouldn't say I've been unhappy or lonely before now. But, somehow, a missing piece to my life puzzle slid into place. I've known her for less than forty-eight hours. It's borderline insanity, but didn't someone tell me things happen faster on the relationship front for single parents? I like having her here.

I press a kiss to her forehead and pour us both coffee. I happen to have soymilk in my fridge, thanks to Mom. Dee's wearing the flannel shirt I wore yesterday, and from what I can tell, nothing else. Ah, crap. Look at me. I've already given her a nickname. Her blonde hair's all kind of messed up from our night. Without make-up, her eyebrows are much lighter, in a way that frames the aqua color of her irises and her golden skin tone. Her natural beauty shines through when she's put together, but I think I love this undone morning version of her more than anything I've seen so far.

She peers up at me, and a bit bashfully, says, "I used your toothbrush. I hope that's okay." Her nose wrinkles as she confesses.

Hell, yeah, that's okay. In answer, I give her a long, slow, deep kiss. By the time we break away, my lightweight pajama pants do a poor job of hiding the beast she's awoken. She smirks with an oh-I-know-what-you're-up-to expression as I guide her to the sofa

Delilah curls up beside me as I grab the throw lying on the back of the sofa, a Disney princess furry blanket my mom gave Kara years ago. It's ugly as sin, but it's super soft, hence its permanent inclusion in our den. Well, that and the fact Kara is largely responsible for the decor in the apartment. And she's four.

And she'll be home this evening. I toy with Delilah's fingers, contemplating my options, and determine I have no choice but to talk. Communicate. "So, I really like you." Light blue eyes, lighter than the sky outside, stare at me over the rim of her coffee mug. I pause, waiting for the mug to drop lower so I can see her whole face and better judge her reaction.

When she lowers the mug, she murmurs, "I really like you too."

I exhale. First part, done. "I'm not exactly sure how the whole dating thing works now. From what I understand, I should probably date you while dating others and take it slow and see how we evolve, but I have a daughter." Her fingers weave through mine. "It's why I haven't dated."

As a vet, I understand when a physical action is meant to comfort. I often place a hand on a client's shoulder. Her action causes me to pause and appreciate her innate kindness.

I inhale and attempt to slow my speech so my fears don't seep through my words. "I want to see you again, but Kara lives with me." My gaze roams the ceiling until I pinpoint what I need to say. "She's a big part of my life. If I'm not at work, she's usually with me." I wrap a piece of her hair around my index finger and admire the smooth lines of her clavicle, unsure where I'm going with this. I do want to see her again. I'm nowhere close to having my fill of her. But the reality is that I have such a small amount of free time in general.

She sucks in her bottom lip, and I'd give anything to hear the thoughts running through her gorgeous blonde head right now.

A pop sounds as she releases her pink, swollen bottom lip. "Mason, I'd love to meet your daughter. I can tell she's an artist." She bites her thumbnail. Then, softly, almost to herself, she adds, "A kindred soul."

Her words knock air out of my chest. I didn't mean to imply I'd introduce her to my daughter.

Sensing my hesitation, she continues. "Why don't you introduce me as a friend? She's four. That's all she needs to know, anyway, right?"

"I suppose." What we did last night was way out of the ballpark of friend territory, but she's right. There's no reason to dissect adult relationships for my pre-K kid.

She smiles her giant, radiating smile. "And it's the truth, right? We're friends, and I'd love to be her friend."

Her phone vibrates on the wooden floor where it's been plugged in all night below the window. She ignores the sound and loops her hands behind my neck and pulls me down to her for a soft, comforting kiss. I massage down her smooth skin to cup her naked ass and squeeze. I glance at the clock. Thirty minutes before I need to be out the door. "Any chance you're available for dinner tonight after work? Kara will be home. But if it's too much—"

"Tonight?" She pushes away from me, and her question hangs in the air. I follow her into my bedroom. What's wrong with me? She must think I'm crazy. I should know better. Wait a few days to call. Or a week. Then make plans. But those are games, and I've never been much for games.

She pulls on her clothes, moving her hands in the air, her lips moving every now and then as if she's having a conversation with herself. I've pushed too far, jumped in too quickly. It's something I do. Or did. "Forget about tonight. I'll give you a call. We can figure something out."

She trails a finger through my chest hair then stands on tiptoes to press her soft lips to mine and makes me second guess the last twenty-four hours when she quips, "Tell you what. Let me consult the Magic 8-Ball."

SEVEN

Delilah

As I step out onto Pierrepont Street for the second time in one day, my phone vibrates. I keep the thing on vibrate during the day at work, and then more often than not forget to turn it off. When I flip it over, I see the name Melinda Daniels. Mom. I click to decline the call and stride with purpose to the door. I've declined a lot of calls—she's going to slip into hysterics soon, so I shoot off a quick text telling her I'll call back tomorrow, then press the button for 8D.

In my office earlier today, I consulted mystical, magical Magic 8-Ball. Anna gives me crap for consulting the fates, but she lacks faith. I let the die roll through the dark waters after vigorous shakes. The answers I received, in order, were Signs Point to Yes, Reply Hazy, Try Again, and Outlook Good. Clear guidance to return to his apartment this evening.

The buzzer sounds, and I step into the marble foyer. I bounce from foot to foot in the elevator, humming the tune to a random Shin's song called *New Slang*. The phrase *life-changing* pops in my head as the elevator doors open. Mason stands in the hall, to the side of the elevator, and a young girl peeks out from behind his legs. She's barefoot and wearing a silk pajama dress designed to imitate Cinderella's gown. Wet, brown hair grazes her shoulders, and she twists back and forth, one arm firmly wrapped around her daddy's thigh.

I bend down to her height and hold out my hand. She stares at it. I'm a moron, trying to shake hands with a kid. I drop it and give her my biggest, warmest smile while looking into her doe-like brown eyes. "Hi. I'm Delilah. I love your gown. It's beautiful."

A glow spreads over her aura as she grins so big I can see dark gaps from the teeth she's sacrificed to the tooth fairy.

"It's Cinderella."

"I love it." I smile and shift forward onto my knees. "Are you Kara?"

She nods and peers down to the floor. Then, as if she's come to a decision, she lifts her head and steps away from her daddy. "Wanna come inside? We made dinner."

"You did? I'd love to come inside!" I've spent tons of time around kids. First, at summer camp, helping out with the younger girls. Then as a camp counselor, working with all the campers. Plus, my mom's cousins live nearby, and they're all younger than me. This should be easy, but this uber happy cheery voice of mine comes across a bit like I'm one of the lollipop kids from *The Wizard of Oz.*

As I push off my knees to rise, Mason offers his hand to help me up. His touch calms the fluttering inside. I've known him less than three days, yet a déjà vu sensation surrounds me, as if I've seen my hand in his a thousand times. It's only the two of us in the hall. He holds the door cracked open, ensuring us both privacy and that we aren't about to get locked out in the hall, and presses a soft kiss to my lips. A thrill courses through me.

His breath tickles my ear when he leans to share, "My mom's here too. She was dropping Kara off, but she'll be leaving soon."

There's a hint of concern in his tone. I get it. Meeting both his daughter and his mom in one day is a lot. But I can do this. He's introducing me to his daughter as a friend, for crying out loud. It's not like I'm dreaming of forever, but our new little thing rocks amazingly good vibes. I do my best to beam positivity up at him and let him know I'm more than okay and excited to meet the other woman in his life.

As I step through the door, a tall, attractive woman with dark hair and familiar emerald eyes, the exact color of Mason's, loops the strap of a beaten-up leather handbag over her shoulder. She smiles at me and extends her hand. "Hi. I'm Cindy, Mason's mom."

She has a warm handshake, and every part of me joneses to pull her in for a hug. At first, I hesitate, then I jolt forward and wrap my arms around her. She laughs for a second, a bit surprised. I'm not. We southerners often embrace, but I've gathered not all New Yorkers are as into skin to skin contact greetings.

She recovers and pats my back. Then she addresses Mason. "So, what are your plans with Amber?" She's frowning, and her arms are crossed. It's as if I walked in in the middle of a conversation she has no intention of dropping. I step back to give them space. Kara's on the sofa, oblivious to the conversation around her, watching a cartoon.

"I'll let you know." He sounds like he's attempting to appease or comfort her.

If that's the case, he misses his mark. Her lips are tucked in so tightly, little lines run above and below her lips.

"Okay." She doesn't sound okay with whatever they're talking about.

It's a private conversation, and, yes, I am listening in. *Who is Amber?*

When she steps back, she pats my upper arm and offers, "It's nice to meet you, Delilah." Then she adds, "Hope you all have a nice dinner."

Mason's deep voice resonates from behind me. "Mom, you don't have to leave. You can stay and eat with us."

"Oh, no. I've got to get home and unpack. Get ready for the rest of the week. Returning on a Monday has me feeling behind schedule." She walks in front of the sofa, bends down to Kara's height, and holds her arms out. "Give Ama a hug."

Kara falls forward into her arms and wraps her grandmother in a super tight squeeze. Then she sits back on the sofa, attention glued to the television. "Love you, Ama." I smirk, thinking to myself that what she's not saying is, *Get out of the way so I can see my cartoon.*

Cindy drops a kiss to the top of her head then makes her way to the door. She waves farewell to me as she offers a polite, "Hope to see you again."

Mason gives her a hug then opens the door for her. She flattens her palm on Mason's chest and says in a low voice she might think I can't hear, "Please, think of Kara."

Mason mumbles something before kissing her on the forehead and closing the door behind her.

Kara pounces on the sofa like a kangaroo. The screen on the TV is still. Her show must have ended. "Daddy! Let's see if it's ready." Then to me, she announces with glee, "We're having spaghetti and meatballs. My pick."

I grin. "Perfect."

From behind me, I hear Mason add, "I hope you don't mind."

I wave him off as I grab Kara's hand and bounce with her into the kitchen to assist with dinner preparations.

The three of us set the table and carry the food from the kitchen as if we're repeating a daily activity, like a seamless team. Kara counts out three napkins and three forks and directs me to the heavy plates she's not allowed to carry because they are so big. As she and I set the table, Mason enters with a steaming mountain of pasta covered with red marinara sauce and meatballs.

Kara sprints to the kitchen and comes back with the breadbasket. She beams up at me. "Garlic bread." Her eyes light up as if she's offering the best food on the planet.

As Kara rattles on about the sandcastles she saw at the beach and the live sand dollar she'd saved by returning it to the ocean, Mason's eyes catch mine. Sometimes he winks, sometimes he reaches out and plays with my fingers. At times, his fingers wander up and down my thigh. Our legs touch the entire dinner. He's not particularly great at the stealth business, but Kara's oblivious, so it doesn't really matter.

A mixture of happiness and peacefulness swirl through me. Borderline bliss. The table doesn't have decorations. No candles or flowers. My table growing up would have been adorned with both. The napkins would have been cloth. We would have had a lot more utensils on the table. But every little thing, from the frayed rectangular placemats to the freshly scrubbed chubby cheeks beaming back at me from across the table, smack me as perfect. If anything, my mind reels and goes a tad fuzzy from the perfection of it all. It's a moment in time when I find myself taking a mental photo so I'll never forget it. I want to bottle this emotion and place it on my memory shelf to never be forgotten.

"Do you wanna color?" Kara asks me at the end of dinner. When I tell her I'd love to, she squeals and runs to get crayons and a coloring book and crawls into my lap. She rips out a page for me to color my own picture, but within minutes, she and I are both working on her black and white image of the prince bending to slip the glass slipper onto Cinderella's dainty foot. Kara informs me she will do the princess, but she really doesn't like coloring in the prince, so, "You wanna do him?"

I am diligently coloring in black boots when Kara wails, "I messed it up." She's one of those kids. It's gotta be perfect. I lift a blank piece of construction paper from the table and sketch the outline of her princess.

She looks at me with awe. "You can do that?"

Such a cutie pie. "Yep. Want me to teach you how?"

She nods vigorously.

"I'll hunt down some learning to draw books.

They make them for different levels. How does that sound? I'll find a good one, and we'll do it together."

Mason clears the table and cleans the kitchen while she and I color between the lines. When he finishes, he steps up behind the sofa, a dish towel between his hands, and announces, "Squirt, it's time."

"Noooooo," Kara wails, squirming in my lap and leaning back into me as if I can save her from Daddy's rules.

Such a cute little stinker. Every kid pushes off bath and bedtime. Or at least, I did.

He grins, and the amount of love shining through when he looks at his daughter brings on a wave of emotion. He looks at Kara the same way my dad used to look at me. His steps alter, and he lumbers over, monster style, until he scoops a squealing, giggly girl off my lap and twirls her through the air, spinning around and throwing her up in the air. Peals of laughter fill the room along with squeals of "Daddy!"

He carries her to her bedroom, throwing her in the air every step or two. How in the world is that child going to go to sleep after being thrown around like a ball? As they disappear into her bedroom, I lean back in my chair and pick up my phone. A text from Mom flashes on the screen.

Melinda: Did you meet someone?

I roll my eyes. I've been living in Manhattan for four years now. All four of those years, I've been hounded by the question, "Did you meet someone?" Her entire prayer group prays I will not fall in love in New York and will return home soon. I rub my finger over the rounded corner of my phone. My finger hovers over my mail icon, and I tap it.

The email from one of my dad's business partners sits below a new email from Anthropologie. I swipe to remove the junk then open the business email. I reread it. He wants to schedule a meeting. He would prefer an in-person meeting, but if not, he'd like to schedule a conference call. I stare at the *to* and *cc* fields for the tenth time. My father is not included.

Mason's head pops out from the doorway. "Your presence is requested, if you don't mind."

I drop the phone on the coffee table and jump up. "Absolutely."

Mason lies down on one side of the narrow bed, and I snuggle next to Kara on the other side. A stack of books sits on the end of the bed. Mason reads through them all, animating his voice to match characters. Kara giggles for each and every female voice and monster voice. By the time he's flipping through a well-worn copy of *Goodnight Moon*, Kara's eyelids are half closed, and Mason's voice has lowered to a barely audible level. By the time he's breathing the words, "goodnight moon," she's off in dreamland.

He bends over her, places a kiss on her forehead, then her cheek, and tucks the covers in all around her. Everything about Kara's bedtime routine reminds me of mine growing up, and I'm filled with a desire to call my parents to tell them how much I love them. I have no business dodging Mom's calls.

Mason wraps his hand around mine, glancing over his shoulder one more time to take in his sleeping daughter, then flicks off the light as he pulls the door closed.

When we reach the sofa, he lifts me onto his lap. He brushes my hair off my shoulder before bringing me in for a long, slow, kiss. He tastes like garlic and mint. He squeezes my ass, and I kiss his neck.

He fingers my hair then gently rubs his thumb across the edge of my lower lip. "How was that?"

"Good." I curl up onto the sofa beside him. "You are so sweet with your daughter." I rub the stubble on his jaw and stroke his hair. "She's wonderful."

He smiles. "She is. She likes you."

"I like her."

"It's not too much for you?" His forehead wrinkles as he asks the question.

"What?"

"All this. Family life. We don't bore you?" His hold on my hips tightens.

"Not at all. I guess I might have a thing for older men." He pinches my thigh, and I squirm. "No. Art is my shindig. And I have fun with kids. I've always enjoyed spending time with them. That's probably why I was a camp counselor for so many summers. This is good. I had fun tonight."

"Yeah, but she can be exhausting. When she's awake, she's non-stop."

"Unless she's watching a show." I place a soft kiss on his knuckle. His hands are weirdly fucking hot. Those long fingers.

He sighs, and guilt flashes across his face. "I try to keep the electronics to a minimum."

"You're a good dad."

Mason dimmed the lights when we re-entered the den after putting Kara down, and the reflection glows on the posters of puppies, kittens, and horses intermixed with Kara's artwork. The walls are an unfettered declaration of his love for Kara. A weight presses on my chest, a stark contrast to the lightness and almost giddiness of the last couple of days.

Mason pulls me close and tilts my head up for a kiss. As the kiss deepens, my need for release grows, but then a colored Winnie the Pooh taped on the wall behind Mason's head enters my peripheral vision. I break the kiss.

In a whisper, I ask, "Should we be doing this? She's right there." I point where I can see the visible gap below her door, meaning there's a space where nothing blocks noises from in here, or from his bedroom, for that matter. I glance at my watch. It's after nine p.m. I've got at least a thirty-minute cab ride to get home.

He caresses my hip and thigh. "You can stay the night, but if you think it's too soon, I get it."

"It's just, don't you think that's a lot for her? She just met me today. Aren't there guidelines we should follow? How would you explain a friend sleeping over?" Kids have friends sleep over. But would she see it the same way? And I told him my life was complicated, but I haven't fully downloaded. This whole thing between us, it might feel good for right now, but it's not going to go anywhere.

A low chuckle rises from his chest. "Are you asking what the parenting rulebook says? As opposed to the Magic 8-Ball?"

That comment deserves a tickle. I grab for him, and we laugh.

When he has me in check, he continues. "There are about a million parenting books on the shelves, and they all say different things. I stopped reading them somewhere around year two or three when I realized no one recommends the same nap schedule, but they are all quite firm in their beliefs."

His fingers play in my hair as he stares off somewhere over my shoulder. I relax into him and revel in the tingling sensation dancing along my scalp as he toys with my hair. He seems to have a thing for my hair.

A long, loud exhale flows out of Mason. It sounds like he's thought things through, and he doesn't like his conclusion. "As much as I want you to stay, it might be confusing to her in the morning. I've never dated anyone since...well, since Amber."

I lift my eyebrows. Amber. Yes, I had wanted to ask about her, but we'd been entertaining Kara for hours.

He answers my unspoken question. "Kara's mom. Amber is Kara's mom. Dating. It's new. For me. For Kara. Let me do some research on this. Figure out what those books say to do."

"So, when you said your life is really complicated, were you talking about Amber?"

"Yeah. She's recently returned to New York."

"Don't feel pressure from me. You take care of you and Kara."

He kisses me then rests his forehead on mine. "Thank you."

"For what?"

"For caring. For coloring. For being fun." His thumb rubs over my knuckles as he holds my hand. "I haven't had this much *fun* in ages."

I can't suppress the grin on my face. I run my nails over his scalp then shift over him to straddle his lap. In the dim light, the green in his eyes darkens to a mossy brown. "I do date a lot."

He frowns.

"I mean, I go on a lot of dinner dates. A lot of nothing. Get to know you, like a speed date but longer. It's usually over by date three. I've lived in Manhattan for four years, and I don't think I've made it past date three the entire time I've been here. You're the first guy I've dated that I do want to see again. You're the first guy I've cared enough about to make a voodoo doll for."

The corners of his lips round up ever so slightly. Not a smile, not quite a smirk. But no longer a frown. "Aren't voodoo dolls a bad thing?

"Oh, yeah. Almost always. So, take heed." I tap his nose with my index finger. "One wrong move, mister, and you've got a black magic mistress spinning her wares."

He smiles then squeezes my hand. "There's nothing for you to worry about. At all." He traces the outside curves of my breast and adds, with a low, guttural sigh, "I'm the one who should be worried."

My chest tightens and constricts my ability to breathe. Once again, he kisses me, and the clamp on my chest lightens. If emotions were color, then at this moment, every shade of blue, yellow, and red would be swirling through, with bright specks of white thrown in as a safety to keep it all from blending too dark. He stills my hips and slides me toward his knees, away from his crotch. "Let me walk you out. If you stay longer, I'm not going to be able to stop myself."

I leap at the chance to break away from these

intense emotions and climb off him. "I'll head out now."

"Let me slip on my shoes."

"What? No way. Stay here with Kara."

We have *fun* in the hall while awaiting the elevator. Nibbling and kissing, restrained because we're both aware one of the other apartment doors could open at any moment. And the elevator is coming. When it arrives within minutes, I'm out of breath, warm and giddy.

The elevator door closes, and on my own, my insides sink as the elevator descends. I'm hazy with where we left things. We were skirting the idea of more. Of dating. And dating is probably asinine. It's a nonsensical option. I smash my head against the wall of the elevator as my emotions swirl and my vexing conscience flares to life.

———

Nestled into the back of the yellow cab, I stare at my dark phone screen. Have I met someone?

Yes, Mom. I have. Holy Mother, Mary, and Angels, I have. And oh, sugar magnolia, am I confused.

· · ·

I press my mom's name in my contact list, and within the first ring, she answers. "Delilah, where have you been? It's been days." There's a pause, and before I can get any words out, she repeats her texted question. "Have you met someone?"

I hear my dad's stern warning in the background. "Melinda."

I exhale, and a damn breaks and words gush uncontrolled out of my mouth like a river after a hurricane. "Yes, I've met someone." There's a faint gasp but I plow on, an unfettered, overflowing flood of information. "His name's Mason. He's a vet. Mom, he's amazing. He has a little girl. She's four years old. You'd adore her. She has art all over her walls. Like, in a way you would never have allowed. Unless it was in your art studio. And even then, it's over the top. Art everywhere. She loves all the princesses, but her favorite one is the one with red hair and a bow and arrow. She also says she likes *Princess and the Frog,* more now because I'm from New Orleans. How cute is that? She's just the cutest little sweetheart with chubby cheeks and hands. And, Mom, he's the kindest guy. He's raising this beautiful little girl, all on his own, while running his own veterinary clinic. His motto in life is to be kind to all things. I mean, have you ever? He's good. He's just...he's really...

he has the most beautiful eyes. Like, such a unique color you'll want to paint them, but you probably won't be able to get the color right."

A memory of him over me in bed, taking me in, thrusting deep inside streams through my head, and I stop talking as heat warms my cheeks. I cross my legs and stare out at the blur of the city lights as the cab whizzes through the streets.

My mother's voice brings me back. "Delilah, how did you meet him?" She sounds markedly reserved. It's the same tone I hear her use when she needs to commandeer the garden club ladies.

A vision of Chewie dry heaving plays through my mental video, making me wince. "Well, that's a bit of a story. You see, I was dog sitting for Anna, and Chewie had some issues." I pause. "And Mason is her vet. He saved Chewie's life." My tone lifts at this last point. For constellation's sake, he's a hero. It hits me then that the last time I tried to talk up a guy to Mom was when I was in high school and I tried to convince her to let me date Luke Nollen after he'd been written up in the paper the week before for drinking underage.

"Dear, he has a child."

"Yes, I know, Mom. And you'll love her. She's adorable."

"I'm sure she is. But, honey, a different dating

etiquette is required for single parents. You can't lightly date someone when you have a child. And you will be moving home soon."

"Yes, Mom, I am eventually going to move home. But I have time." For crying out loud, twenty-six is the new sixteen. There's no rush. I will move. One day. I'm not being that bad, am I?

"Delilah, we agreed. No serious relationships. Your time in New York is meant for you to spread your wings. And it's been four years. We agreed on three. Don't you miss your home? Your family?" The unspoken phrase I hear is, *Don't you miss me?*

"Oh, Mom. I promise, I will come home. As planned. This isn't a serious relationship." The automatic denial flows out while, inside, nausea rises.

"He has a child."

I squirm like a kid who asked for king cake instead of dinner and is at the receiving end of the smackdown glare. "But, Mom, when you meet them, you're gonna love them. Really."

"There is no reason for me to meet someone you're not going to marry, Delilah. And a child. You need to end this. End it before it starts. Listen to me on this. For all your sakes, end this before it starts."

EIGHT

DELILAH

Mom's words bounce through my head Monday night and follow me to work Tuesday morning. On one hand, she's probably right. There's no long-term future. I'm an only child. Of course, I'm not leaving my parents to fend for themselves. And then there's Bayou Development, our multigeneration family company. But there's no deadline to make it home. And how often does someone like Mason come along? He's gorgeous, and the sexual chemistry is out of this world. His tongue, and his thumb, and his fingers, and Jesus, Mother, Mary, and Angels, he knows what he's doing with his manly part. Love comes in all shapes and sizes. What if Mason is supposed to be my love right now? What if he's part of my life's journey, and he's a critical part in my personal development?

My phone vibrates, and I reach over to grab it from the charger on my desk.

Olivia: SOS. Need you both to meet me for lunch. Little Beet? Noon?

The text is to Anna and me. After double-checking my schedule, I agree to meet. A lunch with friends is exactly what I need. I haven't been particularly productive this morning, anyway. I completed some mindless work, adjusting a few layouts to additional sizes for the new media plan, but I need to do some concept development. But before I can create, I need air.

Little Beet is right around the corner from our office. It's a quick lunch spot with windows everywhere. Clean white tile covers select walls, adding to the modern, bright aesthetic. Anna and I arrive together. Olivia's waiting outside by the door. The wind whips around a few dried, crumpled leaves, and random pieces of trash, as we approach.

It's a struggle, but I figure out the odd menu options and make my way to the table with my orange plastic tray of food. Anna and I don't say anything as we wait for Olivia. My confusion over Mason has me moody and down and a touch cross, an overall emotional space I don't frequent often. Right now, I want to slam my ass down at a table and dump all the crap running through my head and vent like an angry madwoman, but this is Olivia's SOS.

She sits down, presses her shoulders back, and sits straight as if she's an account director starting a status meeting. I tap my fork and foot in rhythm and wait. She squares her shoulders and announces, "I moved in with Sam."

Whoa. Not expecting that one.

Anna's eyes go wide like saucers. I push my plate away, and say, "Let's hear it." Olivia jerks back at my statement, so I continue. "That's the emergency, right? What you need to talk to us about?" How can she be so crazy to move in? They just met. It takes time for relationships to develop into serious mode. More than a few weeks.

"Yes and no," Olivia says, her words slow, as if she's thinking about what she wants to say. "It's so crazy, I don't know where to begin." She twiddles her fingers around her coffee.

Oh, Olivia, sweet Olivia. She's Anna's old roommate. She up and left for Prague after one guy hurt her. I didn't meet her until she returned from her sojourn, and we've hung out quite a bit. She seems strong and in a good place. The last thing she needs is to get strung up on yet another dud.

Her eyes glaze over, and she gets to the point. "Sam has a stalker."

Anna says nothing. It's clear she is trying to figure out how to talk her out of moving in with a brand-new guy in a diplomatic, warm, happy way. An Anna technique my mom could benefit from adopting. I roll my hand dramatically, gesturing for her to continue, so Olivia will spill the rest of what she must recognize borders insanity.

"It's crazy, but she's stalking me now. My choices were to move in with him or have him hire me a full security detail. So, I moved in with him."

Stalker? So, there's more to this. She hasn't decided she's fallen in love and is on a forever plan. Stalker sounds bat shit crazy. But at least she's not falling in love overnight. I'm not crazy to think that simply does not happen. A sense of relief sweeps over me. I exhale and attempt to focus on the matter at hand. "Do you want this or not? Because if you don't want to move in with him, he can totally afford a security detail for you."

"How do you know how much a security detail costs?"

What the feck does it matter how much a security detail costs? She's dating a freaking billionaire. I huff. "I do know a thing or two. And I don't know exactly how much one costs, but Mr. Megabucks can afford it. Well, do you want to move in with him? Are you that serious about him? How long have you been dating?"

Anna wakes up out of her shocked stupor and gets all defensive of our whackadoodle friend. "Hey, chill. Sam's a good guy. They'll work it out."

"I am chill. I'm asking a question. It's an important question." *To me.* It's an important question. No one falls in love that quickly. Jeez. She's in the enjoyment phase. The period of time where they enjoy each other, learn from each other, and grow. Maybe it's love, but it's way too early to know it's a forever love. Sometimes love lasts, like, a week. Sometimes it lasts a month. We fall in and out of love all the time. Right? There are songs about this. Who dates someone for a month and then says, 'This is it for me?' The whole idea makes me want to throttle someone.

"Sshhhh." Olivia hushes me. "I want it, okay? Yes, it's moving our relationship to another level, but I'm ready. And I was looking for an apartment anyway."

"When, exactly, were you apartment hunting?" This is such bullshit. She's lying to herself.

"Well, it was on my to-do list." Olivia sounds like a spoiled kid defending her purchase of a chihuahua she can fit in her Louis Vuitton pocketbook. I should know. I've been that kid with an Elle Woods crush.

"How long have you been seeing him? Like, a month? How can you know he's the one after a month?" She's practically glaring at me now, but I don't care. Someone has to be a good friend here. That's why she called this emergency meeting and invited yours truly.

"I didn't say he was the one. I said things are good, and this feels like a natural progression." She straightens her napkin and fork and lifts her head as if daring me to continue *being her friend*.

Anna, ever the mediator, jumps in. She places her hand over mine, and says, "Hey, calm down." I huff and stare down at the table as she attempts to coax me. "It's okay. If anything goes wrong, we'll be there for Liv, okay? And if things are still progressing, then she's right where she needs to be, and she's safe. Safe. Okay?"

Anna then shifts her focus to Olivia.

"Now, tell us more about this stalker. And are you in any real danger?"

"Well, you remember the dark-haired girl I met at school? She's hung out with us some? Lindsey?"

Lindsey? I've met up with her a few times since Olivia introduced us. "Yeah?"

"She's the stalker. She's not a student at Columbia after all. She's been stalking Sam for years." I stare out the window, and Olivia's voice kind of floats in and out as she continues her explanation. She hasn't threatened Olivia, so that's good. It sounds like she's been obsessed with her billionaire boyfriend for years, like a celebrity kind of fatal attraction.

"Holy shit," Anna responds. "That's insane. Do you think she'd hurt you?" she asks. Sweetheart Anna. Nurturing to the core.

"I don't think so. I mean, did either of you get that vibe from her?" Olivia asks, her question directed more to me, given I spent time with her.

No, I don't think she'll hurt Olivia, so I slowly shake my head. Lindsey's a wild child for sure. Lots of fun to go drinking at the bars with. Dang, this means one less friend to go bar hopping with. All my friends are coupling off. Did someone decree everyone has to pair off after twenty-five?

"What's worse is...he hooked up with her," Olivia blurts.

Okay, so this drama is straight out of *People* magazine. I twirl my fork in my fingers. "That may be what kicked the obsession off. But who knows? Do you remember the stalker who killed that girl on that TV show? *My Sister Sam?*"

Anna twists in her seat and kicks me under the table. "Delilah, please!"

I tune out and eat. I should care more, but I can't get out of my head. It sounds like her boyfriend's got it under control, and there's no real danger. And this craziness has Olivia leaping over a hundred relationship milestones and into his home. Moving in together is a huge decision. One she shouldn't take lightly. And it doesn't seem plausible she could develop deep emotions for someone within a few weeks. Not let's-move-in-together emotions. It's one thing to have let's-have-sex-frequently emotions, but moving-in-together emotions? Come on, now, peeps.

I stare out the window and flip my plastic fork through my lunch as annoyance and anger simmer. I'm not sure where these emotions are coming from, and that fact alone is not sitting well with me. I should be concerned for Olivia, but instead, her jumping into a relationship is all I can focus on, and the idea really ticks me off. This isn't me. I'm not the judgmental sort.

I try to focus back in on the conversation but can't. Mason keeps infiltrating my thoughts. His smile. His touch. Our night. And morning. This is normal. But then there's something else. This knot in my stomach and a heaviness on my chest. I'm uneasy. I am not one to get emotional over a guy.

I still want to see Mason. Is that so bad? Can't I enjoy a few relationship milestones of my own before I end my "me" time? He might have a kid, but it's not like I'm going to pull an Olivia and move in with him in the next two months. From Kara's perspective, I'm a friend. And what Olivia is doing is just off the charts insanity. I'm not like her at all. She's one of those girls who jumps from serious relationship to serious relationship. That's not me. As a matter of fact, I am her polar opposite.

NINE

The chalkboard sign reads *Your Pets Will Love Us. We Shih Tzu Not.*

Sleep-deprived, a perma-frown has been sitting on my face all morning. But this chalkboard sign. Bet has me smirking before I pull open the door. Whatever they are paying their magenta-haired receptionist, I'd bet it's not enough. Bet's got it going on. They need to keep this marketing genius.

Two dog owners, one cat owner, and someone holding a cage with a towel over it, containing what I hope is something harmless and feathery, like a parakeet, sit spaced out among the chairs in the waiting room. Bet's face lights up when she sees me. Mason said he eats lunch at one o'clock. The waiting patients have me second-guessing my surprise, but there's no packing up now. I've been spotted.

Bet slides the window open and leans over the slim counter. "Hey, there, sweetheart. How's your baby?"

"She's doing good. All better. Home with her mommy now and happy as can be."

The door behind Bet opens, and Ashley's head pops out like she's searching for someone, then disappears behind the door again.

Bet's oblivious to the action to the side of her, as she smiles at me with a hopeful expression. "Are you looking to adopt? I can help you if you are. We have the most adorable puppies right now at the humane society where I volunteer. There's this one puppy, oh, my goodness." Her hands go to her heart, and she rocks her entire chest left and right as if hugging the referenced bundle of joy. She's a hoot.

"I'm not sure I'm ready for that kind of responsibility. Need I remind you? I almost killed a dog recently. Let's give it some time. I stopped by to see if Mason is around."

As the words stumble out of my mouth, the door behind her opens once more. Mason steps out, and the moment he sees me, those enigmatic orbs shine and a smile spreads across his face. Within seconds, he's through the second door into the waiting room and his arms are around me, circling my waist and pulling my body close to his.

"To what do I owe this pleasure?"

His instant warm embrace fills me with a bubbly, fizzy sensation. The warmth from his touch and the low rhythm of his heartbeat also soothe as I return his hug, blinking away my awe at my physical reaction. I whisper, fully aware we have an audience, "I thought I'd surprise you for lunch."

He pops a quick kiss on my lips and spins me toward the door. He's in scrubs, and the way he ushers me out, situating my body in front of his as a shield, has me giving him the side eye. As soon as we spill out to the sidewalk and the chilly winter air, his fingers weave through mine. "Don't you need a coat?"

He grins. "Nope. I wasn't prepared for my reaction to holding you. These scrubs hide nothing. Had to get out of there fast. Trust me. The cold air is a good solution."

He runs his thumb over my knuckles as we

charge New York style down the sidewalk. "Are you guys busy today?"

"Normal day. Lots of check-ups. You okay with a deli?"

I nod, and he ducks into a deli with a back area of tables for eating. There are no windows, and it's a little dark and cramped down toward the back, so not my first choice for lunch, but I'm with Mason, so it'll do. And he doesn't have much time.

We stand at the counter, and I order a Greek salad and sparkling water. He orders a Philly cheesesteak and grabs a root beer out of the nearby refrigerator. Before Mason finishes ordering his lunch, my requested salad, taken straight out of a refrigerator, is pushed across the counter to me. The plastic top condenses from the change in temperature. Salad may not be the specialty here. Small pink square tiles dot the floor of the back room, and blackish grout fills the gaps. I check out the table, and it looks clean enough, so I sit. One bald man with spectacles, the *New York Post* in one hand and half of a giant sub in the other, sits in a back table.

"Do you come here a lot?" It's not the kind of place I'd pick, but some of these little hole-in-the-wall delis pack a surprise with insanely delicious sandwiches.

He shakes his head, both arms resting on the table with his gaze fixed solidly on me. "Nope. I'm more of a street vendor or pack my lunch kind of guy, but I figured you'd want to sit. And the PB&J I packed from home can be my afternoon snack."

A man with a heavily stained white apron steps into the dining area and delivers a foot-long sandwich wrapped in shiny silver foil. The enormous sandwich could feed a family of four. When Mason sets it down on the table, it almost spans the entire length of the brown plastic top table, but Mason expresses zero surprise or dismay in the size. I sit, gobsmacked, as he unwraps the top portion and prepares to bite into it. He glances at me, sets it down, unrolls it, then picks up half. That's good. Watching him hold the equivalent of a loaf and eat it with two hands left me unsettled, if a bit mesmerized.

"They have the best Philly cheesesteak. Want a bite?" He pushes the greasy, cheesy concoction my way, and I lean over for a small bite. I close my eyes in ecstasy because, holy moly. The cheese and meat and crispy white toasted bread with a hint of butter blend seamlessly. I moan, and his eyes darken. I know that look. "Do you have plans tonight?"

I flip the plastic lid off my salad. It's drenched

in dressing and feta cheese. Digging my plastic fork through the lettuce, I search for any brown edges. "Yeah, I do. Wednesday night is my yoga class. I've already signed up."

He pulls two napkins out of the container on the table and sets them up like a placemat then places half his sandwich on them. Maybe it's a good thing he has a PB&J for an afternoon snack, because I'm totally eating his half of the sandwich he laid out for me.

"Tomorrow night?"

"Nope." I shake my head. "No plans."

"Come over for dinner again."

"Will Kara be there?"

"Yeah, she wants to see you. She's been thumbing through our cookbooks searching for the right recipe to make for her new friend." He flicks his finger on my nose. "You."

"Are you sure that's a good idea? I mean, I don't know. She's a kid." The sandwich attracts my focus, and I momentarily forget what I'm talking about as I take a big bite of buttery, cheesy goodness.

"She is a kid. She's my kid. And you're my girlfriend. Right?"

I almost choke on the meat and cheese I hadn't quite swallowed. Girlfriend? "What?" I grab my

Diet Coke in an attempt to help the sandwich go down. Once I'm safe from requiring the Heimlich maneuver, I set my drink down. "Girlfriend? That's a compound word."

He squints, and he's kind of smiling, but I'm not. No, not at all. "So, not ready to take it there yet?"

"No. That's big. That's huge. It's a double. It's two words." I thrust two fingers in the air. He has to understand. He has a kid. This can't be what he wants. I'm his kid's friend.

He takes an enormous bite of his sandwich, and we both sit in silence. He sets the sandwich down and wipes the grease off his fingers with a napkin. "Are you seeing other guys?"

"Mason, it's been less than a week. When would I see other guys?"

He peers up at the ceiling then back at me. "Yeah. You're right. You're absolutely right. Sometimes I jump into things. It's a problem I have. Sorry." A sheepish, barely there smile appears. "No double words. Got it."

Doubt fills me. Oh, Mylanta, was Mom right? How is Kara gonna feel when I move away? And what is up with Mason? Guys don't jump in like this. This is not normal behavior. I shift in my seat. It's this hard plastic seat, and it's impossible to sit comfortably with a bony tush like mine.

His knees nudge mine. "Hey. We'll take it day by day. Okay? And to Kara, you're a friend. She doesn't know what dating is. Not really. She's happy to have a new friend." I shift my feet so they cross with his below the table, and my muscles relax. "She hung your art up on the wall. The drawing you sketched and she colored."

Those verdant eyes stare into mine, and he reaches under the table and squeezes my knee. A frisson of energy passes through, and I have this odd desire to push back the table and climb on his lap, to pretend we're all alone and the bald man in the corner doesn't exist. "I'd love to come over tomorrow night to hang out. Have Kara pick out a recipe and then send it over to me. Tell her the two of us are going to cook for you. Oh, I forgot. Here's some lotion." I pull a tube of hand lotion I brought for him.

"Thank you?" he asks. There's no telling what he's thinking.

"For your hands. You wash your hands so much. Dry skin. Use it."

He pulls me close and kisses me. It's one of those kisses that leaves you stunned, and warm, and filled with happy. He murmurs in my ear, "Are you still asking that 8-Ball about us?"

I slowly shake my head and smile.

He pops a quick kiss on my lips. "Good."

I'm still replaying our lunch date when I return to the office. One particular word keeps coming to mind. *Girlfriend.* I haven't been someone's girlfriend since college. There I was, so critical of Olivia, and I'm getting compound-worded within a week of the first date.

I round my desk and find a tangerine Post-It note affixed to the front of my monitor. It's from my boss, Maxwell, asking me to come to his office when I'm back from lunch. I glance at my watch, immediately calculating to determine if I've overextended my lunch hour. It's no secret around the office that I take my hour for lunch. I'm not like Anna. The whole 'first to the office and last to leave' thing never worked for me. I'll work hard during the day, but I'm not going to kill myself trying to climb the proverbial ladder.

I lift the Post-It and head to his office, fiddling with the paper as I round the cubicle maze to his office. When I tap the frame, he peers over his monitor. "Hi. Can you close the door?"

Well, goosh ah tah. That's never a good sign. I close the door and drop into one of the seats across from his desk. He steps around and takes the seat next to mine. I shift, sit up straighter, and inch my chair a few inches away from him. Body space and all.

Maxwell smiles, then leans across his desk for his notepad and pen, drops back into his seat, crossing one leg over his knee, and places the notepad on his thigh. He's a good guy. We've never had any issues. I thought he liked the work I'd done recently for Heineken.

My fingers tap out a beat on the armrests while my knees bounce. "Am I in trouble?"

He laughs out loud. "No. Exact opposite. I called you in here with good news. You have earned a promotion."

"What?" I exclaim. I was promoted from assistant art director to art director about a year ago.

"Yes. As you know, Laura is leaving. You're already doing the same kind of work Laura did, but you aren't managing anyone right now. I believe it's a good point in your career development to gain experience managing others." He flips his notepad around so I can see it. It has the names of the different groups in Creative with circles around them and his name is in the center of all the circles like the sun. So, he's showing me how my group would theoretically fit into his world in some kind of creative person's version of an organizational chart. He continues explaining what the senior art director role would mean, which accounts he'd have me working on, and which employees, meaning physical, live human beings, I would manage.

"I don't have any experience managing people." He pauses in his monologue with a quizzical expression, like I just announced I can't do basic math. Maybe I interrupted him. Probably another reason he should give this idea serious consideration. I hear myself breathing in rapid breaths as if I'm having an out-of-body experience. "Do you offer training?"

He chuckles and sits back in his chair, then lowers his resting leg to the floor. With slow, steady words, he says, "You will be a good manager. You're great with people. Everyone loves you. But why don't you take some time to think about it?"

I enthusiastically nod, my movement so strong that my chest rises and lowers as I rock my body. Yes. Time. Time to think about it. It's a big step. I've been pretty happy with my worker bee status. This whole notion of being responsible for a team, for people's growth and development, nurturing someone else's creative skills, that's a whole big shebang.

Phrases come out of nowhere, my motivational Pinterest board come to life.

One foot in front of the other.

Just keep swimming.

From the acorn grows the tree.

It is only the first step that is difficult.

My bouncing knees still, and I pull my shoulders back, resting my hands on my lap. "I would appreciate some time to consider the promotion. I am grateful for the opportunity, but I do not want to accept the promotion unless I can commit to being in the role. I have some...responsibilities that might require I return home. I would like to give this opportunity the serious consideration it deserves." Yowza. I wish I'd been recording myself. Give it up for sounding professional and adult-like.

"Absolutely. I had heard someone mention you had plans to move home one day. I had hoped this promotion might persuade you to stay." He tosses his notepad onto his desk as he stands, and it lands with a thud. "But I do appreciate your taking this seriously. If you take this position, while we obviously can't require you remain with us for any specific amount of time, we would appreciate it if you planned on committing to remaining in the role for at least another year."

"Of course. Completely agree. Thank you." A massive shock of pain reverberates through my shin, and I shriek, "Mother!" I grip my shin, and see I collided with his ultra-low glass coffee table.

Maxwell peers over at my huddled form. "You're not the first person to do that."

I hold out my index finger, pull back my thumb, mimicking a gun, and cluck my tongue. "Thanks, Cheech." He chuckles again. The man has a low laugh. I force a smile then limp down the hall into Anna's office to debate the merits of accepting an increase in responsibility while squelching that nagging guilt about an ancient promise.

TEN

Kara and I FaceTimed yesterday evening after my yoga class. Her bright, happy face at times filled the screen as if she was an inch away, and other times her iPad would fall, and I'd have a view of the ceiling as she babbled away. She colored in pictures from her Princess coloring book, and I used my set of colored pencils to doodle, and we'd show each other our finished creations. Kara's grandmother, Cindy, flitted around in the background, periodically coming into the screen, but she never joined the conversation.

Kara also planned our menu for tonight. She

chose macaroni and cheese and sausages for dinner. As it turns out, I have a stellar, gooey, yummy family mac and cheese recipe, and I stopped by and picked up a variety of sausages. It's kind of an odd meal, but I did leave the menu up to a kid. I also picked up a nice cabernet for the adults and sparkling grape juice and plastic champagne flutes for Kara because of how much I loved sipping out of them when I was little.

The elevator door opens, and Kara stands before me in the middle of the hall, a huge grin on her face. She leaps forward, arms wide, and gives me a super big hug. I drop my grocery bag on the floor and pick her up and spin her around. She giggles, which gets me all kinds of riled up, and I set her down, grab her hands, and spin so her feet fly out in the air behind her. We go around and around and around with her giggling and me laughing until I come dangerously close to crashing her feet into the side of the hallway, and we both fall down, overcome by dizziness.

I close my eyes, willing the hall to stop spinning but loving the sounds of Kara's laughter. It's like none other. Carefree and full of joy. When I open, Mason crouches in front of me, one hand tickling the little girl on the floor while the other rests on my knee. He's wearing faded jeans, a black short sleeve t-shirt, and a huge smile. He smells freshly showered, and his hair appears damp. He squeezes my knee then straightens to a standing position and helps me up, before scooping a giggling Kara over his shoulder and leading the way down the hall.

Mason holds the door for me, Kara over his shoulder like a sack of potatoes. The moment I pass through the doorway, he closes the door, flips the lock, and wraps an arm around my waist to pull me in for a covert kiss while Kara hangs upside down. The soft press of his lips against mine sends tingles through my whole body. I press a light kiss to his neck and breathe in his earthy musk scent. Then I break away and dart behind him to take over tickling Kara until she's squealing, "Stop! I can't breathe!"

I place a soft kiss on her chubby cheek and head toward the kitchen, calling out, "Come on, girl. We're gonna cook your daddy dinner."

I'm at the kitchen counter unloading the groceries I bought when she catches up with me, her cheeks bright red and her dark pigtails sticking out from the side of her head. I pull one, and she giggles and reaches up, trying to grab the massive messy bun on the top of my head. I did blow out my hair in preparation for tonight, but somehow, my hair always ends up piled on the top of my head by the end of the day. I laugh and pick her up with one arm while dragging out a step stool I spy in the corner. I set it out and place her on it then tap her nose with my finger. "You're gonna be my sous chef."

Mason stands to the side, watching us, a goofy smile plastered on his face. Kara beams. "I'm gonna be the oo chef."

I lift the wine bottle out of my bag and hand it to Mason to put him to work, then I set out the ingredients and help Kara measure and pour it all into a big mixing bowl. As we mix away, I ask Mason to boil the macaroni noodles. Within fifteen minutes, our mac and cheese is in the oven and we're cleaning up the kitchen mess.

"All right, team. Hands in the air!" We high-five, and Kara leaps off the stool, cascading off the counter, and I catch her in mid-air and twirl her in the middle of the cozy kitchen. "What are you doing, little one? You don't hurl yourself into the air." I set the giggling handful onto the floor, and we all high-five again.

Mason's hand rests on my hip then dips slightly lower and squeezes my ass. "You two head into the den. I'll be in with our drinks, and then we can play a game."

Kara opens her mouth wide and gasps, "Candyland!" With big eyes, she asks, "Have you played Candyland, Deelah?" She scrambles from my clutches to the floor and drags me into the den, eager to play.

We spin our way through two loops on the Candyland board before the oven buzzer sounds, and I jump up to check on our cheesy concoction and roll the sausages in the oven. Kara and Mason busy themselves with setting the table.

I show Mason and Kara the champagne flute I brought for her, and her mouth drops open. "So pretty!" she exclaims. "Can I use it, Daddy?"

Mason grins down at her before answering my questioning glance. I drank from these as a kid, and they're plastic. "She usually has to use what we call sippy cups. Or cups with lids." He pours a small amount into the bottom of the flute and guides her back into the main room with the kitchen table. I hear him say, "I need you to be very careful with this, okay?"

"Pomise, Daddy."

I'm opening cabinets searching for a platter for the sausages when Mason comes up behind me and places kisses on my neck. Chills create goosebumps all up and down my arms, and I squeeze my thighs together, attempting to keep the sensations in check. He twists me around and lifts me up on the counter and steps forward between my legs. Then his mouth is on mine, and our tongues are colliding, and he's grinding into me. I forget everything, my mind gone, lost in the physical sensations, until he takes a step back and holds me in place on the counter as if I am the dangerous one.

His chest heaves as he breathes out, "She goes to bed soon. Thirty minutes." He says it low, as if he's talking to himself. Then he holds his hand out, helps me off the counter, opens a cabinet, and pulls out a platter for the sausages. He stares at me like I'm dinner, and yeah, it's not sexy at all, but his hungry, dark stare brings out my giggles.

When we enter the great room, each of us carrying a steaming dish of food, Kara sits at her spot in a raised chair, a smile on her face as she glances between us and her big girl glass. She doesn't say a word, but pride the adult glass remains upright shimmers around her.

I scoop a pile of mac and cheese on her plate, and her mouth opens into a little 'O.' "Dat's a lot!" I look to Mason, wondering if I messed up again somehow.

He chuckles and spears a sausage and deposits it on her plate. As he cuts it up into incredibly tiny pieces, he says, "You don't have to eat all of it, sweetie. Only eat what you want." Then he glances up to me, a bit of a smirk on his face. "I'll eat whatever you don't, baby girl."

She nods as if that makes complete and total sense. She's only four. Of course, she needs a smaller portion. I'm such a dumbnut. He probably tells her she has to eat everything on her plate or some other grown-up nonsense. I can hear my Mom's voice in my head, *'Delilah, if you want dessert, you need to finish what's on your plate.'* Dessert. I remembered sparkling wine but didn't remember dessert. Oh, sugar. I may have rocked it as a camp counselor, but my little kid skills need dusting off.

Mason's hand covers mine. "It's the best meal I've had in a long time. Thank you." He shifts his gaze to his daughter, and she beams, pride and love flowing. She bestows her huge smile on me, and I fight to control the urge to reach out and pinch those chubby, angelic cheeks. They are just so freaking squeezable.

"Can you come tomorrow night too?" she asks in a high-pitched begging voice.

I lean in to pop a kiss on her cheek. I can't help it. Her chubby pink face draws me in. It's yummier than candy.

"Maybe?" I glance at Mason, looking for him to take the lead on this one.

He returns my gaze then raps the table with his knuckle to gain Kara's attention. He bends down slightly so he's closer to her eye level. "Tomorrow night, you're going on a playdate, remember? You'll be with your mommy. Without me?" He's studying her, and his brow wrinkles.

Her eyes sparkle. "My sleepover." She aims her bright smile at me. "It's my first sleepover!" The lines on Mason's forehead relax, and he nods his agreement.

He grins as he glances between the two of us. "If Delilah will agree, while you're at your sleepover, I'd like to take her out to dinner since she's been so nice to cook for us." He looks over to me, and as our eyes meet over her head, adds, "If she's free?" My insides whirl, and my cheeks burn from the constant smile on my face. Gah. Is there anything sexier than a single dad? A single dad veterinarian with dark hair, enigmatic eyes, and earthy good vibes to boot?

"As luck would have it, I am available tomorrow night." I chew on the corner of my lip, playing with it, as I sit, mesmerized by those eyes. For a moment, the art-filled walls slip from view, and all I see is him.

Then Kara's bubbly voice breaks through. "But you won't play games without me, right? Can you play with me dis weekend? When will Mommy bring me home, Daddy?"

"We're gonna play it by ear, pumpkin, remember? If you want to come home, you'll come home Saturday. If you're having fun, then we'll make it a double sleepover and you'll come home Sunday."

Kara reaches out and clutches my index finger. "Can you play Sunday?"

"Of course! Maybe I'll bring my yoga mat over, and we can go to the park and do yoga together."

"Yoga?" she asks with a skeptical squint.

"Yeah. I'll teach you. Oh, girlie, you're gonna love it. Trust me."

"I play soccer." Her eyes go big as she proceeds to tell me about her soccer team and how she scored last weekend. Mason pulls out his phone and shows me photos. There are hundreds of photos, and while it's impossible to tell because they're in uniform, I'd bet all those photos are from one game. She's as cute as can be in her royal blue jersey that almost comes to her knees and her pink shin guards and knee-high socks.

In less than ten minutes, Kara declares herself done, and even though my glass is still almost full of wine, Mason jumps up and carries her down the hall to run the bath. I've eaten enough, but the speedy dinner has my head spinning. I leave our wine glasses on the table while I clear the dishes and tidy up in the kitchen. My phone vibrates. It's Mom calling once again. I hit decline. She would not be happy if she knew I'm here.

When I have everything stowed in the dishwasher and the counter wiped down, I step out into the main hall and spy Mason carrying a toweled-up, giggling burrito into her bedroom. I fall in step behind them and stand in the doorway as Mason rolls open the towel and blows air bubbles all over her belly. Her laughter rings through the room intermixed with, "Daddy, stop!" and "Stop it!" followed by, "Stop!" and then, "I can't breathe!" She's laughing so hard, and the precious sound has me wrapping my arms around myself as my cheek muscles incinerate from my too-wide smile.

After pajamas are on, Mason tucks her in then sits to her side on the bed. She taps the other side of her narrow twin bed and says, "Come read."

I join them, taking the vacant side of Kara, so Mason and I create a Kara sandwich. His arm goes behind her, and he fondles my shoulder discreetly behind Kara's head. We each take turns reading.

She studies each page and sometimes runs a finger over the picture or the words, while Mason and I steal glances over her head. As we read, her eyelids droop, and our words are said more softly until we whisper. Mason lifts the book from her lap and tucks her in. His hand goes to my chin, and leaning over Kara's sleeping form, he places a soft kiss to my lips then we tiptoe out of her bedroom.

He pulls the wooden door closed, taking care to be as quiet as possible, and my gaze once again falls to the two-inch gap below the door. His bedroom door stands directly beside hers, with yet another two-inch gap. Why on Earth did he pick an apartment with his bedroom so close to hers?

The proximity doesn't seem to be what's on his mind. He pulls me into his bedroom, where he slowly closes his door with as much care as he closed hers, then he flips the lock. His eyes darken as he guides me backward to the bed. He caresses my backside, cupping the curve of my ass.

"This dress." He snatches the hem, lifts it up my body, over my head, and tosses it to the floor.

I stand before him in a white lace bra and matching thong. He blinks as if he can't believe what he's seeing. His awestruck expression does all kinds of good things to my insides. I lift my hands to my hair and undo the bun, letting my hair spill down my back. In that moment, under his yearning gaze, I feel alluring and sexy. So often, I round my shoulders to suppress the bulge of my breasts, a habit since middle school, but this time, instead of shame, I revel in knowing that at this moment this man appreciates not only my body, but also me. His bold, hungry gaze fuels my confidence as I reach behind to unsnap my bra then shift to let it drop slowly to the floor.

He swallows as my fingers trace the scruff lining his jaw. I hear him exhale, and in a low strangled voice, he says, "You are so beautiful."

Cool air surrounds my bare nipples as they harden. He feathers his fingers down my shoulder and across my breast then flicks his thumb across the peak of my nipple. I shudder, relishing his rough, warm fingers on my sensitive skin.

A soft tap sounds on the door. We both freeze. "Daddy, I'm thirsty."

Mason swallows as he caresses my breast, and he calls, "Just a minute." Then he whispers in my ear, "Do not get dressed." He crosses the room in broad steps then pauses with his hand on the door-knob as he glances back. I unfreeze and pick my sundress up off the floor and hold it to my chest then slide against the wall, so he can open the door while I remain unseen, assuming she doesn't enter.

He twists the knob and uses his body to shield Kara's view as he closes the door behind him. Nothing suspicious about that at all. He's lucky. Well, we're lucky she's four and not thinking through Daddy's weird behavior.

I climb onto his bed and shift his pillows against the headboard so I can rest my back, clutching the sundress over my breasts self-consciously, fully aware I'm in my panties sitting on a man's bed while he puts his daughter back to sleep in the next room. The whole situation is a bit naughty, and I caress my breasts as I wait. My center throbs with need. I spread my legs and use my fingers over the apex of my thighs, the slight pressure over my clit sending familiar sensations through all my girly parts. I usually masturbate in private on my belly for better pressure. But right now, I'm picturing him walking in on me, lying on my back in full view, bringing myself to climax.

The crotch of my panties is damp. I apply pressure with my thumb, while my finger flits inside, playing along the soft, smooth slickness. The doorknob rotates, and I leave my right hand in my panties but use my left to pull back the sundress.

When the door opens, I'm leaning against the

headboard, legs pressed together, wearing only my lacy white panties, and my hand in the cookie jar, so to speak. Mason stands in the doorway, stupefied. I roll my hips against the pressure, and he springs to action. He closes the door, reaches for a basket of laundry, and dumps all the clothes against the bottom of the door, locks it, and then basically leaps onto the bed.

His lips find mine, hungry and possessive. I am bare, open to him with the exception of a thin strip of fabric. He's fully clothed, an issue I plan to resolve, pronto. I need his clothes gone, his skin against mine. I yank the hem of his t-shirt and pull it up. He breaks from our kiss long enough to rip it off and throw it. My hands shift to his belt and jeans as he takes over, shoving the pants and boxers to the floor. He stands before me, naked. It's impossible to not admire the lines of his pecs over his sculpted, toned abs. The dark hairs trailing down to his swollen, waiting erection. I reach out, my thumb circling the tip, smearing the juice already there, and, with my gaze locked on his, I raise my thumb to my mouth and suck.

Within seconds I'm pressed against the back of the bed. His body covers mine as his mouth claims me, our hands frantically searching and grabbing as I shift to center him between my legs.

His head drops to my breasts, lavishing attention on each nipple, suckling and twirling his tongue as I arch into him.

He growls, "My God, I love this body." I could say the same of his lean, muscular form. He continues sliding down, kissing and licking, until his tongue dips inside, setting me off, and I cry out, overwhelmed with ecstasy as his palm falls over my mouth. "Shhhhh. You've got to be quiet, baby."

"I want you. In me. Now," I gasp.

He trails kisses between my breasts and down my stomach. "No. I want you coming on my mouth." He dips his head and lets that magic tongue free, sucking on my clit as his long finger joins in, and I detonate. My toes curl, and I reach for the pillow on his bed to cover my mouth as I close my eyes to see bright yellow spots behind my lids.

He reaches past me, and I hear a drawer opening, then a rip. He lifts the pillow from my face and lowers to kiss me, our tongues colliding and dancing as he hovers over me, between my legs. I taste myself mixed with him, and I dive in, loving the moment.

In one thrust, he enters me, and we both moan, then it's my turn to say, "Ssshhhhh."

He growls. "Fuck you feel good. So warm. Tight. Perfect."

"You. Too." I thrust up with my hips as I push him to the side. He understands and flips onto his back as he reaches for his cock to re-enter me, letting me ride him the way I want, the way I need.

His hands glide up my stomach to my breasts. "So beautiful."

"And you. So sexy." I angle my hips until he's ramming against my cervix. "Your cock."

He gasps a questioning, "Yeah?"

"I really, really like it."

He grips my hips and slams up into me. "Really likes you too."

My fingers press against my clit as I ride him to my second orgasm, then he flips me once more and thrusts so hard that the headboard hits the wall. I giggle and repeat a "ssshhhh" as he slides out of me and picks me up. The next thing I know, I'm on the floor and he's deep inside, thrusting, chasing his release. His hand dips down, pressing against my clit, mimicking my actions from earlier as he pounds, his movements becoming erratic, and within moments, my legs are shaking as I arch up, my muscles quaking as my cosmos spins out of control. He collapses onto me, sweat covering his torso and dripping down his forehead. I wrap my arms and legs around him, holding him tight.

He pulls back slightly so we can kiss. A slow, deep kiss. My fingers run through his hair and down his arms and back. "I love doing that with you."

He whispers back, a slight sound so subtle the breeze sends chills across my entire body. "Ditto." Minutes pass before he asks, "Shower with me."

I nod my agreement as he picks up a towel from a stack of towels on a nearby chair and wraps one around me. Then he wraps a towel around his waist and reaches into his bedside drawer and fists a handful of condoms.

I squint and wrinkle my nose, a silent question.

"I went shopping." He's wearing his perma-grin as he tracks through the apartment to the bathroom on the opposite end.

It turns out we did need them. Not in the shower, as we did other intimate things, but later, quietly in the kitchen as we replenished our wine glasses, and then a final time in the bedroom, much later in the night, this time below the comforter.

I set my phone alarm for 5:00 a.m. and was out the door, unobserved by Kara, when the city still lay covered in darkness. What a perfect night. The way he looks at me, holds me, and—blast it all —the way I feel around him, I'd have to have my head up my ass to not see this is growing into something. I'm a fizzy, bubbly, whirry mess. And then there's the rub. I'm going to have to say goodbye.

One day, not today. This is all new. I simply need to enjoy it. There's no point in focusing on where this is going. In that alternate universe, where I stayed here, I'd still need to focus on the now. It's a day by day thing. And everyone knows the quickest way to kill a budding relationship is to focus too much on where it's going.

Life is a journey. And it's a one day at a time kind of thing. In the words of my favorite large turtle, you've just gotta go with flow. And live. *Carpe diem* and all that jazz.

ELEVEN

Mason

I wander down Clarkson Street, searching for the door to enter. Bare maple trees line the street growing out of allotted symmetrical square gaps in the concrete. The warm red brick apartment building spans the entire block and features arched windows that blend in with the Tribeca neighborhood and are reminiscent of the nicer parts of my neighborhood in Brooklyn. I kissed Delilah goodbye early this morning as she snuck out before the sun rose, barely twelve hours ago. Yet my body hums with anticipation, my cock half hard, joyful at this change of pace after so many years of hibernation. But my need for this blonde free spirit runs deeper than a hormonal need. She's beyond amazing. She brightens a room. Her laugh and her glow and how her hands seem to move every time she speaks, as if there's an invisible wire between the two and every time her mouth opens her fingers must react. She's live art in action.

Her fondness for my daughter, well, I imagine anyone would feel a warmth and gratitude for anyone who treated his child well. But it's more than that. She's filling a void I hadn't recognized in my life, and now that she's filled the void, I find myself wanting to see her every single day. Thinking about her all the time. Checking my phone for texts. Smiling as I type to her.

I locate the heavy glass door and pull back on the antique brass pull. White marble graces the lobby floor, and pristine white sofas and a rectangular white pine table with white chairs fill the expansive room. The only color comes from the green base of a sizeable white orchid plant centered on the expansive piece of furniture.

It's a beautiful lobby, but I've lived in New York long enough to know a beautiful lobby doesn't mean spacious, gorgeous apartments. A doorman standing behind a coordinated white pine desk greets me with a professional, "Good evening, sir."

I ask for Delilah Daniels, and after giving me a polite nod, he picks up a phone on the desk. He speaks then listens. After setting the phone down, he points to the sofa area and says, "Please have a seat, sir. She'll be down momentarily."

I head over to the sofa section but hesitate before sitting on the pristine white sofa. I did shower before coming over after work, but years of dirty, stained scrubs has trained me to be conscientious before sitting.

I flip through email while the doorman fixes me with a judgmental stare. Since I've been relegated to the waiting sofa, he's probably thinking this is our first date. I open an email from a pharmaceutical rep in an attempt to avoid thinking about why she didn't ask me to come up. Of course, if she did let me up, we might not leave. I stop reading email and stare at the elevators, but what I see is a play by play of last night. Her heavy, full breasts. Driving into her on the floor. I remember the way she looked with her hand down those white silk panties. I shift in my seat, grateful for the heavy denim.

I hear the click of heels on the marble floor before I see her. She rounds the corner, passing by the elevators. Her long blonde hair cascades around her, flowing over her shoulders. She's wearing a black, off-the-shoulder sweater over faded jeans and brown suede heeled boots that expose the tips of her red painted toes. Looped over one arm rests a camel coat and a black handbag.

I know the minute she sees me because she smiles so big a flash of white catches my eye, and her hair bounces higher as her pace picks up. Those bright blue eyes sparkle, and she charges right into me. I catch her and hold her close, breathing in her flowery camelia scent. I never wanted to leave Minnesota, and as I hold Delilah, I'm hit with the idea that I'll never want to leave her. I didn't have a choice back then.

My lips brush hers, and as her body presses against mine, I fight the urge to ask her to show me her apartment. This is a date. Our first date outside of my home. This could be the start of something really good.

I twine my fingers with hers and lead her out the building and around the corner to 7th Avenue. The restaurant I picked is about a twenty-minute walk away, but those open-toed high heel boots have zero grime around the edges. They are either brand new or they aren't comfortable walking shoes.

There are many things that come with being a momma's boy. My dad used to scold Mom, telling her she was spoiling me, making me too sensitive and too soft. He may have been right. My love for my mother has no bounds, and I do believe I owe her everything. Anyone raised for years by a single mom working two jobs would likely share the same level of love and devotion. She taught me so many things, among them respect and concern for women. And she taught me some women's shoes are inexplicably created with form over function in mind.

"Are you going to be okay in those shoes?" I specifically picked a restaurant we could walk to, but those boots have to have a five-inch toothpick heel.

She angles her head up to me and smiles. The lamp light shimmers on her lip gloss as she pulls her coat tighter around her. The winter air whips blonde strands behind her, and a few strands fly around and stick to those wet full lips. "Where are we going?"

"Marc Forgione. My mom suggested it."

Her hold tightens on my forearm, and she bounces slightly on her toes. "Oh, I *love* that place! He's one of my favorite chefs. No, let's definitely grab a cab." She steps past me, arm in the air, and a cab stops within seconds. She opens the passenger door and smiles at me as she waits for me to join her. Cab it is.

The cab delivers us moments later to 134 Read Street. I told Mom I wanted a romantic restaurant but nothing stuffy. I don't particularly care for formal, stiff settings, but putting my preference aside, Delilah's energy and joy shouldn't be restrained in a place requiring hushed voices and still hands amongst a symphony of forks, spoons, and knives.

She bounds out of the cab as I pay. I follow the bouncing blonde into the restaurant. We take our place in the short line behind the hostess stand. The brick walls and warm, golden lights offer an upscale tavern atmosphere. The chef here has a stellar reputation, and the restaurant has great reviews, so I'm expecting the food to be phenomenal.

We're seated in a back corner. A waitress stands at our table within seconds of us sitting. She reaches out to shake my hand, and I sit back, stunned by our unexpected VIP reception.

She laughs and says, "You're Mason, right?

I'm Leigh. I absolutely love your mom. Cindy's so great."

I relax as I put all the pieces together. Of course. Mom's my source for our reservation, and she's the reason we have the best table in the restaurant. "It's nice to meet you. My mom has had great things to say about you." In reality, I don't think Mom has ever mentioned her, but I do appreciate the last-minute reservation.

Within minutes, Delilah owns the conversation, and I learn all about Leigh. She's a cellist and waits tables at night, but also plays for weddings and gives cello lessons during the day. Delilah and Leigh exchange phone numbers because it turns out they like some of the same bands, and they agree to meet up at a show a couple of weeks from now.

Leigh speeds away after I request a bottle of the recommended white. I expect she didn't budget twenty minutes of talk time for our table, and she has yet to get our food order. I waited tables all through undergrad and through vet school, so I'm in tune with what she's up against. She's friendly, but this is a high-end restaurant, and while she's expected to spend time at each table, she's also expected to meet all of her tables' needs, and with a quick scan, I'd bet she has at least four tables in her section.

Delilah beams at me, and our waitress's challenges fall from my mind. Her golden skin glows against the candlelight. I reach across the table to hold her creamy, smooth hands. She's beautiful, stunning. Large diamond studs sparkle in her ears, and I notice she has chunky silver bracelets, several dotted with diamonds, as is her Cartier watch. The mix of diamonds speaks to the wealth Ashley bashed when she first came into the clinic.

She's completely out of my league. There's a sophistication to her that can't be ignored when she's dressed in something other than ripped jeans and t-shirts. Even her dainty rose gold nose ring bears an air of sophistication tonight. She's probably aiming for a lifestyle far beyond anything I'll be able to afford as a single dad struggling to buy his way into a veterinary practice and pay off student loans. I swallow hard as reality punches my gut. I've introduced her to my daughter.

The sommelier arrives with our wine and interrupts my downward spiral. After he leaves, Delilah and I raise our glasses. I search for the words for our toast, and Delilah speaks.

"To new beginnings," she supplies, her candy pink lip gloss glimmering in the candlelight.

My phone vibrates in my coat pocket, and I take it out. This is Amber's first time having Kara on her own, without me, so it won't be surprising if she has to reach out with a few questions. It is Amber. I swipe to answer, but I'm too late. I wait a moment and watch the phone to see if a voicemail comes through. Or a text.

I offer Delilah an apologetic smile. "Sorry. Amber has Kara. She called. Do you mind if I step out to call her back?"

"Not at all! Do you want me to order for you?"

I tell her I'll have the cioppino, and she asks what I want to start. The prices in this restaurant are unreal, and I don't want anything else, but I tell her I'll take the stracciatella and charge out the door to see what Amber needs.

The temperature has been steadily dropping since sunset, and I don't have my outer coat since we checked them. I shiver on the sidewalk as I wait for Amber to pick up the phone. She doesn't pick up. She didn't leave me a message when I missed her call, so I text her.

Me: Everything okay?

· · ·

I wait a few minutes. No response. Call again. Voicemail. My mom is out of town, back at the beach with her friends, or rather, with the guy I suspect is her new boyfriend. If she was in town, I'd have her stop by Amber's to check in.

My gut tells me something isn't right. I stare through the window into the restaurant. I can barely differentiate Delilah's blonde hair from the sea of heads. Leigh is back at our table, presumably taking our order, or maybe sharing her childhood history.

I call Amber one more time and get voicemail. I grip my phone and return to our table.

Delilah twirls a strand of hair around her finger, watching me as I approach. I exhale with a huff and sit.

"Everything okay?"

I nod. Her wide eyes stare at me, expectant, so I augment my response. "Yeah. I couldn't reach her." I place my napkin in my lap as I consider how much to share. She doesn't have kids. I can't expect her to understand. And if I tell her about Amber, she'll think she's listening to a jealous ex. In reality, I couldn't care less what Amber does and who she does it with. For our daughter's sake, I wish she wanted to be an involved parent. I've been reaching out for years, in the hope that one day she'd decide she was ready to be a mother. When she called and suggested we get together the next time she was in town, I jumped at the chance. For Kara.

I place my phone on the table, screen side up so I can see if any texts come through.

Delilah studies me. "Are you worried?"

Hell, yes, I'm worried. Why isn't Amber picking up her phone? She lives in a studio. There's no way she can't get to the phone in four hundred square feet of space.

Damnit. I'm derailing this date. I don't like this, but short of leaving the restaurant and heading to Amber's, I can't do anything. I have a choice. Trust the mother of my child with our daughter, and force myself to relax and enjoy this date, or pack it up and head back to Brooklyn, knowing chances are I'm going to interrupt mommy-daughter bonding time? Bonding time I pushed for so my daughter won't go through life yearning for a missing parent.

Delilah's hand slides over mine, and the tension in my shoulders eases. I close my eyes, inhale deeply, and decide. "Sorry. What did you order?"

She grins, and in her natural, animated way, tells me all about how she was torn between the swordfish or the short ribs, fingers fluttering around her as she talks, exuding energy and youthfulness. I rest against the back of my chair as she shares more about her thought process on food selection, and she's updating me on Leigh's, our waitress's, upcoming weekend plans when a long text appears on my phone.

Amber: Hey, you won't believe this, but I got called in to sub as backup singer for Craven Five! Shelley's sick. Holy shit!!! I took Kara back to your place and set her up with a Disney movie. She's all set with popcorn. She promised me she's gonna go to bed once the movie is over. Such a sweetie. Enjoy your date. Wish me luck!

A vision of Kara sitting in my apartment alone haunts me. She has never been alone in her life. I jump up and send my chair flying backward, crashing back onto the floor. Delilah, along with everyone else in the restaurant, stares at me.

"I've got to go." Standing, I frantically search the restaurant for our waitress so I can pay and leave.

Delilah reaches across the table, concern

etched into the corners of her eyes. "What's wrong? What happened?"

I scan the restaurant for our waitress. "Kara's at home. Alone. Amber left her." Delilah gasps. My heart races, and I clench my fists. When I glance down, I see Delilah holding my phone and reading.

She thrusts the phone to me and says, "Go. Go. I'll get our food and meet you at your apartment. Go." She pushes my phone into my hand, and relief floods my center.

I take out a credit card and place it in her hand before rushing out, yelling "Thank you," as I run toward the door.

I leap into a cab. I don't have a landline phone and have no way of reaching Kara. The sense of helplessness overwhelms me. I lean forward on the seat and tell the cab driver it's an emergency, and I need to get home as quickly as possible.

The driver jabs the steering wheel and mutters something, then throws his arms up and says, "Traffic."

Friday night traffic in the city is hell. The cab stops and starts. Red taillights flash up the streets. The thick slow stream of bridge traffic has me wondering if the subway might have been faster. I tap on the CityMap app to double-check my choice, and it confirms cab is the fastest way home by five minutes.

Uncontrolled panic floods my system. I run through my options. I could call the police. They would go to the apartment. But what if they called social services? What if social services decided Kara wasn't safe? Chances are all fault would lie with Amber, but who knows what she would say if the police questioned her? And who knows if they wouldn't find some fault with me, her primary caregiver? Or if they might take her away from me while they carried out an investigation.

I'm not a religious man, but I do send out prayers to the universe. *Please let her be okay. Please let her not be scared. Please let her be happy and watching a happy princess movie.*

The cab stops, and I throw cash up front and leap out of the cab, sprinting into my building and running straight to the stairs. I don't stop running, taking the stairs three at a time until I'm throwing open the stairwell door and running down the hall to our door. My fingers quiver, forcing me to use both hands to guide the key into the lock. When I finally get it in the keyhole, I twist the knob and throw open the door. The TV plays, the blue light the only light in the room. "Kara?"

Her little head rises from the sofa. I pick her

up and squeeze her, and she sniffles. Then I hold her out and search for injury. Her cheeks are damp from tears.

"Daddy." She points at the screen as tears fall faster. "He lost his daddy." I watch the screen until I recognize the animation. *Lion King*. She hasn't seen this one before. *Damnit, Amber.*

I reach forward, grab the remote, and flick the TV off. "Honey, are you okay?"

She sniffles and nods. Then she reaches forward and wraps her tiny arms around me and presses her wet face against my neck. My heart melts. I will never trust Amber with her again. Never.

TWELVE

As I approach, arms burdened with take-out bags, the wooden door at the end of the hall opens. Mason greets me with Kara on his hip, her sleepy head tucked against his chest. Kara smiles when she sees me, and she wiggles to get on the floor, but Mason holds her tight. He kicks the door to keep it open for me to enter.

I drop the brown paper bags on the bare kitchen table.

Kara squeals, "Deelah," and holds an arm out to me. I step forward and wrap an arm around her and kiss her chubby, pink cheek. Mason's arm loops behind me, and the three of us stand in the great room, holding on to each other. The slow burn in my back muscles subsides, and my eyes go all misty. The little bug is okay.

Mason had texted when I was in the cab, so I had read that she was okay, but seeing her means so much more than words on a phone. I mean, I figured she would be fine. In theory, she was safe, locked in her apartment. But she's so little. Too little to be left alone. There are knives and sharp objects and scary thoughts if you let your mind wander. I breathe in deeply and sniffle to keep my swirling emotions in check. Kara doesn't need to see me cry, even if the tears are of the happy sort.

Kara breaks the silence by slapping her hand against my cheek and saying, "You came!"

I break away from our threesome hold and empty the bags of food. "I did. And I brought food. Are you hungry?" I had the foresight to order a few desserts to go, as well as some buttered pasta and marinara sauce on the side in case Kara hadn't eaten dinner yet.

I glance over my shoulder and meet Mason's blank stare. He continues to hold Kara tight. She wiggles a bit to get down, but he shows no sign of letting her go. I head into the kitchen to grab plates and silverware and to give him a moment.

Within minutes, I have the table set, food out of the bags with serving spoons, and I shift to Mason. Cold, dark green orbs track my every movement. Other than squirming to get down, Kara seems somewhat content in her daddy's hold, but Mason's tormented countenance troubles me. Kara doesn't need to pick up on it.

I stand next to Mason and stroke his shoulder and bicep until the muscles beneath his shirt relax, then I loop an arm around Kara to shift her from Mason's hip to mine. His jaw muscles ripple, as if he's grinding his teeth.

"Let's get Kara seated so we can eat." I say it softly, searching for some sign he's okay. He's rattled, but he's got to get his feet back on the ground, for Kara's sake.

He blinks, like he's coming out of a fog, and releases her to me. I get her set up in her booster chair, a plastic contraption that sits her higher to the table, and buckle her in. "Did you eat, honey?"

"Mommy gave me popcorn!" She says *popcorn* with a high pitch and with the same enthusiasm I used to say *cotton candy* when I was a kid.

I open the container of angel hair pasta, some Leigh found in the kitchen for me, and ask if Kara would like marinara sauce too. I urge her to stick her finger in the sauce to taste it, and she giggles because she's breaking a rule. I explain it's take-out, and our manners can slide when it's take-out. As I pour the sauce she declared yummy onto her food, I glance back at Mason. He's still standing in place, but the harshness has softened.

I guide him to his chair then take a moment to knead his hard shoulders and press a soft kiss below his ear. As I step away to my chair, he loops an arm around my waist and pulls me close. A soft, "Thank you," escapes.

At bedtime, Mason and I surround Kara with each of us on one side as we take turns reading books to her. Kara holds my fingers but snuggles against her daddy, her body partially lying on his. I pick up a well-worn copy of *Goodnight Moon* and hold it up as a suggestion for our next book, and she gives her approval.

Then softly she says, "No *Lion King*. The daddy gets hurt."

She's such a sweetie. I brush her hair back and kiss her forehead. Mason's eyes glimmer in the lamp light. It's one thing to have an illustrated book where a character gets hurt. It's quite another to watch the movie in action with dramatic music and vivid, moving color. And for his baby girl to take that in, I know he's got to be swimming in a well of emotion.

When she succumbs to sleep, I squeeze her precious little hand and lay a soft kiss on her forehead, then lean over further and press a kiss to Mason's jaw. As I leave Kara's bedroom, Mason lies on the bed, eyes closed, one arm possessively draped over his daughter. His concern and love are so apparent, it warms the soul and twirls about nostalgic memories and feelings. I swallow back my emotions and pull the door closed as tears glide down my face unchecked.

Minutes pass, and I sit on the brown leather sofa, wrapped up in the fuzzy princess blanket. I'm stroking Belle's image when Kara's bedroom door opens. Mason slumps down on the sofa beside me and pulls me next to him. I snuggle into his side, much the way Kara did tonight in bed.

Mason threads his fingers through mine and exhales. "Dee, you have no idea how scared. How many scary scenarios crossed my mind. Fire. Her falling. Scissors. She's barely four! How could she leave her alone?"

On my cab ride over, I had similar thoughts. I also called Jackson, since he's a lawyer, to learn more about Mason's options. "Has Amber done this before?"

"Never. But she's never had the chance." He gazes out the window into the night. "Amber wouldn't even hold Kara in the hospital. She was afraid she'd grow attached. She was determined to not give up her dream. Probably would've had an abortion, but she found out too late. Her plan was to place Kara up for adoption. As you know, I told her no. I told her she could still pursue her dreams, and I'd raise Kara. For years, she wanted nothing to do with her. But I've pushed and pushed."

"When did she start spending time with her?"

"Recently." He rubs his forehead hard, as if he's trying to remove a memory. "I always sent her pictures. For years, Amber wouldn't respond. This past year, she thanked me. Then, a couple of weeks ago, she finally called. I wanted Kara to have her mother." His voice cracks, and I lean over and place a soft kiss on his neck, the only place I can reach.

Still holding him, I tell him, "I called a friend on the way over. A lawyer. He suggested you report this to the police so you have it on record."

Mason recoils but keeps me tucked into his side. "I'm not filing a police report. Too many unknowns. Social services could take her away while they investigate. I can't risk it."

"Jackson's specialty is corporate law. He suggested you retain a family practice lawyer. He said it's important for you to get full custody so you can control how much contact and what kind of contact Amber has in the future." I'm speaking in a low, quiet, calm tone, but Mason reacts as if I'm shouting, squinting and jerking back, shaking his head.

"No. I don't need to get lawyers involved. Amber wants as little as possible to do with Kara. I've been the one pushing for their relationship. I won't push anymore."

I don't argue, although I don't agree. But there's too much emotion to push on this right now. Sometimes life throws curveballs that require a good night's rest and a stable heart before we can catch the ball and spin it back out into the universe.

Mason tugs my hair and in a gruff, broken voice says, "Thank you for being here."

I place a kiss on the corner of his lips. "Any time."

He exhales. "About that, before Amber did *that*, it hit me I let you into my daughter's life. She's my world. I'm not sure I'm making the best decisions right now." My chest constricts, making it a bit harder to breathe. He runs his thumb across my knuckles. "You make me happy. I love spending time with you. You fit into our world easily. Make it better. But it's not just me. And it's not fair to you. It's not fair to ask you to make a commitment so early on. But I can't let you get close to her and then..." He stops speaking, but he's said enough.

I reach up and angle his head to mine, forcing him to look me in the eye. "I can't promise *us* forever. But I can promise you I'll be there for Kara for as long as you want me to be in her life. I didn't know I could love a little kid. Not now, at this stage in my life. But I do. I was so scared in the cab ride over here. All I could think about is what she needs, and what you need." I hated the sense of helplessness. I called Anna and had her put Jackson on the phone. Probed him with questions about legal rights and what we should do, gathering information for Mason because it felt like the only action I could take while stuck in the back of a cab in Friday night city traffic.

Mason's strong arms wrap around me in a cocoon, holding me close. His heart reverberates, and I press closer to the sensation. "I'm falling for you, Delilah." He runs his fingers through my hair and repositions me on his lap. "But I get the feeling I'm out of my league here." His thumb lightly runs over the earring in my ear, a gift from my parents. "I don't think I can afford to give you the lifestyle you're used to on what I'm going to make as a veterinarian—"

"Mason, if you think I care about money, you've got it all wrong. I don't need you to provide for me." His brow wrinkles as his thumb and index finger caress my chin.

I run my fingers over his stubbled jaw and gently pull until his eyes meet mine. "I'm falling for you too. I've never been in a real relationship before. Nothing serious, at least. I'm probably going to mess up. But if you're okay with being with someone who doesn't know what she's doing, someone who has a whole lotta shit to figure out...I want to be with you. And I want to be there for Kara too. I'm falling for both of you." I hold my breath. I need to tell him about New Orleans. About my obligations. What I've been putting off. What I can't put off forever. But he's not responding to me. He may not want this. Me. I'm a lot to take. I get that. And I definitely don't have my shit together. He'd probably prefer someone who is buttoned up and organized and even-keeled and...

His strong hand cups the back of my neck, and he pulls our heads together, forehead to forehead, while his other arm loops around my back to hold me close. We sit there, holding each other. I close my eyes while breathing in his earthy, clean scent. The tender moment stirs deep, and novel emotions rise as I hold him and revel in the sensations rippling through my core.

He places a soft kiss on my forehead, then trails light kisses from my cheek, to the sensitive skin below my ear and down my neck. He lifts me off the couch and pulls me into his bedroom, taking care to close the door softly, then lifts me up and carries me across the room. He sets me down on the bed and unbuttons his shirt, his eyes never leaving mine. His movements are slow and precise. Measured. With gentleness and care, he discards my clothes. There is a heaviness in the air, a seriousness. Neither of us speaks, but we swim in each other's eyes.

I love this man. I love how much he loves his daughter. How he stepped in to take care of her when it would have been so much easier to put her up for adoption. How he cares for every living being in his path. How he studies a problem and finds a solution. I love how much he wants his daughter to have what he didn't have, and how much it's breaking him that he can't give her her mother. I love those jade eyes, an ever-changing hue I have yet to pinpoint, and I love how I get lost in them. These may be fleeting emotions, or they may be as permanent as the sea, but for now, my love for this man is deeper and more intense than anything I've experienced in my life.

When he spreads my legs and lifts my hips and thrusts deep inside, he fills me, physically and emotionally. His tongue caresses mine as our bodies join. Tonight, we are making love. Comforting each other. Reveling in the newness of something that feels right. He brings me higher and higher until I detonate, shuddering around him as my orgasm rips through me, leaving me bare and vulnerable, clinging to him as if he's my lifeline.

A nagging worry gnaws at my newfound bliss. Guilt. My life here is temporary. We are temporary. But as I snuggle into his side, I tighten my hold on him and will my negative notions away, to be dealt with another day.

THIRTEEN

MASON

Saturday morning, I wake with a hard-on and my hand cupping her full breast. I have less than sixty seconds to revel in my position before I hear soft tapping on the bedroom door and my baby girl questioning, "Daddy?"

I leap out of bed and grab my boxers from the floor. Delilah's golden hair drapes over the pillow, and the sheet falls below her waistline. She's gorgeous, but there's no time to appreciate her. I pull the comforter up to her shoulders and charge to the door, thankful I locked it after my last trip to the bathroom last night.

I open the door, and an inquisitive face peers up at me. "Why's the door locked?" My door is always open, but with a glance back at Delilah, I realize that's a part of my routine that's going to be changing. And I couldn't be happier about it.

I scoop my baby girl up into my arms, closing the door behind me before heading to the kitchen to get coffee started. Kara's arm points back to my bedroom as I'm carrying her away. "Did you have a sleepover?"

I flip the kitchen light on then set her onto the counter and set about grinding the coffee beans. I learned a long time ago that sometimes silence leads to an easier question.

"Can I play with Delilah today?" she asks as she kicks her feet back and forth against the counter.

After I press brew on the coffee machine, I squeeze Kara's cool bare foot. "If she can."

She beams a smile up at me, and my heart warms. "Yes. We can paint. And she can teach me to do the yoga."

I kiss her nose. "I'm not working today, so we can do whatever you want to do."

"Yay!" There's a slight pause as I pull down the coffee mugs before Kara drops her bomb again. "Did she sleep over?"

There's a sadness to her tone that has me twisting around to face her. "Yes, baby. She's my girlfriend. We're going to be spending more time with her. Is that okay?"

She toys with the edge of her nightgown. "Yes. Can she sleep in my bed next time?"

"You wanna to have a sleepover, pumpkin?"

She nods. "I'm not sure what age kids start doing sleepovers with friends. Let me ask some of your friends' parents and see what they say, okay?"

"Why not Deelah?" she asks with her adorable little girl plea. I grin as I pour my coffee.

"You want a sleepover with Deelah?" She nods. "Tell you what. Why don't we ask her?"

She leaps forward off the counter, and I barely catch her in time. "Kara! Careful."

"Aw, Daddy. I can do it." Before I can respond, she's running out of the kitchen.

I follow, a little too slow pre-coffee to anticipate where she's going. As I round the corner, I glimpse a flash of Kara's nightgown heading into our bedroom—my bedroom. Not our bedroom. Not yet. Maybe one day.

I enter the bedroom as Kara jumps up and down, using the bed as an indoor trampoline, and

Delilah ever so slowly reaches for my pillow and slides it over her head.

Airborne, Kara squeals, "Deelah! Wanna sleep over? In my room?"

I catch Kara in mid-air and toss her away from the bed as her peals of laughter cascade through the bright sun-filled room. Delilah lifts a corner of the pillow and peeks out.

"Morning, beautiful. Sorry about this one here. Want me to bring you some coffee?"

She smiles and nods, but the pillow stays on top of her head and the comforter remains near her shoulders. I step into my closet and pull out a pair of my sweats and one of my smaller t-shirts and throw them onto the bed. "Feel free to wear anything of mine you want."

"Where are her clothes?"

I toss Kara in the air a few feet out in front of me and step forward, clearing us out of the bedroom, and continue doing the toss-catch game as I explain we had to rush home last night, and she didn't have time to pack clothes.

"So next time she'll pack clothes?" Kara asks as I set her back up on the kitchen counter.

I grin as I take out a second coffee cup for Delilah. "Yes, next time she'll pack clothes. And when your friends come over, we'll be sure they pack clothes." I supply the next part more to get her brain thinking about future sleepovers with her friends.

Delilah rounds the corner into the kitchen, her hair pulled into a giant pile on top of her head. She's wearing my sweats and a plain white t-shirt, and they swallow her, yet with her bare feet and shiny red nail polish, she's adorable and sexy.

I reach into the refrigerator for the soymilk, finish Delilah's coffee, and pull her body into mine when I deliver her mug. Her hair still smells of flowers, and I relax into her as I kiss her forehead. Delilah stands on tiptoe and places a kiss on my neck.

Kara smiles at us then holds her arm out into the air. "Deelah, wanna watch cartoons?"

"Absolutely." Delilah scoops Kara up onto her hip and carries her into the den as they debate exactly which cartoon they should watch. It was close between *Paw Patrol* and *Doc McStuffins*, but I hear Delilah mention she likes the Doc, and after a squeal from Kara, TV sounds fill the now empty kitchen. I open the fridge and set about making pancakes for breakfast.

I'm lost in the world of flipping pancakes when two arms slip around my waist and Delilah's lips touch the back of my neck. When I twist in her arms to face her, I place a soft kiss on her lips. I want more, so much more. But it's got to be restrained, given we have a child in the next room. Delilah must be thinking the same thing, as she steps away from me and rests her back against the counter.

"Sorry about this morning."

I tilt my head. "Huh?"

"I didn't realize she would wake so early. You could have kicked me out. I would've been okay with it. I know she's just a kid, and it's got to be weird to have me here in the morning."

"Uh-uh," I break in. "Not weird at all." Perfect, actually. "I told her you're my girlfriend and you'll be over. A lot." Blue eyes meet mine. I hold my breath. This is the girl who told me she doesn't like compound words. But surely things have changed now.

Her eyes widen, and she presses her lips together in a flat line. I pause, waiting for her response. We didn't talk specifics last night but...

"Okay." She reaches up and pulls me down to her for a deep, slow kiss that has my heart speeding up and blood rushing to my cock. For once, I'm glad my kitchen doesn't open into the den like so many do in open floorplans.

It's hard to describe the sense of peacefulness

Delilah brings with her. Kara and I, we were happy before. We had a rhythm that worked for us, and my baby girl giggles and laughs as much as any kid. But there's a brightness and energy to Delilah that warms the white walls in our apartment. She's like a pair of Maui Jim sunglasses infusing the world with opalescence. And I am fully aware these thoughts are those of a cheeseball, and I don't care. Not at all. Kara adores her and seems thrilled to have her around. Last night's events with her mom seem to be forgotten. Kara's beaming and giddy. All the happiness I see in my daughter is what I'm feeling on the inside.

After breakfast, we all bundle up to head to the park. It's a chilly early December day, but the skies are blue, and red and green holiday decorations appear on every street and in most store windows. I hold Kara's left hand and Delilah holds her right, and we swing her along, down the city sidewalks until we reach the park entrance. We're the picture of the perfect family, the family I yearned for when I was a kid. The mother, father, and child. It doesn't matter that Delilah isn't Kara's biological mother. But having someone in that role for Kara is something I've always wanted for her. Maybe I should have tried to date years ago. It's almost as if I was trying to hold this spot for Amber, should she change her mind, even though she couldn't have been more clear about her wishes.

In the park, Delilah finds a dry, sunny spot in the brown winter grass and proceeds to teach Kara and me a few yoga poses. I snap loads of photos of the two of them giggling and laughing and rolling around on the ground. Delilah's phone is charging back at my apartment, so every now and then she reminds me to send her some of the photos.

After we've spent a couple of hours outside and our exposed skin turns pink from the cold, we duck into Colonie for lunch. As luck would have it, there are three open bar stools at the counter. Kara loves sitting at this neighborhood restaurant because she can watch the cooks prepare all the food. She sits mesmerized by the action, glued the way some kids focus on an electronic device or the television.

After lunch, we head home down Montague Street. Shops and restaurants pack the commercial thoroughfare. Kara begs to pop into a toy store. Delilah tells us to go ahead, and she walks over to a clothing store across the street. The toy store is small, but packed floor to ceiling with all kinds of toys and stuffed animals. She drops some silver marbles on a display, and we watch them roll down a sort of roller coaster. The display model shows what the plastic pieces inside the $180 box can build.

"Do you want to add it to your Christmas list?" From about September on, Kara doesn't get new toys. Anything she shows an interest in gets added to her list. It's what my mom did to me, and now I fully appreciate her brilliance. Wandering through a toy store adding to a wish list is so much easier than tears in response to being told no.

Kara plays with the marbles a bit more, watching them roll through the downward maze, before she says, "Let's go find Deelah."

We look both ways, cross the street, and peer through the glass of the shop Delilah entered. The door to the boutique chimes as we open it. Delilah stands at the register, chatting with the shop girl as she checks out. I see piles of clothes on the counter and can't help but hope Delilah's planning on storing some of her new purchases at my apartment.

Delilah drops down to her knees as Kara approaches and asks, "What'd you end up getting?"

Kara wraps her tiny fingers around two of mine, and her eyes grow big as she sees the large shopping bag by the register being filled by the salesclerk. "We was just looking."

I scoop her up and kiss her cheek. "She added a few things to her Christmas wish list, right?"

Delilah frowns and reaches out to squeeze Kara's thigh as if she's comforting her. Kara pushes against my chest to get down, then scrambles up Delilah's thigh to sit on her hip. She's tiny, so she can get away with being carried, but those days are coming to an end. She's about one growth spurt away from being too long and gangly to easily carry around. I take the shopping bags and reach for Kara, but Delilah twists away and exits the store.

When we get back to the apartment, Delilah and Kara immediately dig into the craft buckets. As Delilah plays art instructor, I grab my laptop to finish up some patient reports from Friday. There's a surreal quality to the moment. I can't remember the last time I had the chance to get work done in the middle of a weekend afternoon, at least, not since Kara dropped her afternoon nap. It's also a little too perfect and dreamlike. *This* is the life I wanted when I was a kid.

When I turned fourteen, and yet another birthday went by without a call from Dad, I asked Mom what had happened. Asked why we moved away, why they got divorced. I'd been so young when it happened, it never occurred to me to ask why they were getting a divorce, and then as I grew older, it felt like the business of grown-ups.

We were in Joe's Pizzeria on Montague Street. It was there, sitting on a round black leather stool, that I learned my father had an affair and she became pregnant. We lived in a small town, and she couldn't bear to stay and watch this other woman grow large with his baby. He could've stopped her from moving to New York, but she offered to waive child support, and he chose money. Ultimately, he chose money over me. She never told him he couldn't have anything to do with me. He simply got busy with his new family. So many years I would hope for a phone call or for him to ask me to come out and visit for a week over the summer. Then, eventually, I stopped hoping.

When I asked Amber to marry me, if I'm honest, I did so because I wanted the family I didn't have as a kid. I told myself I could be there for her as she finished growing up. It didn't matter that I wasn't in love with her. I loved her carefree spirit. The opposite of mine. Paying for college and grad school, getting good grades, that required discipline. Constant work. Amber chased her dream without any care for anything else and no discipline to hold her back. She had a passion for music. For her, nothing was better than being on a stage.

It never occurred to me to question how that selfish quality would play out in a mother. Or wife. I believed I could give enough for both of us.

I still remember the hardness of the floor underneath my knee when I proposed. Her panicked expression as she backed away and the desperation seeping from every crevice as I saw the family I craved backing out the door. Then Kara arrived, and I fell into survival mode. Intense workdays as I struggled to remember everything from years of vet school, working to build my confidence in my ability to diagnose correctly on everything from snakes to parakeets to bearded dragons, while at night I was up with a colicky newborn.

When I first met Delilah, those crystal blue eyes and blonde hair caught my attention, but I was out of practice. It had been years since I took the time to look at women or to think about dating. Even with Delilah, when I first met her, my focus automatically shifted from the beauty in the room to my patient. That had been another manic day, but I still noticed the concern and care Delilah had for the creature under her care, a dog that wasn't hers. One of my favorite quotes from Immanuel Kant is, "We can judge the heart of a man by his treatment of animals."

Delilah held the dog's head in her lap, massaged her ears, spoke to her, and provided her undivided attention. She treated her like she was human, actually better than some humans treat each other. She pushed me. Wanted to get her way. And she was cute. She flirted. Didn't back down. And she pushed open the door to a possibility.

Delilah's energy makes me smile. There is a literal bounce to her step that sends her hair billowing along her back when it's down or jiggling when it's wrapped up on the top of her head. She's carefree, but she's also stable and down to earth. She's an artist, but her drive doesn't stem from a desire to be worshipped on stage. She loves being around people and appreciating color and creativity. I love all those things about her. But seeing her with my daughter? Nothing could prepare me for the powerful emotions ripping through my body. The warm sensation in my core when they hold hands, when she does something as simple as cut up broccoli for her on her plate and then play a game to tempt her to eat it. I don't know how to navigate us forward, to go from our initial dating to having her in our life each and every day. I don't want to scare her away. But I have an idea of my ultimate goal.

She agreed to be my girlfriend. She wasn't exactly joyous about it, but she agreed. That's a step in the right direction.

FOURTEEN

DELILAH

Snuggled into Mason's warm chest, the sounds of birds infiltrate the cocoon I've created beneath his thick navy comforter. Rain patters, softly at first, and increasing into a heavy crescendo against the window. I sigh, place a kiss on his nipple, and stretch for his one bedside table to reach my phone to turn off my alarm. My movement wakes Mason, and his arms wrap around me, pulling my body over his and his oh-so-awake anatomy. I trail kisses down his throat then push up and leap off the bed to find my clothes.

In a throaty, sleepy, and extremely sexy voice, Mason says, "Hey, get back over here."

I giggle as goosebumps from the chilly air form all over my naked body. I clutch my arm over my bulbous breasts to keep them from swinging as I step around, searching for my clothes. Last night, when I snuck in after Kara fell asleep, he didn't waste any time tearing my clothes off and sending them flying against various walls.

"Do not cover those up."

I glance up, and those emerald orbs are tracking my every move. His bicep flexes as he adjusts himself in bed for a better view. I shake my head. Guys have always loved my boobs. I wish I felt the same way about them.

As a teen, I'd worn giant sweatshirts and blamed the strong indoor AC to hide these melons, then when older I graduated to loose, flowing, hippie wear in the form of shapeless dresses and tops. For whatever reason, when I gain weight, I gain it in my boobs first. I'd seriously considered breast reduction surgery but had been scared to go under the knife. Meanwhile, I have these big boobs and a somewhat flat ass. It doesn't make sense, but Aunt Josie used to tell me not to worry. She'd say, "Once you have kids, your ass'll come in." Not exactly the most comforting idea, but by ninth grade I had implemented a gym routine to stay healthy and strong. One thing about big boobs, they require a strong core for carrying these puppies around.

Mason watches my every move as I slip on my lavender silk panties and growls as I pull his t-shirt over my head. I can't stop my smile. I might have had issues with my boobs in the past, but Mason being really into *my* puppies leaves me tingly and giddy. And it makes me less self-conscious about the slight pudge on my belly that I can't seem to flatten.

I flutter my fingers at him, a goodbye gesture. "I promised Kara I'd be in her bed when she wakes up. I'm not breaking my promise to her." I slide his sweatpants on as his hungry gaze follows my every move. I want to crawl back into his bed, but Kara comes first.

He groans and falls back against the pillows. Then he snaps his head back up. "Wait. Before you go," and he curls his index finger repeatedly.

I don't understand, so I tilt my head. "Huh?"

"Let me see. One more time." I laugh out loud but give in. I take the hem of my shirt and pull it over my breasts, flashing him. He moans and laughs, and I shake my head at his ridiculousness before slipping out.

I fall back asleep, warm in Kara's bed, and wake with her on top of me, her dark hair dripping over my face. "Wake up!"

I flip her onto the bed then tickle her like crazy. Mason enters her room, and within moments the three of us are a human pile of ticklers and gigglers. I have no idea how they recommend a girlfriend be introduced into the fold, and if someone came and told me we were doing it all wrong I'd probably go pink in shame, but right now, there's no rule book, and this feels pretty right to me. Well, *girlfriend*. It's still a big word. Hard to swallow. But I'm getting there. I mean, surely after getting cold busted in the morning, it's better to say we're dating and not simply friends.

When we return to the den, Mason tells Kara and me to sit while he goes in to whip up a batch of scrambled eggs and hash browns. Our plan for the day is to go and buy a Christmas tree after breakfast, and to make ornaments, since Mason doesn't have many. I'm thinking popcorn garland and tinfoil stars. And I'll check Pinterest for more ideas.

Kara gets settled on the sofa and starts an episode of *Doc McStuffins*, and I pick up my phone from the floor where it's been charging since sometime yesterday. Mason's extra charger plugs in against the wall. I tend to forget it since it's partially hidden by the massive, ugly, brown La-Z-Boy chair.

I wrinkle my brow. Thirty-three missed texts and three voicemails. Two texts from Anna, a couple from random friends checking in for weekend plans, and twenty-six texts from my mom. I scroll through all the texts. Most tell me to call her, then a few ask if I'm with *that* man. The last text sends my heart racing.

Melinda: My flight leaves at 7:20 a.m. I should be at your apartment by 11 a.m. See you soon.

Jesus, Mother, Mary, and Angels, what the heck is going on?

I call her, and it goes to voicemail. I check the time and realize she's in the air. I stare out the window. The sky is overcast, gray, and dreary. I stand by the window, pacing, and watch pedestrians bundled in coats and scarves scurrying down the sidewalk as I listen to the ringing on the phone, waiting for my father to pick up. It goes to voicemail, and I don't leave a message. He could be on the flight with my mother. I call Aunt Josie and get voicemail. This time, I leave a message, "Aunt Josie, Mom's on her way here. Is everything okay?"

Under normal circumstances, I'd assume she was simply being Melinda Daniels and hopped a plane when I didn't answer at her first call, afraid I was falling in love and making plans to remain in the big, bad NYC. Her repeated texts of "Call me now" and "I need to speak to you" have me tapping my finger on my phone and pacing by the window, fear rising as worst-case scenario ideas come to mind. A car accident. Something so bad she can't tell me on the phone.

I spin in a circle, trying to corral my thoughts, as Mason sets out the breakfast on the dining table. A worried sensation settles into the pit of my stomach. I need to get back to my apartment and find out what has Melinda sending twenty-six texts and hopping a plane.

After breakfast, Kara and Mason bundle up in coats and scarves and follow me out onto the sidewalk. Mason slips his arms into my coat as Kara hugs my thigh, and Mason's kiss slips into borderline inappropriate-in-front-of-kids territory. Concern radiates through his features, his wrinkled brow, and angled eyes. He offered to come with me, but that's not a good idea.

If Melinda Daniels flew here to stop this relationship before it gets going, then he doesn't need to face her unchecked fury when he shows up with his daughter in tow. One thing about my mother, she's used to getting her way, and if she flew here to inquire about my relationship status, she won't handle it being thrown in her face well. If she flew here with demands, Mason's presence will make her less flexible, not more. There are ways to manage Melinda, and they require delicacy and the intrusion of spirits, often of the Earth-dwelling variety in the form of one Aunt Josie.

I stare out the window on the way to my apartment. The city speeds by in a blur, the cold gray winter day outside present in the blaring dry heat from the cab and the bundled pedestrians. The pit in my stomach grows with each bump over the Brooklyn Bridge and with each pothole the cab driver slam dunks. Yes, my parents purchased the spacious condo I now reside in so they could have a bedroom when they visited, but in the four years I've lived in it, every visit had been prepared long enough in advance for theater and dining reservations and, at times, a personal shopper. My mother's happiest place on Earth is the private room at Louis Vuitton and the accompanying "free" champagne. Almost everything she loves to do requires advanced planning.

There's no way she had time to pull together her preferred New York City experience. She could have bad news. News so bad phone or text couldn't be used. I squirm in my seat and pick at my nail polish then force my hands to still as I stare out the window at the passing stores, restaurants, and delis. She could be coming here to get a handle on the boy situation. I should have answered the phone. Leaving the unknown out there for her frantic mind to unravel wasn't wise. And if this trip's purpose is to put an end to Mason and me? Then I'll tell her no. I'm not going to leave her and Dad stranded in New Orleans. I will eventually return, as agreed, and step in as a partner. But I've never fallen for someone before, and the emotions he has unearthed in me, emotions I didn't know I could possess, aren't something to walk away from. I need to see where this goes. I owe myself that much. It's part of my personal growth.

My heel raps on the floor of the cab as I think of Mason and Kara. His kindness and thoughtfulness. His tender touch and the mischievous sparkle in his eye. His devotion to his daughter. He stood up to me and didn't let me have my way.

And I still like him. Maybe even more. No one tells me no. That's got to be a sign. An omen.

Then there's Kara. My little dark-haired soul mate, an artist to her core with unhindered joy and happiness. I found these two, and for the first time in my life, I crave a real relationship. An adult relationship with commitment and responsibilities. Even the prospect of countless dinners at home and TV afterward doesn't scare me away. If anything, a night of roaming bars and clubs has lost its appeal. I don't need to hunt for the next guy because the only guy I want to see and spend time with is Mason.

For years, I'd go on a date and find something wrong. Maybe his hands were too sweaty. One guy had this white gunk on the edge of his lip. He'd wipe his mouth, and it would still be there. *Goodbye.* Another guy mentioned Harvard, pronounced "Hahvard," at least once every minute. Before dinner concluded, I had created a game to see how much time would lapse before he name dropped his alma mater. The gap maxed out at a hundred twenty-four seconds. *Buh-bye.* More than one guy got the boot when they couldn't look at my face. It's one thing to have a thing for boobs, but it's another when an entire meal is spent ogling my chest, which I never, ever put on blatant display. My friends told me I'm too picky, and I had started to suspect they might be right.

Then I met Mason, and it didn't hit me right at first, but somehow, I found someone I want to spend time with. Yeah, he's a good-looking guy. And we've never discussed it, but his well-developed, lean muscles show that he, like me, values the importance of incorporating some sort of fitness into the daily routine. He must do push-ups or something. Burpees and planks. Probably after she goes to bed at night.

The whole single dad situation. That's like a revelation. I would have never thought I'd be into the parent thing, but the way he looks at her, with so much love, turns me into a puddle. And he cares. He's into me. He's made it clear he wants this relationship. With me.

As an only child, it's not like I didn't grow up with people caring about me, but the way he looks at me, holds my hand, feeds me, checks in during the day... Yes, the relationship is new, but it's good. Mason defines a good person. I'll never wonder if he's with me because of my family's money or our New Orleans heritage because money isn't what drives him at all. The man uses his daughter's artwork to decorate his walls. He's driven to care for others. The man is an animal doctor. That's got to be a sign his soul is good. And I'm not going to give him up. Not yet. Not when I just found him, and we are still at the most fantastic stage. When something happens to you that hasn't happened before, don't you at least have to find out what it is?

A calmness sweeps over me as the cab approaches Clarkson Street. I refuse to let her break us up. For the first time in my life, I will stand up to Melinda Daniels.

I take the elevator to the fourth floor, which is the floor my bedroom is on. It's 10:30 in the morning, and I don't have much time to shower and prepare for my mother. I charge down the hallway to my bedroom, and as I pass the staircase that connects all three floors of my condo, I hear my mother's voice from above, echoing through the stairwell.

"Delilah, is that you, dear? Come up here, darling. I'm in the kitchen."

I exhale and pause in front of one of the hallway floor length mirrors. I pulled my hair up into a bun this morning, but flyaways dart out all along the sides. I'm wearing a gray plush sweatshirt and jeans I purchased yesterday in the little Montague Street shop, and my brown boots with the peekaboo toes. Shoes meant for warmer fall days than today. Mom will either critique the boots or the hair. Since the hair speaks to my not having stayed in my apartment last night, I'm betting on the hair.

I smooth my palm over the flyaways, although without hairspray it's a fruitless endeavor. Might as well face the demons, as they say. I pull my shoulders back and climb the stairs. She must have landed earlier than estimated and has already had time to get settled in one of the guest rooms on the sixth floor, which means she's already scoped out the entire place.

As I reach the fifth-floor landing, I face my mother. She sits on a stool in front of my kitchen bar, her straight, angled bob absolute perfection, not a hair out of place. Tears run down her cheeks. Her mascara doesn't run, and for one bizarre moment I want to ask her what brand she uses, but I blow out air to clear the inane thought. "Mom, what is it?"

She lifts her head, and light blue eyes, replicas of my own, shimmer through the tears. "Oh, honey. It's your father." Tears gush forth, and I wrap my arms around her. She rests her head on my chest as she sobs. "Honey, he's dying."

FIFTEEN

Delilah

The brown cardboard box human resources offered sits on my desk, empty. I stare at it, numb. In
another life, this box held wine bottles. Judging by
the shape and size and the circular indentations
on the bottom, it held a dozen. A spiderweb
crosses from one side, covering a corner. The thin
strands can only be seen when light reflects on
them, and the pattern breaks near the center. A
soft tap on my door tears me away from my deep
box inspection.

"How'd it go with Margaret?" Anna stands in

the doorway, her brow furrowed in concern. I wave her into my office.

"Fine. She wouldn't let me resign. Talked me into a personal leave. Three months, and then we regroup. The senior art director position may be filled if I come back, but they will hold my current position for me."

I pick up a silver bamboo frame from my desk. The picture's of Moxie, my childhood dog, an American Water Spaniel. She was a good dog. Come to think of it, she never, ever overate. I place the cherished memory in a large cardboard box. "I don't think I'll be back, but Margaret wouldn't listen to me. She said it's all too new, and if I need to resign, then she understands, but for me to go home and find out more before making any decisions."

Anna perches awkwardly on the arm of an office chair across from my desk. "What can I do?"

I pull my desk drawer, which requires jiggling because it's crammed with Post-It notes, pens, receipts, paper clips, gum, hair ties, rubber bands, and a gazillion other objects. I stare at it and think I see the corner of a tarot card. "If I don't come back, maybe clean out this office for me?"

She drops into the seat and pulls one leg up to

her body. "What does he have? You only told me he's sick."

Tears build up as I stare at the framed picture of a slow loris, a type of small, endangered primate, hanging on the wall behind her. The round black glass pupils speak to me. I adopted one, not for real adopted, but sent money in to save one on the island of Java in Indonesia, hoping to remove it from the endangered species list. The other framed picture in my office is of Chevy Chase circa the seventies, and a framed photo of Nina Simone hangs closer to my desk.

"Mom couldn't stop crying, and I stopped asking. She told me I have some time, that I could wrap up this week, but they need me. My plan is to get home, see my dad, talk to his doctors, then do research. New Orleans is great and all, but depending on what he has, he may need to see doctors from a larger hospital. My folks tend to refuse to believe you can do better than New Orleans— well, for most things. Mom's full-on accepted there's better shopping in New York." I force a smile until Anna steps up and wraps her arms around me, causing me to completely lose it, crying so hard snot drips from my nostrils.

Anna grips my hair bun, placed low on my head because the high bun didn't feel right this morning, and she tugs hard to get my attention. "I want to tell you he's going to be okay."

My bottom lip quivers because all I can think is, *he's not going to be okay.*

Anna holds me as she continues. "But you still have time with him. Go home and be with him, okay? Be there for him. Share memories. Talk about the good times. Enjoy the time you have left. And know he will always, always be in your heart. He's a part of you, for always."

I nod and reach for a tissue. The loud *wonk* of my blow forces me to laugh, then the snot spilling out from the sides of the tissue has me spurting out, "Eewwww." Anna laughs as she passes me the tissue box.

My phone vibrates.

Mason: Up for company tonight?

I told him about my dad via text. Mom and I spent yesterday in the apartment. At first, we cried. We cried so much. Then she orchestrated plans for my transition to New Orleans. She sent off text messages to Realtors, picked a pack-and-ship moving company, and quizzed me on where I'd like to live in New Orleans. I told her I'd stay in the carriage house to start. If Dad's going to be sick, being as close as possible makes sense. The carriage house, which only carries the name due to its history, serves as a guest home overlooking my parents' swimming pool. Governor Kennedy and his wife once stayed there. It'll work for me. Besides, I can't fathom house hunting while Dad is sick.

Me: Sure. I need to pack but would be good to see you. My flight home leaves tomorrow morning.

Mason: I'll bring dinner. What's your favorite comfort food?

Me: Chicken and dumplings

Mason: On it. Mom's keeping Kara.

I type out my reply.

Me: Bring her. I have to tell her goodbye.

Then I erase before sending. I haven't made it clear to Mason that I'm moving yet. Packers are in my apartment today boxing up clothes. Mom stayed this morning to get them started before returning home to Dad. When Mason gets to my place, it'll be obvious this isn't a short visit.

Anna has her arm wrapped around my shoulder. She's reading the text exchange and squeezes when she sees me erase my words. Tears fill my eyes once again. It's difficult to swallow through the emotion.

"Hey, it's not goodbye. You can come back to New York."

I shrug. "Maybe. But I can't imagine leaving Mom alone in New Orleans once he passes. And I was going to move home one day, anyway. It's always been the plan."

"Do you think you'll try long distance?"

My chest aches. I have no idea if the pain ripping through my chest is from the prospect of ending things with Mason or my father. But, my god, it hurts. My whole chest throbs. I exhale, then sniffle, then grab a tissue and blow. "Long distance. How would that work?"

"However you two decide you want it to work."

I shake my head. "I don't know, Anna. He has a child. He couldn't very easily take off for a weekend, and I don't know if I'll be able to get away.

And this isn't a temporary move. I mean, after my dad..." A sob breaks out, and I can't say the words. "I won't leave my mom alone."

An email notification catches my eye. It's from a secretary at Dad's office. I scan the formal, curt meeting request. His partners want to have lunch with me. And Dad's not included on the email. It's as if the sharks smell blood in the water, so now there's a new level of aggression.

"Don't make decisions right now. This is all new and fresh. You don't know what you're dealing with. Go home, get the information, let all this settle before you do anything. Promise me, okay?"

She tilts my head and forces me to look at her. Then, with one hand on the top of my head and the other on my chin, she forces me to nod.

"You are agreeing. You are promising me. You are not going to make any decisions today. You have time."

Everything in the room blurs once again, as tears blot my view, but the heavy, excruciating pain in my chest lightens ever so slightly for the first time since yesterday. The notion that nothing is final, that no decisions have to be made soothes my aching lungs. A sliver of hope breaks through the surges of pain weighing me down.

SIXTEEN

Mason

A strong, cold wind gusts down Clarkson Street. The bare tree limbs bend under the force of the wind, and I clutch my scarf and coat. The walk from my clinic to Delilah's isn't a long one. I lower my head as I barrel forward headfirst into the night. Delilah hasn't shared much, she doesn't seem to know much, and she needs me.

My mom graciously agreed to let Kara stay with her tonight. I can't imagine how I would handle this single parent thing without my mom. It's a wonder to me she managed as a single parent, always there for me but also working multiple jobs at times to keep a roof over our heads and food in the refrigerator. Then, less than ten years after I'm out the door and she gets to live her life for herself, I get drunk, don't wrap it up, and she's re-arranging her life for me, yet again, helping me out. If anyone has ever owed their mother, it's me.

I open the heavy metal and glass door to Delilah's apartment building, and dry heat blasts over me. As I loosen the scratchy wool scarf, I stride to the reception desk where a uniformed doorman in a pressed navy jacket with a narrow brass nameplate greets me. The nameplate reads T. Reids.

"How can I help you, sir?"

"I'm here to see Delilah Daniels."

"One moment..." He dials the phone. "Ms. Daniels, there is a gentleman here to see you." He listens for a few seconds. "She says for you to come up to the fifth floor."

When he hangs up the phone, he directs me down the hall and around the corner to the Penthouse C elevator bank.

Penthouse? I've lived in the penthouse a few times myself, but always in a fifth-floor walk-up, without a doorman, and where we applied the name penthouse because it was on the top floor. As I follow the directions, ignoring the row of elevators for the masses, I mentally catalog some of the finer points of her building. Doorman. White marble everywhere. White lobby furniture. Fresh, white orchids. These details didn't strike me exactly the same way when I didn't associate the words *penthouse* and *private elevator* with Delilah.

A raised plaque and the words "Penthouse C" in script identify her elevator. Looking farther down the long hall, I see additional elevator entrances. Presumably other private elevators. I step into hers, and the panel offers a 4, 5, 6, L, P1, and P2. I press 5 and wait.

When the doors open on the fifth floor, I step out into an apartment. To my right, there's a wall and a small table with a massive white orchid, and to my left is a long hall that opens into a haze of light. I turn left and follow the hall, bypassing a long built-in for coats, scarves, and a bench with a basket of gloves.

"Hello?" I call.

Delilah rounds the corner at the end of the hall, a small smile on her face. "You're here. Thanks for coming over."

She places her hand in mine, and I pull her close. I've been worried about her all day. I busied myself with patients, mostly a non-stop rush of well-checks mixed in with a few geriatric animals fighting the wear and tear of age. In between each patient, I'd check my phone for any new texts.

Color left her face when she read the text yesterday. The moment I stepped into the den, hot scrambled eggs steaming in the bowl, I sensed something was wrong. She clutched her phone, shoulders down, looking like someone sucker punched her.

I wanted so much to follow her home, to be there for her as she met her mother and learned more about what was going on. But I had Kara, and the scene that was bound to play out between Delilah and her mother was no place for a child. It also wasn't the time or place for Delilah's mother to meet Kara for the first time. These things I understood, but understanding didn't make letting her leave any easier.

The tension in my shoulders subsides as I inhale Delilah's floral aroma. Her long blonde mane sits at the nape of her neck today, instead of piled on top of her head, as if she's signaling to the world it's not a top bun day. Her gray sweater bears holes around the seams, and her jeans are riddled with artfully places tears, as if she bought them ripped. She's wearing thick socks instead of shoes, and she falls much lower to my chest. She holds on to me as if she's clinging to me for life. I want to wrap her up and promise to take care of her, to say her father will be okay, and we'll find a cure. But, as a veterinarian, I know all too often there is no cure. All too often, the strategy shifts from seeking health to lessening pain and making the most out of the gifted days that remain.

In my practice, we light a candle when it's time to say goodbye, so others speak in low voices. A lighted candle is our silent way of sharing what is happening behind a closed door. Someone is saying goodbye to a family member. It happens too often, and it's never easy. I'm always grateful when an owner stays while I inject the medicine to end the pain because I know when they leave the room, their pet searches for them. In my core, I believe it's so much better for a pet to be held by their owner as they fall asleep for the last time.

We stand there, holding each other. She rubs her face into my shoulder, and as she pulls away, I notice dark, wet marks on my shirt. She tugs my hand, and I follow her around the corner then stop. Outside, it's gray and dreary, but her kitchen is enormous and bright. White, shiny cabinet doors with silver pulls offset by a navy tile backsplash run down both walls of the kitchen with an enormous gray island in the middle. The end of her kitchen boasts glass sliding doors that open onto an outdoor terrace ensconced in floor to ceiling glass. Oversized rectangular gray ceramic tiles line the floor. An abundance of green plants fills the room at the end and provide the only source of non-white, gray, silver, or navy color. This one area might be larger than my entire apartment. She has not one, but two stainless steel chef kitchen refrigerators. Not one but two white porcelain farm sinks. The ceiling in the kitchen curves upward into a dome, and prominent silver pendants fall from the middle, cascading light throughout the spacious kitchen. The kitchen could easily grace the pages of *Architectural Digest*.

"Nice place." No wonder she seemed so puzzled my bathroom wasn't attached to my bedroom. Her reality differs dramatically from the majority of New Yorkers. And mine.

She points me to a stool and wordlessly offers me hot tea by picking up a white ceramic mug and angling her eyebrows at me in a questioning manner. She speaks volumes with her hands, eyebrows, and head. I nod to indicate I'll have some.

With her back to me as she pours hot water, with a defensive air, she says, "I know. It's a lot. My parents bought this place when I moved here.

Or, well, my dad's business did. My dad views it as a real estate investment. And any of the partners can stay here if they come to the city." She opens a cabinet and pulls out a flat wooden box. She pushes the mug of water and the box toward me across the island. The box holds a restaurant's worth of teabags. I pick Moroccan mint and close the box, sliding it back to her.

"What does your dad do?"

"Real estate. It's a second-generation family business, but he's taken it to the next level. He's kind of big shit in Louisiana. But no one cares here. It's nice."

I take in the kitchen as she talks. I will never, ever be able to afford a place nearly as nice as this one in Manhattan. Ever.

"Did your Mom make it home okay?"

Her lips turn downward, and she sniffles. "Yeah. She texted right before you arrived."

I rap my fist against the counter. "I didn't know where to get chicken dumplings. I thought we could order dinner in. Maybe I should have picked up something and brought it with me." She stares at me with a blank expression. "Do you have some menus?"

She leans across the counter, and the giant bun on the nape of her neck shifts. I miss the top of head bun and grip my coffee mug to prevent myself from reaching over and re-doing her hair.

"Oh, yeah, here are some menus." She pulls out a jam-packed drawer stuffed with menus and flips through them. "Do you mind if we order Italian? I'm kind of craving chicken parm. This place, Mama's, you'd never want to eat there because it's kind of a hole, but, oh my, they have the best marinara sauce. Buttery garlic knots too."

When she locates the correct menu, she whips it out, victorious, and catches my eye as if to ask if it's okay. I give her a nod, and she tosses the menu my way.

"They have an app. It's easiest to order on the app. They have so many freaking options, ordering by phone can take forever. Drives me bonanzas." She flicks away on her phone then glances up at me, waiting. I tell her I'll have whatever she wants, and she half waves her hand and shifts away from me as if she's having an entire conversation in her mind, and something about the twist of her head and the attitude as she pounds on the phone has me suspecting I'm not faring well in the conversation.

She sets her phone down on the island and says, "Thirty minutes. Want any wine?"

I haven't had much of the hot tea she fixed me,

so I decline. She disregards me and opens the wine refrigerator, removes a bottle of red, and pours two glasses.

I frown as she slides the glass my way and says, "You can have it with dinner."

She picks up her glass, leaving mine on the counter for me to take or leave, and strolls into the glassed-in room at the end of the condo. I follow. Lush, healthy plants fill the space. I estimate it would require at least thirty minutes to water all the plants in this room.

"So, how big is this place?" So far, I've seen a long hall, an enormous kitchen, and a glassed-in room, but no den or bedrooms. I did see a stairwell to the left of the kitchen farther down the hall. There are three floors, or, at least, three access points.

She shrugs and fidgets, bouncing her knees rapidly. "Fifty-five hundred square feet. Five beds, five baths. I can give you the tour if you like?" Her toe taps, defiant, as she awaits my response.

"No, that's okay. It's gorgeous." I continue looking around. This place has every appearance of being professionally decorated. Yet another stark contrast between her home and mine.

She sighs and sets her drink down on the coffee table. "Yeah. Surprise." She holds her arms out and shakes her fingers doing her jazz hands wave.

I squint, studying her defensive posture and half-hearted attempt at lightening the awkwardness between us. "Did you mean to keep this from me?"

She takes a sip of her wine before responding. "Maybe. Back home, everyone treats me differently. When I moved here, everyone assumed I was just like them, the same kind of background, living with roommates, struggling to make ends meet in an entry level position. I hardly ever bring anyone here. It's not like having all this makes me different from everyone else, but I guess I've always assumed some people back home were nice to me because of my parents. And that's not a whacked assumption. People did a lot for me because of them. Because they wanted something. People kiss ass when they want something. Moving to New York gave me a clean slate. A chance to be normal. Where my name didn't automatically fill in blanks for people about who I am or what they could get from Dad by being nice to me."

I swallow my tea as she takes long swallows of her wine. I lean back on the sofa and observe her, sitting across from me. Red eyes and swollen cheeks give away she's been crying, but she's stiff, and her shoulders are back. Her posture reminds me of an animal that hasn't yet decided if I can be trusted. "How much does a place like this cost?"

Her cheeks flush, a vibrant pink tone overtaking the pale cast of white skin. Her chin juts out as she answers, "Ten million. My dad believes Manhattan real estate holds its value."

"So, this is your parents' place, then? You rent from them?"

Her gaze finally meets mine. "No. Technically, it's the firm's. Decorating it, being allowed to live here, that was a graduation present."

I cough. "That's a really nice graduation present."

"Yeah, it is. So what?" she snaps. "Having money doesn't make me a bad person. Nor does it make me different."

Anger seeps through her words as they fly out of her mouth. I put my palms up in the air, defensive. "I didn't say it makes you different."

She stares at me for a moment, then puts her elbows to her knees and rests her forehead on her palms. "I'm sorry. I'm emotional. You haven't done anything."

"But you expect me to do something? What do you expect me to do? Has someone done something bad to you because your family has money?" I don't say because she has money, because while she probably has a ton in her bank account, all signs point to it being her parents' money. Something she grew up with but didn't earn.

"No. If anything, good things have happened because of it. I was invited to every birthday party growing up, accepted onto every sports team, even if I'd never held a lacrosse stick or had any experience in the sport, almost never had to introduce myself because everyone seemed to know me. My parents can be generous, and they make the party rounds, and I was always in tow. It wasn't bad." She pauses and releases a dramatic sigh. "But moving here, being a nobody, I loved it. When I say my last name, no one bats an eye. The friends I make here, they see me, not my family. When I enter a party, people don't crowd around to greet me like I'm the guest of honor."

"I have no idea what any of that would be like, but I believe it's possible for someone to know about your family and still see you for who you are."

The buzzer sounds, and she gets up. I take my time following her back into the kitchen. She's on the phone, an old model hanging on the wall, similar to the one used by the doorman downstairs. I wander into the hallway over to the stairs. *Holy shit.* The sleek, black banister curves gracefully at each landing, and where I'm standing on the fifth floor, I can look up and see the sixth and down and see the fourth. This unit has three floors, a rare find in New York. Her palatial pad is on the fourth, fifth, and sixth floors of this building, and I can't help but wonder how extravagant the penthouse on the top floors must be.

Hand blown, teardrop lights cascade in a chandelier with a triage of lengths so bulbs artfully scatter the entire way from the sixth floor ceiling to below, extending the length of three floors. I hear Kara's voice in my head. "Daddy! Look! So pretty!" She'd go bananas over this, and rightfully so. If someone snapped a photo and showed me, I'd assume it was from a museum or possibly a high-end hotel, and this is Delilah's *home.*

Delilah calls from far away, "Let's eat in the kitchen."

I head farther down the hall, past the staircase, and peer up to the landing above, then down. Moving boxes are stacked all around the landing downstairs. I head back into the kitchen. "Are you moving?"

She focuses on setting out the food, plates, and

dinnerware. "Movers are coming tomorrow. I'm only packing clothes and personal items. We'll leave the furniture in, as it will sell better furnished. People can envision the space better when it's furnished."

I pull a chair out and sit down. I didn't pay for this food, and I meant to, but it doesn't really matter, so I don't say anything about my meaning to pay. I stare at my empty plate. There's a thin gray line traversing the white china plate, and I focus on the crack.

Delilah says, her voice shaking, "My parents need me."

I close my eyes and breathe then flex my jaw. "Right." I understand. She needs to be there for them. "What's going on with your dad?"

She fills her plate with chicken parmigiana and angel hair pasta. "My mom was too emotional to answer my questions." I snap my head up and watch her as she picks at the melted cheese. "I gave up on getting answers from her. It hurt her too much to tell me. She did better once we started making plans on moving forward. That's the way she is. She does better when she's focused. Once I get home, I'll sit with Dad. Find out more."

"But you've already decided you're moving home? For good?"

She sets her fork down, and the sound of the utensil hitting the glass table echoes through the quiet room. "My mom and dad need me."

We eat in silence. I decide I do want wine and keep our glasses filled. Her father is dying. If it was my mother, I'd be a wreck. I would rush to be by her side. Like a methodical scientist, I run through the indisputable facts. We haven't known each other long. We've barely had a conversation about where our relationship is going or what it means. Yes, I did use the girlfriend word. She agreed. I introduced her to my daughter. I opened the door into my life.

I flex my fingers wide then ball them up into a fist, examining the veins lining the back of my hand. I opened the door into my life, but as I'm seeing now, she never opened the door into hers.

It makes sense she wouldn't discuss her moving plans with me. For her, we've had a fling. A temporary relationship. One in a string of relationships. It's called dating. I stand and pick up my plate, heading to the kitchen and searching the bottom cabinet doors for one that might house the trash.

"But I'd like to still see you. And keep in touch with Kara."

"How would that work?" I ask as I continue my quest for the garbage.

She toys with the cloth napkin in her lap, twisting it between her fingers. "You have, what? Thirteen years before Kara goes off to college? And it's not like you could move to New Orleans. Her mom is here."

I mutter, "*My* Mom is here."

She continues. "It's one thing to try long distance if there's an end in sight. But thirteen years, that's not an end. That's..." she trails off and doesn't finish her thought. I understand what she's saying, though. Thirteen years is an eternity. "Friends, though?" she asks in a high-pitched voice, a tone that rings unnatural and immature.

Friends? She can't be serious. I want to take this pain in my chest and rip it out and toss it away. Throw her away into the distant recesses of my memory. Forget all about this girl and my short time with her. I huff. But she's hurting. She's going to need a friend. And Kara isn't going to want Delilah to disappear altogether. Kara will be happy with FaceTime calls. "Yeah, friends. I can do friends."

I stumble out into the hall. I can do friends, but right now, I need to get out.

"I'll text you, okay? Or you, you text me. Let me know when you've landed tomorrow. And when you find out more about your dad's situation."

I press the elevator button, and she joins me, hands down by her sides, and a lone tear runs down her cheek. I surge forward to close the distance and comfort her.

"I'm so sorry. I'm sorry about your Dad. I'm sorry you have to move home. I hate it. But I understand it. If it was my mom, I'd do the same thing. I would." My shirt pulls tight as she grips it, hard, and buries her face into my chest, sobbing.

Somehow, I'm kissing her and pushing her back against the wall. Frantic. She wraps her legs around my waist as I lift her and rut into her like a wild animal. She kicks the table, and the orchid goes crashing to the ground, sending brown bark across the white pine floor. The contrast of dark and light catches my attention and slows my breath, then I kiss her slowly. Her thumb wipes a tear from my cheek.

She pulls back, caressing the edge of my jaw. "Bedroom." Her feet fall to the floor, and we step around the broken mess down the spiraling stairs to her bedroom.

She unbuttons my shirt and tugs it off my shoulders. I lift her sweater, and she raises her arms as I raise it over her head. I unsnap her bra, and it falls to the floor. Her breasts—god, those breasts. I fondle one, my thumb brushing her nipple as she works my belt buckle and unzips my jeans and pushes them down to be trapped by my boots. I step back and sit on the bed to remove each shoe, then the jeans. My erection sticks out into the air, painfully hard and stretched. She stands still, watching as I rid myself of clothes. Then it's my turn to unzip her jeans. I maneuver her to the bed and have her sit as I kneel on the floor before her, naked, cock in the air, fumbling with the side zipper on her high-heeled boots, then pull at her jeans.

Tears fall on both of our cheeks. I reach back for my jeans, pull out a condom, spread her legs, and claim her. Her nails scrape my back as I drive into her, and she cries out. The emotions eat at me, tearing me up from the inside. She hurts. I see it in her glassy eyes and tearstained cheeks. I hurt. Her teeth sink into my shoulder, and I welcome the physical pain because I can't bear the emotional. It's too much. We take and take and take from each other, twisting on the bed, and I bleed from her nails and her teeth until we both tremble and cling to each other long after our orgasms rip through us.

Trickles of blood stain her sheets. My blood. She rains soft kisses and apologies as her naked body presses against me. "I was falling in love with you."

Her lower lip slips out in a pout, and tears rush down. I don't expect a response, but when she says, "Ditto," her confirmation is a balm to my pain, and I cling to her, pressing kisses over her hair and forehead as I hold her.

Eventually, she slips out of bed to go to the restroom, which is naturally conveniently located a few feet away in an en suite. When she returns, I head into the bathroom. The marble space is enormous and mind-blowing. Again, white shines everywhere. The shower is enormous, the freestanding tub something Kara could swim in.

I slide back into bed and pull her naked body to me. She rests her head on my chest and drapes a leg over mine. I play with her hair which flows down her back, free. I'm not sure when it fell out of the bun, but I love it like this. Soft, golden silk. I love this woman. It's an impossible situation. We live on two different planes, and soon to be two different states. But I can't bear to let her go. Not today.

"We could try long distance. See how it goes?"

She kisses my chest and fingers the dark brown curls. "For thirteen years?" Her soft breasts press against my side, and I reach around to cup her smooth ass.

"As long as it takes for us to find a solution. It'll take time. I can't move in a day. The clinic is expanding, and we're in the process of taking on more debt. One of my partners is planning for a round of friends and family financing. I don't know how many weekends I'll be able to get away for quite a while. Finding someone to buy me out at this stage would be tough, and I can't leave my mother. But none of that means we can't find a solution eventually. And, you don't know what's going on with your dad. It's possible the best doctors are here in New York, and it would be better if they moved here."

She rests her head on my chest, but her muscles are tight. I work the knots with my fingers. "I have to return to New Orleans. It's always been the plan. My dad's business? I'm his successor. If I don't step in, it falls out of the family."

"You said it's a real estate firm?"

"It is. I'll hardly be an asset. But Dad's partners are already reaching out to me. Probably because he's sick. It's kind of a done deal. Mom thinks I can manage the marketing."

"Is that what you want?"

"Mason, what I want doesn't matter. I've been postponing the inevitable for years. This has always been the plan. It's time I grow up, enter that adult world that everyone with half a brain always bashes."

I chuckle. "Mmm. I've been living in that adult world for quite a while, and it's not all that bad."

"Yeah, says the guy who hadn't been out on a date in four years."

I kiss the top of her head. "This sucks."

Her full, swollen lips curve into a slight smile. She leans forward and presses her lips to mine. "Let's try long distance." She places her index finger over my lips, as if shushing me. "I can't make any promises, but let's see. You can't easily get away, but maybe I can. For weekends. It's not like you had this raucous social life a long-distance relationship is going to impact."

I hold on to her, grateful for the chance. Grateful for another day with her. Even if she's far away, she'll still be mine. And maybe, in a couple of years, the clinic will be in a better position for me to find someone to buy me out. Then I remember Amber, and it hits me that I'll be taking my daughter away from her mother if we move. My daughter would have her own back window moment, watching her mother drift into the distance. And there's my mother too. A woman who has given me so much when I had no one, as a kid and as an adult. I should be making love to Delilah one last time before she's gone for an unknown length of time, but instead I lie with her in my arms, sleepless, staring at the white ceiling, running through options in my head.

As morning breaks, I find myself selfishly hoping the best doctors for her father are in New York. Because while I'm grateful Delilah and I haven't ended everything, I find it hard to be optimistic about a long-distance relationship without any sort of path to close the distance.

SEVENTEEN

Delilah

After collecting my luggage from the carousel, I pull my two oversized suitcases outside, texting my mother to coordinate her picking me up curbside. I tug off my thick cotton sweater, thankful I had the foresight to wear a t-shirt beneath it. It's a blue sky, seventy-two-degree day here in New Orleans. A stark difference from the forty-two-degree temperature I left behind.

I was supposed to visit in October for the VooDoo Music Festival but changed plans last minute. If I had come home then, would I have known he was sick? I don't speak to him enough.

So often when I call home, I speak to Mom and get the briefest of updates on Dad. *Oh, he's fine. Playing golf. Working. In the garage. Watching the Tulane game.*

My mom pulls up in Dad's black Range Rover. She drives a sky-blue Porsche convertible, which while a design marvel, wouldn't hold one of my suitcases. Dad isn't in the car with her, which can't be a good sign. Is he so sick he can't ride to the airport?

"Where's Dad?" I ask as she hugs me in greeting.

She pinches my arm. "What kind of greeting is that? What am I? Stale king cake?"

"Mom." She's unbelievable. "Dad's sick. He's the reason I'm here. Where is he?"

Mom sticks her chin out, and for a second I fear she's going to break down crying. Maybe reminding her of Dad's illness isn't a good idea. I squeeze her shoulder and change the subject.

"Looks like it's going to be a gorgeous day today."

She smiles and situates herself in the driver's seat. "Yes. Oh, and you're in luck. The Christmas decorations are everywhere. Of course, they've been up since before Thanksgiving. Yes, it's true, they've been doing it for years, but it's simply too early. Now, I'm always torn at home too. Do I keep out my fall decorations, or shift to Christmas?"

The familiar streets of New Orleans pass by as Mom continues about this annual conundrum and how retail stores are rushing all the seasons. On the bright side, it sounds like I'll be home to help decorate the tree. I haven't done that since college.

The conversation has shifted to plans this afternoon, and how she hopes to throw a 'welcome home' party for me. Of course she does.

I interrupt her as she asks if this weekend is too soon. "I'm sorry, but I don't feel like celebrating. Not right now. You understand, don't you?"

She swallows and stares at the road. Her slim, pale hand flexes on the steering wheel. I'm all down for her denial. I get where she's coming from. It's always been easier for me to smile and put a bounce in my step than to explain to someone else what I'm feeling, to share anything other than a happy face. But I can't be the happy she hides behind. She's going to need to launch a new gardening club initiative or volunteer to be on the decorating committee for the Annual YaYa Arts Center Christmas Gala.

We pull into our driveway, and I watch the

front door, willing it to open so I can lay eyes on Dad, see him and wrap my arms around him. Pull him into his study and find out everything Mom can't bear to say. If it's cancer, I'll need to evaluate his doctors and make sure he's on the best treatment plan. If it's some strange disease, it's the same strategy. Google the hell out of it until answers, or at least experts, are found. Maybe we can get him into a medical trial.

She parks in the driveway and pops the rear open. We each lug a heavy suitcase out and onto the pavers. Dad still hasn't come out. One glance at Mom, and it's clear she's not expecting him. Either he's not home, or he's incapacitated. This is not the Dad I grew up with. He's always the one to pick me up at the airport. "Is Dad at work?"

"No. He'll be home for lunch. He had something to do this morning."

Mom leads the way around the side to the carriage house, intent on getting me unpacked. Marie, my Mom's faithful, cheery assistant, greets us. Marie has worked for Mom for at least fifteen years. She works Monday through Friday and oversees all things to do with our home, from the cleaning of it, to the outside gardening, to helping Mom plan social events.

She wraps her arms around me as she beams.

"Welcome home, Miss Delilah. It's so good to see you." She pulls away and pinches my cheek, a move that used to annoy me to no end. "I was absolutely delighted when your mother told me you're returning home. I'm gonna get you unpacked, okay, dear? I have the master bedroom outfitted for you, but if you want any changes or need anything at all, you just let me know."

"Thank you, Marie. Has your granddaughter arrived yet?" Mom mentioned Marie's daughter had announced the gender of her baby, and Marie was over the moon with excitement about her new grandbaby's upcoming arrival. Mom disappears as Marie and I lug the heavy suitcases up the narrow staircase to the upstairs bedroom.

"You go spend time with your mother," Marie tells me. "I'll get you unpacked and settled."

I give her a hug before departing. "You're the best, Marie. Thank you." Unpacking happens to be one of those activities I rather dislike, so I'm quite happy to leave, knowing she'll iron any clothes that are wrinkled and restock any items she believes I need more of. Growing up, all my clothes were perfectly ironed and my closet expertly organized. She's a wonder, and I've no idea how much my parents pay her, but it most certainly isn't enough.

Downstairs, I notice the fresh vase of hot pink roses on the circular kitchen table. There must be thirty-six flowers in the vase, and on a whim, I snap a photo and text it to Mason.

Me: Home. Please share with Kara. These flowers remind me of her.

I step outside, taking a moment to stretch as I meander around the swimming pool. The French doors in the main house are open, and white gauze curtains hang straight, flapping slightly from the breeze of the overhead fan on the wide porch.

I enter the house, calling, "Mom?"

She rounds the corner, arms full of newspapers and mail. "I'm going to put this down in your father's office. He'll want to go through it all when he gets home."

I follow her into the office. It has a distinctly different design aesthetic from the rest of the house. My mother loves bright colors and wallpaper, and my father lets her decorate however she desires. However, he designed this room. The walls are painted a forest green on the top half, and the bottom half is a dark mahogany. Dark leather club chairs and a sofa fill one side of the room, and his commanding walnut desk almost fills the other side. That desk serves as command central.

I settle into one of the well-worn club chairs and watch her arrange the mail neatly into specific stacks. "Mom, what's going on? Where's Dad?"

Her shoulders lift, and her busy hands pause for a second, then she resumes her work. Once she's satisfied with her stacks, she sits back into Dad's office chair. The desk envelops her slight frame. She bows her head, stands, and moves over to the club chair near me.

"Your father has multiple sclerosis."

The name of the disease doesn't mean much to me. I sit there trying not to twitch. The name of the disease doesn't register, but my heart still thumps in my chest. I've donated for MS events before, if I knew someone running or biking a race, and an image of someone in a wheelchair comes to mind.

"We were going to tell you when you came for the festival. Then we were going to tell you at Thanksgiving." Her tone smacks of a reprimand. I deserve it. I've been canceling visits with increasing frequency over the last couple of years. Thanksgiving was a big one. She smooths the fabric on her skirt flat as she sits with perfect posture. Her lower lip trembles, the one visible sign she is struggling to hold back her emotions. I lean over and reach for her but can't quite touch.

"The disease, right now, it's not bad. We were shocked by the diagnosis. I went to my first support group last week." Her voice cracks as she weeps, the same tears she cried in my apartment, and I come to her, scooting her over to make room for me in the club chair and I hold her as she cries. She sobs into my chest, and I run my fingers through her hair to soothe her. She pulls a tissue out of her skirt pocket, and once the tears have stopped and she has her emotions in check, she curls the used tissue in her hand and continues. "Sweetie, it's going to get bad. So bad. Thank you so much for coming home. I can't do it on my own."

"Mom, of course I'm here. You don't have to do anything on your own. But I don't know anything about MS. I can Google it, but what did his doctor say?"

She dabs her nose with the tissue. "When the disease progresses, it will be bad. Wheelchair, maybe confined to bed. He'll need help with basic care like dressing and feeding and...toileting. Oh, honey. This support group. A lot of them are men.

MS strikes more women than men. You should have heard their stories. I'm so scared. So scared. And your Dad, honey, he's in denial. He's working less and playing more golf. Which I suppose is good. He should do that while he still can. But it's like he's refusing to believe he has this disease." Somehow, hearing that Dad isn't being the ideal patient doesn't surprise me. I can help with that. Dad and I are similar in nature, and when Mom gets to be too annoying and doting, which is what Dad might be reacting to, I can whisk her away.

Mom pulls my arm away from my face, and it's not until her hand closes around mine that I realize I've been chewing on my thumbnail. "Okay. So, what did the doctors say? What is his life expectancy?"

"Oh, honey, they don't know. They don't know." Her voice quakes, and I hold her and kiss the top of her head.

The click of the front door opening sounds, and I leave my mother to compose herself as I go to see who is entering our home. My dad beams when he sees me. He's in full-on golf attire, but his right hand rests on a cane. "Dad?"

"Delilah! When did you get home?"

"Just now. How are you?"

"Good. Tony and I hit the back nine this

morning after a breakfast meeting at the club. Your mom tells me you've had enough of the Big Apple and you're moving home. Come here and give your old man a hug. I knew you'd get sick of the big city one of these days."

He steps forward to wrap me in his arms, and I gladly go to him, but I can't stop staring at the cane and the trembling, veiny hand pressing on the cane. For the first time in my life, or at least the first time I've ever noticed, he gives me a one-armed hug, and the entryway blurs as my eyes fill with tears. I swear the man has shrunk.

"Come with me, sweetheart. Let's catch up."

My heart cracks as I study my father. He's lost weight, and the lines on his face seem deeper. He doesn't look like he's going to die tomorrow, but something in his posture or demeanor paints an older, more frail appearance. With each slow step, his hand wobbles on the cane for support on his left side.

I follow him to his office. My mother stands by the door, watching us approach. When I enter the room, Dad steps behind me, his body blocking my view of my mother. "Let me spend some time with my daughter, Melinda. You picked her up from the airport." I can't see her reaction.

In a low murmur, I hear her respond, "She

needs to be here, Hoffman." In a louder tone, directed at me, she continues, "I'll knock when lunch is prepared."

My father closes the heavy solid maple wood door and makes his way to a leather wing back chair, his left hand vibrating through the entire journey. I watch his progress, stunned.

Before he has situated himself into his favorite office chair, I ask, "Dad, Mom has not been a good source of information. Can you tell me more about MS? About what your doctor is saying?"

He gestures to his liquor cabinet, a massive built-in that features a full bar and a glass pitcher of fresh water at all times. "Would you mind getting me a glass of water?"

I get up to pour him a glass, deliver it, and sit on the edge of the chesterfield leather sofa. He drinks the cool water, and I tap my toes, impatience building. My mind is a blur. I need Google.

"Sorry, sweetie. Yes, you see, your mother and I were going to tell you, but then you didn't come home."

"Tell me what, Dad? About MS? Mom was crying so hard when she came to visit me, I couldn't get any info from her. She said you are *dying*."

He grimaces as I tell him about Mom, swallows, and tells me, "I'm not dying. Any more than you are. But, if you remember, I've had some strange symptoms for years. Tired, and your Mom was convinced I was working too hard. I'd fall down. Strange falls. At times, it felt like my muscles weren't responding, but my blood pressure and cholesterol were good each year. Then my vision, well, I started having problems. Some pain too. A few months ago, a brain scan confirmed I have multiple sclerosis, but multiple sclerosis hits people differently. I didn't have any symptoms at all until my late forties. And my flareups, that's what they call it when the disease acts up, have been pretty far apart. Far apart and mild enough that I've been able to ignore it for a long time. Until my vision issues. Now I'm on medication. Here's the thing I need you to understand, sweetheart. Your mom, she's worried. She went to a blasted MS support group, and I think they scared her out of her cotton-picking mind. Dr. Steiner had no business sending her to that group, but what you need to know, sweetie, despite what she seems to believe, it's not a terminal illness. On average, an MS person's life expectancy is maybe five to ten years shorter than a non-MS person. They make treatment advancements every year. More medicines are available. If I take care of myself, I might never be as bad off as some of the spouses in your mom's support group."

"But you don't know?"

"No. But, honey, I could be in a car crash next month too. So could you. Life is full of unknowns. For my part, I've decided to live more while I can still walk. I play golf almost every day. I'm stepping down as CEO. I'll still have a seat on the board. Now that you're back here, we can find you a role that you like in the company. It's time to implement the succession plan."

My forehead rests in my hands, my elbows on my knees, as I absorb everything he's telling me. "So, you call it Mom's support group. Is it a support group for caretakers?"

He swallows his water, licks his lips, and nods.

"What about you? Do you have a support group for people with MS?"

His hand trembles on the top of the cane, and he kicks his right leg out straight and shifts, grimacing as if his hip is hurting. "Dr. Steiner recommended one. I haven't been yet."

"Why?"

"Honey, I don't need it. I might not for another twenty years. And look at your mother. She's been a train wreck since she went to that damn group."

The library door swings open, and Aunt Josie, a tall, beautiful woman with thick, long, mahogany hair, bursts in. "There she is. Come give me a hug!"

I step to her, and she wraps me in her arms then pulls back and glances at my father as she squeezes my hip. "What's going on here? Why the serious faces?"

"Dad's telling me about his MS."

Dad speaks up. "Melinda told her I'm dying."

Aunt Josie's mouth drops open. "No. She. Did. Not."

I hug her more tightly because her expression is what I'm feeling.

"Josie, what are you doing here?" Mom's shrill voice rings behind her.

"Melinda, what have you done?" Aunt Josie places both hands on her hips as if she's scolding one of her kids.

If Mom's eyes were loaded with bullets, Josie would be on the floor in a puddle of blood. "We need her here. Do not interfere, Josie. I'm sure one of your three children or your grandchildren could use your services, so why don't you run along to where *you are needed*."

"Don't be ridiculous, Mom. I haven't seen Aunt Josie in a year. Can you stay for lunch?"

"I only had lunch prepared for three," Mom says, her lips in a tight scowl. Dad, Josie, and I stare at her. She adjusts the glasses on her nose. "I'll have an additional place set. Of course, you're welcome to stay, Josie."

My gaze follows Mom's retreating back. She's on a roller coaster of emotions, evident by all the tears. I have more to research, but it does seem she's latched onto the worst-case scenarios. She could also be correct that Dad is in denial, and whatever just happened between Aunt Josie and Mom, I can't even process. Those two are inseparable. My sleep-deprived brain is on overload, smooshed down and trampled.

"Well, I'm home. Let's go get lunch. Aunt Josie, I want to hear all about the new school you're working on opening."

Holding her hand, we walk together to the screened-in porch by the pool where my parents love to take lunch. My father ambles to the kitchen, presumably to find Mom. Marie steps onto the porch to offer us a beverage, and a young girl I've never seen before steps out to add an additional seat at the table. For a moment, I wonder what Mason and Kara would think. Setting the table, or at least the silverware and placemats, is Kara's responsibility at home, and my lovely mother has hired help to do almost everything.

Lunch passes with small talk. Mom's garden club is still struggling with the strange rose disease that travels from bush to bush. My aunt has broken ground on the new art school she's been advocating for years. The school will use art and music as therapy for children with developmental issues. Dad and I eat quietly, listening to the two women as they dominate the conversation.

In one tense moment, Aunt Josie asks me to tell her about New York. My mother interrupts in a clipped tone. "Instead of talking about the past, let's talk about getting her settled here. Why don't you ask her what neighborhoods she might con- sider moving into, so we can keep our ears open?"

I remain silent as they go back and forth. I need a nap.

When our plates are cleared, Dad asks if I'd like to go sit out in the yard with him. Toward the back of our property, behind the carriage house, my parents built a fire pit surrounded by a brick patio. Spanish moss falls from the tree limbs in long, graceful streams. The tree line camouflages the alley that runs behind our property. Dad and I each take a seat in the comfortable chairs, and he pulls out a joint.

I sputter. "Dad? You smoke pot?"

He shrugs. "Medicinal purposes. Technically, the prescription is for the MS, but I find it helps me to better deal with your mother."

As he lights up, I pick up my phone. I've missed a text from Mason.

Mason: Flight okay? What have you learned?

Since my father seems to be somewhat preoccupied, I respond.

Me: He has multiple sclerosis. Do you know much about it?

Mason: A little. Is he in the middle of a flareup?

Me: No. He's not on his deathbed. Did I mention my mother can be a drama queen?

Mason: So, he's okay?

Me: I think? I've still got a lot of questions.

Mason: Can we talk tonight?

Me: Yeah. I'll be here. Smoking medical grade ganja with Dad.

Mason: I'll call later

Dad watches as I type into my phone. When I set it down, he asks, "Who's that? The young gentleman you're seeing?"

"Yeah. I mean, for now." I reach out to take the joint from my Dad and suck on it, inhaling the sweet aroma.

"Your mom guessed something was different about this guy. That's why she pulled this stunt of hers."

"Dad, it's not really a stunt, is it? Yes, it sounds like she greatly exaggerated the situation when she flew down and told me you're dying. That's a bit of a pisser. But she's genuinely terrified. And you don't seem bothered at all. I'm having a hard time figuring out exactly what the fuck is going on. Unless you start telling me more, I'm going to spend the night on Google, and then I'll probably be more terrified than Mom is."

Dad scratches his leg. "I'll tell you whatever you want to know. But, honey, if you moved back home because of my MS, then you didn't move back for the right reasons. Yes, our dream is for you to move into a house nearby so we can see our grandbabies each and every day. But the last thing

I want is for you to be my caretaker. And to be frank, if it comes to me needing a caretaker, Melinda is not going to be my nurse. We're lucky. I have money to hire whatever help I need, plus long-term care insurance. The absolute last thing I want is for my disease to become a burden to you. Or your mother."

"Dad, you wouldn't be a burden. I want to be here for you. And for Mom. You've been there for me my whole life. I love y'all. I owe you everything."

"We love you too, sweetie." He exhales and situates himself in the Adirondack chair, shifting his legs while grasping the cane for support. Once situated, he resumes. "While I disagree with your mother's methods, your return is good timing. Frank, Todd, and I are looking to step out of the business, pass it onto the next generation. If you don't step in, the whole plan gets dicey."

"I'm meeting them for lunch next week."

"You are?"

"Yeah. I'm surprised you don't know."

"Well, everyone's been treating me like a goddamn invalid, but I suppose it's good for you to meet with them on your own. It's a good start. They need to see you can take over our third of the business. You let me know, though, if they aren't treating you like a partner. I'll be damned if I'm going to let them force my family out of a business that was my family's to begin with just because they each have sons who already work there."

The topic clearly pisses him off. Deep lines form all around his mouth, and the flex of his jaw looks like he's grinding his teeth. "We've had this succession plan for decades. It was a mistake to invite them into the business as partners." He sucks on the joint and rests his head on the back of the chair.

"I still can't believe your mother. Using my illness." He shakes his head and scowls then passes me the joint. "Sometimes it's like I don't know her anymore. She and I...we agreed we'd talk to you. About the business, not about this." He waves over his stomach and chest, making it clear by *this* he means his health.

I reach out and hold his hand, resting my head on the back of the Adirondack chair as the effects of the ganja begin. My muscles relax, and a calmness sweeps over me. The anger, confusion, and pain in my chest dissipate. I watch the clouds float by as my father does the same.

EIGHTEEN

Mason

Kara and I stroll down Montague Street to the park. My thick coat does a poor job of blocking the cold winter wind. My hands, the skin raw from frequent washing at the clinic, ache in the bitter cold, a reminder I need lotion. Kara chatters happily beside me as I pat down my coat and discover I do have a pair of gloves stuffed in the oversized pockets. I'm pulling them on when Kara leaps ahead of me shouting, "Mommy!"

I quicken my pace to minimize the distance between my daughter and me. Amber waves, a huge smile plastered across her face. Her dyed hair, a mix of black, purple and white-washed violet, is pulled back tight in a harsh ponytail. As I get closer, I notice her hair is matted and needs to be brushed. If it weren't for having a four-year-old girl, I'd probably never even notice something like that. Amber has three nose rings, and I suspect she's added to the collection of ear piercings. Her ripped jeans, black leather motorcycle jacket, and red Doc Martens scream *band girl*.

I wrap her in a hug when I reach her. Every time I see her, full of big dreams, guilt gnaws at me for knocking her up when she was so young. I remember that Saturday like it was yesterday, when she appeared at my door and asked, "Hey, do you remember me?"

I absolutely remembered her. I met her when I'd first arrived in New York after vet school and had two weeks of freedom before getting my ass handed to me as a first-year veterinarian. I had two weeks to get settled and blow off steam before starting my new job. She'd been this nineteen-year-old dropout, full of life and all about letting loose and having fun and pursuing her dreams of being a musician. We met during my first night of freedom and were inseparable for the next two weeks. I went all out, telling myself it was the undergrad life I denied myself as a driven, competitive student aiming to be a vet. We had an unforgettable two weeks, then I started a new job, and she disappeared.

That first year as a vet threw me hard. I aced vet school. But real-life practice was anything but textbook. I found myself second-guessing every diagnosis, referencing books, and spending too much time per patient. That first year was brutal.

When she didn't return my texts, my ego took a hit. I thought of her a lot. Our two weeks of unfettered freedom. Sex every day. At clubs in the bathrooms, in my apartment. But I'd accepted I'd never see her again. Then she knocked on my door six months later. Crying and showing too much to continue the tour she'd been so psyched to be a part of as a back-up singer and bassist. She hadn't yet procured the four-hundred-square-foot rental she now keeps, more as a storage unit than anything else. With no other option, she came to find me.

I invited her to live with me. I tried hard to make it work with her. One night, I went all out. Scattered roses throughout my studio apartment, lit candles, bought a thick platinum band with tiny diamonds around it. I figured the ring matched her rock and roll vibe. Back then she had jet black hair.

She opened the door, and I got down on one knee. I held out the ring box, nervous as hell, not sure at all we'd make it for the long haul, but every part of me felt asking her to marry me was the right thing to do. The responsible thing to do.

After declining my proposal, she sent a nameless guy from a band to pick up her stuff. She emailed me to tell me she didn't love me, she was too young to get married, and she was putting the baby up for adoption because it would be best for the baby. Maybe adoption would have been best for Kara, but I couldn't.

When Amber scoops up Kara, the worn leather jacket sleeves slide up on her arm, exposing a new tattoo, scrawled across her wrist and onto her palm. It reads *Entertain Us*. Fitting, I suppose, for a band girl, flitting between bands, searching for her big break. Now twenty-three, Amber shows no sign of choosing any other kind of life. If her tattoo accumulation continues, she'll soon be limiting her career options to either band gigs, waitressing, or non-corporate environments. Fuck. I hate myself for even thinking like that. I'm only thirty-two, but damn if being around Amber doesn't make me feel like a stodgy old man.

Amber's piercings glitter in the sunlight when she smiles up at me. "Hi there, stranger," as she slaps my butt in her playful way. She's always been an over the top flirt.

But today, as the three of us walk to the park, the family that could have been, a surreal sensation overwhelms me. As if I'm having an out of body experience, I watch the three of us. Kara between us, a hand in each of ours, swinging. They are singing the song about rainbows, and I stare ahead, physically present yet detached. Fear finds crevices deep within. The intrusion quakes my core. Amber and Kara sing about lovers, dreamers, and rainbows, while a neon yellow sign flashes *caution*.

Amber never wanted to be involved in Kara's life. I'm the one who has been pushing this for years. I'm the one who has taken great care to keep Amber updated, hoping to entice her into her daughter's life, careful to avoid pushing her away. No phone calls for months on end? Never said a word. No birthday phone call? No Christmas present? None were expected. She's been completely absent. As agreed, I've kept the door open, on the chance she might change her mind.

When out of the blue she called and asked if she could see Kara, I didn't hesitate. We haven't talked about Mommy much. Kara couldn't miss what she had never known. I waited until they met to tell her Amber, this stranger, was her mother. She accepted that she travels far away for her job. There hasn't been an emotional attachment. Kara hadn't met her. But now I see it growing before my eyes. *What the hell am I doing?*

I lived the pain of craving a dad. The sadness when a birthday passed unacknowledged. The crush of not being invited for a visit over summer break because of an insane business travel schedule. Reading Facebook posts about his new kids. And here I am paving the way for a repeat life for my daughter.

We arrive at Pier 6, and I have no memory of the way over, other than squeezing my daughter's small glove as we swung her into the air. Amber and Kara run toward the slides, giggling like two little girls heading off to play together. The scene before me is what I've always wished for. Amber enveloping Kara in motherly love. Playing with her. Being in her life.

Awareness of tomorrow looms overhead. One day, Amber will receive a text about a gig, a huge opportunity, playing bars in multiple states that promise tremendous exposure, and she'll be gone. We won't hear from her for a few months. I'll call when Kara asks to speak to Mommy, and she'll decline the call. And I'll say something like, "Mommy's probably working right now. She'll call us back." And I'll tickle her or throw her in the air. But how many more years will tickling and air tossing create a successful diversion?

I find a bench and sit, remove my gloves, and stare at my hands. Delilah might be right. Maybe I should press for full custody now. Amber is a giant wild card in my daughter's life. She could settle down and become the co-parent I hoped for, the loving mom Kara deserves. Or she could follow in my father's footsteps, wave goodbye, and essentially close the door. Or she could become something far worse. She could weave in and out of her life, and eventually arrive back in Manhattan and want her to live with her half the year and parent in a completely irresponsible way, leaving a too-young girl at home alone or taking her out in venues a child has no business in. We might not agree on how to parent *at all*.

As I check my email, a new email from Delilah appears in the list. When I called her last night, it went to voicemail. Like it always seems to these days.

December 1
  To: Mason Herriot

From: Delilah Daniels

Hi - So, my dad's doing good. He's walking with a cane now, which is new. I've been doing research on multiple sclerosis. I'll tell you all about it when we talk.

In some ways - mystical ways - it's good MS hit. He's stepping back from the company and enjoying life. Otherwise, he would have worked hard until he ended up six feet under. At least now he's embracing his next life phase.

Did Kara like the flowers I sent her? Sorry I've missed your calls. I've been falling asleep early.

How are you? How's the clinic? Do you ever watch the clouds? You should. It's sort of meditative.

I miss you. I miss you in a way I didn't think possible.

Love,
Delilah

I lean back on the park bench. The gray sky obscures the Manhattan skyline, wrapping it in fog. I imagine Delilah has a blue sky in her back yard, with the kind of white, fluffy clouds that change shape as they shift overhead. She's already forgotten it's winter, and white fluffy clouds, the kind worth watching, are a rarity here.

"Daddy!" I barely have time to lift my arms before a small body crashes into my torso. Her eyes sparkle, cheeks bright pink from the cold air, and her nose drips a little. I pull out a tissue from my coat pocket and wipe. She grins. "We did all the slides."

"That's awesome. Which was your favorite?"

She whips around to point, and as she does, sends my phone flying. Amber bends and picks it up, glancing at it before handing it back to me. She pauses a moment before asking, "Who's Delilah?"

Before I can answer, Kara's jumping up and down, eager to answer. "She's our friend. She sleeps over. She slept over with me. And with Daddy. But she had to move to New Orens to help her daddy."

I take my phone back from Amber, close out of email, and slip it into my pocket. I wait to see how Amber handles this. Will any mothering instincts kick in? Will she ask me about a woman staying over? Will she connect the dots and remember I had a date the night she abandoned our daughter and that this might be the same woman?

Amber toys with a few of the leather and

chain bracelets on her right wrist. Kara climbs into my lap and cuddles, shivering a bit.

"You're cold, aren't you, baby girl? Want some hot chocolate?"

She grins and nods multiple times in quick succession. I stand and snap open my jacket to tuck her partially inside. I love that she's still small enough that I can hold her on my hip and warm her inside my coat.

I point to a nearby street vendor selling hot chocolate, and she curls into me. "Do you think he has marzmellows?"

I bounce her as I tramp in that direction. Amber steps up beside me, and I almost trip over my own feet when she positions herself under my right arm, the one not holding Kara, and her left hand tucks into my jeans pocket and curves around my ass. She backs away as I stumble then I charge forward to the vendor with a speed Amber's shorter, booted legs can't match.

We've been together countless times over the last four years since my marriage proposal, admittedly when she was pregnant, but not once has she touched me or remotely flirted with me.

My heartrate spikes, and I smoosh Kara closer to me. "Hi. Yes, we'll take two hot chocolates with lots of marshmallows." I turn as

Amber reaches us. "Would you like a hot chocolate?"

She tilts her head and opens her mouth slightly, rolling her tongue against her teeth. I'm hypnotized by a small piercing, the glint of silver against her tongue. "I'll share yours."

I set Kara down on the ground so I can pull out my wallet and pay for our drinks. "Make that three, please," I say as I hand over my credit card.

The three of us meander down the black path in the park, often stepping on the grass to avoid speeding inline skaters and joggers, and the many city dwellers with a faster pace than four-year-old nibbling at marshmallows can muster. Kara stops to pet every single dog we come across, always taking care to ask permission, the way I've taught her.

I scout up ahead, searching for a bench to fit the three of us. There's no top on Kara's hot chocolate so she can access the marshmallows, and the only reason her coat isn't covered in a sticky mess right now is that she's been picking the marshmallows off one by one.

As I point our trio in the direction of an open bench, Amber's smooth, melodic tone interrupts my focus on getting us seated spill-free. "So, tell me about Delilah."

Kara opens her mouth wide, exposing a gooey half chewed marshmallow. "She's an artist. Her favorite princess is Tiana. She looks like Cinderella. She colors good. Her daddy's sick."

We sit on the bench with Kara between us. I slide back, sipping the now lukewarm beverage, choosing to blend into the background as mother and daughter bond.

Amber scoots back on the bench too, angling so she is facing me. "Are you dating her?"

I drink my hot chocolate to buy time for a response. After a moment, I answer, "Yes." I stare straight ahead at the skyline.

"Is it serious?"

I continue staring, annoyed. This isn't the kind of conversation I want to have in front of my daughter, and I make it a point to not ask Amber about her dating life. But, in all fairness, this is a woman in contact with her daughter. If I ever met a man in Amber's life, I'd probably ask questions. If she came around enough for Kara to be involved in her life.

"Are you going to answer me?" Amber reaches out and prods my shoulder in a teasing manner. She's chuckling. To her, it's funny.

"I am serious about her. But she had to move home to help take care of her father. I don't...the future isn't...I don't have answers." I can feel her staring at me. "We're figuring things out."

"Where'd she move to?"

Kara pulls on Ambers coat to get her attention. "New Orens."

"New what?"

I clarify. "New Orleans."

"Wow. That's far. So, you're dating other people too, then, right?"

Technically, we're dating exclusively, but emotions were high when she agreed. All of her actions since landing in New Orleans indicate the 'let's be friends' request is coming. I'm bracing for it. But Amber doesn't need to know any of that. Nor does Kara. "No."

I get up and excuse myself to go to the restroom. I don't need to go, but I need a break from this conversation. When I find my way back to them, Amber's on her phone, and Kara is playing on the dead grass in front of the bench. "You guys ready to go?"

We don't make much headway before Kara yanks at my coat and whines, "Daddy, how much farther?"

We've traveled a long way for little legs, so I bend and scoop her up onto my hip. Amber keeps pace alongside me, and after about a block, she loops her arm behind my back and squeezes or tickles Kara, making her laugh.

Amber's close to my side, and a skateboarder approaches from the opposite direction. On instinct, I wrap my right arm around Amber's shoulder and veer to the right to get out of his way. Within seconds, Amber's hand fills my jeans pocket. She smiles up at me, and it could be my imagination, but I think her fingers curve around my ass cheek again.

I glance down at her questioningly, and she says, "My hand's cold."

I kiss Kara's forehead and continue home. If someone were to take our photograph right now, we'd look like the perfect family, out at the park on a Saturday afternoon.

Amber asks, "Hey, you guys wanna get pizza for dinner tonight?"

Kara bounces on my hip and squeals, "I do! When we get back, can we play Candyland?"

Amber says yes, and the three of us continue down the path, a picture-perfect family.

NINETEEN

Delilah

The clouds scatter across the sky. The fluffy cloudscape exhibits a wide array of shades of white, as if an artist mixed a palette of white, cream, and possibly the smallest touch of black, and with heavy strokes, created the scene. I press my back against the solid wood of the Adirondack chair, riveted.

Dad taps my wrist and gestures with the lit joint, asking if I want another hit. I have a nice buzz going, and at this moment, the sensation that the only thing that matters are the clouds above overwhelms my mind. For some reason, Dad likes to open his mouth and speak when we sit out here. I prefer to commune with nature, to lose myself in the moment.

"Have you heard from Mason lately?"

"Yeah." We email and text. I haven't been able to FaceTime with Kara as much, because her mom has been around on the weekends. I'm happy for her. That's a good thing. I ignore the twisting in my stomach and the odd nausea. *No. Come on, Delilah, her mom should be in her life. I'm here. Studying clouds.*

"He going to come down here for a visit anytime soon? I'd like to meet this fellow."

"Dad."

"What?"

I smash a mosquito on my wrist. One wing sticks out from the gooey black spot. No blood seeps through the black goo.

"Delilah."

"What?"

"Is Mason going to come visit?"

I don't have the energy to wipe the smashed mosquito off. I extend my arm, resting it on the flat wooden arm of the chair, watching the black smoosh spot, half expecting it to regroup and fly away.

"He's super busy. He's adding a new location

to his veterinary practice. They're working with some finance guys on a friends and family investment round, and they may open a third location."

"Has he asked you to invest?"

"No."

"Well, when he does, be sure to run it by our financial planner."

Noises fluctuate in concert from his chair, the grating of wood against brick as he shifts, exhales, and curses. I don't watch him, but I hear him extinguish the joint, but that doesn't make sense because I can't hear that. There's no noise involved in extinguishing a joint. A crash sounds, and I resume studying the smashed mosquito remains. Dad's cane rolls on the ruddy red brick pavers.

"Okay. That's enough ganja for the day. I'm going to get us some water and food." His palm covers the base of his cane, and he maneuvers it off the ground. When he returns, Maria is with him, and he takes a glass of water from her tray and pushes it my way.

"Drink this." He strains and, in slow motion, sits back down in the Adirondack chair while Maria sets down a small tray on the side table between us. The tray includes a tower of small sandwiches that reminds me of the little sandwiches they serve at fancy tea. Pimento cheese sandwiches. One entire sandwich fits in my mouth. All sandwiches should be cut to this size. Maria is brilliant.

"Delilah."

"What?"

"You aren't happy here, baby girl."

Dad's probing gaze studies me. I swallow my third sandwich then swipe the black smudge off my wrist. The mosquito never flew away.

"I'm fine, Dad."

"No. I don't think you are. I've been enjoying our afternoons, but if you're ready, I think it's time for you to find your place in the partnership. You'll be happier once you've got something to fill your days."

Ugh. "I'm having lunch with Frank and Todd tomorrow." Yes, I've rescheduled it a few times. There's a certain finality to joining the firm I've been putting off. Dodging my whole life, really.

These last two weeks the slow days have flown by and blurred together. I email Mason. Sometimes. I go to lunch with Mom and whatever friend she has scheduled for that day. I fend off her requests to get more involved in her gardening club. I don't have an issue with gardening, per se. But, by my guestimate, the median age of the club is seventy-five, and my attention span when discussing rose bush varietals is remarkably limited.

I do read. I've been on a book a day diet since arriving in my hometown, but I didn't move here for an endless vacation. I thought I'd be helping my parents, but my help's not needed.

No, instead, this is it. I promised my dad I'd join his company. One day. And that day is here. "I'll find out from Frank and Todd when they want me to start." Having a place to go, being around people with a purpose, that's what I'm missing. I'm missing the energy. Real estate won't be as vibrant as life in an advertising agency, but it won't be all bad.

"Yes. I like that they're having lunch with you, without me there. They're treating you like a partner. Don't forget, you are an equal partner."

Mom's voice sounds across the back yard. "What are you saying, Hoffman?"

I can't see her because she's standing behind my chair, but she sounds close by. Her hand falls on top of my head, and she pats me like a dog. Yep, close by.

"I have some properties on the computer to show you, dear. Not that we mind you staying with us, but you'll feel more settled once you find your own place." Her firm grasp on my shoulder pushes me forward and propels me to the house. She rambles on about some committee and random things she needs me to do as I survey the well-groomed grass below my feet.

I climb the porch stairs. The dark paint is chipped in places on the edges. The wood below the dark brown paint has a hint of texture, as if a mildew fairy flew by during the night and swiped her mildew brush over that singular streak of exposed wood.

"Delilah, how are you, dear? Come give me a hug." Aunt Josie stands at the top of the stairs, arms wide. She pushes me back and tugs my chin and twists my head left and right, as if she's examining my make-up.

"Have you been sharing your dad's medical marijuana?"

I laugh, a full-on belly laugh. Maybe the first time I've laughed since I arrived.

"Delilah, come and check these listings on my computer. If you like any of them, I'll set up some time for us to go see them." I obediently sit in the chair behind Mom's laptop. As I flick through the properties, nausea rises, forcing its way up the back of my throat. I jump up and rush to the bathroom.

When I return, Mom and Aunt Josie crowd

the computer, discussing the listings in low, discreet tones. I sidestep them and make my way to the porch, where I pick up my phone. I left it on the coffee table out here some time earlier today. I thumb through and re-read my email from Mason.

December 10
    To: Delilah Daniels
    From: Mason Herriot

Hey there, Delilah,
    Are you planning on staying in New Orleans? Why don't you answer when I call? Long distance relationships require communication. Have you decided we shouldn't try? Would you prefer we're just friends?
    I love you and miss you.
    Mason

I press the wide, flat phone to my heart and fall onto my side on the sofa, half lying, hanging my legs over the side in a contorted position. My head's woozy, and the room spins and shifts.

Voices from the kitchen carry onto the porch through the screen door.

"Oh, I like this one."

"I don't know, Josie. Do you think she needs a house? I'm thinking a condo. Until she's married."

"I think she needs to go back to New York. She has a life there."

"Hush. You'll see. She'll reconnect with her friends, and she'll have a life here in no time."

"You shouldn't have forced her to come home."

"I didn't make her. She wanted to come home."

"You keep telling yourself that."

"Josie. Stop it. Now, listen to me. I want you to go with us to Paris, but there can be no more of this. Do you understand me? She is home, where she needs to be. Drop it."

"Was she excited about Paris?"

"I haven't told her yet. She's gonna be thrilled."

"I thought she prefers London?"

"What would make you think that? Paris? Over the holidays? Nothing beats Paris."

The conversation drones on. At some point, I wake, alone outside on the porch, and make my way back out to the pool house and into bed.

In the morning, I go for a long walk through the neighborhood, shower, get dressed, and leave to meet Frank and Todd to discuss this next stage in my life.

When I enter Mother's, a hole-in-the-wall restaurant I grew up coming to with my parents, a wave of nostalgia sweeps over me. Nothing about the place has changed much. It's like walking through a time capsule. Black and white photos from early days line the wall, proving it's a bit of a living, breathing relic. My dad's partners, Frank and Todd, have already claimed a booth.

"Mr. Williams, Mr. Landry, so good to see you both." My heart isn't into being here, but I give them an honest to goodness smile and warm hug. I've known these two for as long as I can remember.

"Delilah, you're old enough now to call us by our first names." Mr. Landry—well, Todd—has aged almost as much as my dad. He's wearing a light blue and pink paisley bowtie. He always wears bowties. He's not related to the Landry family that owns this restaurant, but you wouldn't know that, given he comes here so often he knows everyone's names.

When we're all seated in the booth, Frank adjusts his tie then starts to spread his arm across the back of the booth. He's a big man, and it would seem natural, except his business colleague is sitting beside him, and I stifle a laugh when Frank gives him a glance that communicates *What are you doing?* And he retracts his arm.

"How's Frank Junior?" Frank's son is five years older than I am, so he's never been a close friend, but I've seen him at holiday parties and charity events over the years.

"He's good. Engaged to be married."

"That's great. You and Mrs. Williams must be so excited."

"Oh, we are. She's not you," he says, pausing to wink at me, "but she's a good one. We like her."

Todd interjects, "It would have made things a whole lot easier if it had been you."

In my head, the words, *What you talking 'bout, Willis?* sound out, but my friendly-to-adults smile remains plastered on my face.

Mr. Williams angles his body in the corner of the booth so he's halfway facing Todd and me. "Yeah, would've been a whole lot easier. But you two, well, you're not really each other's type. And he's really into this girl he's got." His lips pucker as if it's a big disappointment.

I smile and politely nod, sip my sweet tea, and lob a question over to Mr. Landry. "And I hear

Teddy and Mary Beth are expecting? You and Mrs. Landry must be thrilled."

"Oh, yes. Not due until spring. They're busy getting ready." He makes a loud noise in the back of his throat, and I look to Mr. Williams for any sign of concern over his friend's choking noises. "He's taken over the corporate development business, and Todd Junior runs the real estate side. You know, the side of the business where they develop neighborhoods and sell houses and stuff."

"That's great." We all nod at each other, bobblehead-like, and smile.

"So, Delilah, tell us what you want to do at Bayou Development." Frank Williams sits up a bit straighter, but there's still a noticeable curve to his shoulders, and he pushes his spectacles up on his nose.

The waitress walks up right then, and I'm filled with gratitude. I haven't yet read the menu, but it's not a problem. I always order the jambalaya.

After she refills our sweet teas and walks away, Mr. Williams continues, as if the waitress never appeared. "It sounded like you were happy up north. What were you doing up there? Art?"

"I'm a graphic designer. I develop advertising. At an ad agency."

"Do you like it?" Mr. Landry asks. He's a friendly man, they both are, but their postures are all off.

Below the table, I wrap the cotton napkin around my index finger, unwrap it, and repeat. Both men scrutinize me, watching my every fidget. It hits me at that moment. Mr. Long Tie and Mr. Bowtie see the same thing I see. There's nothing for me to do in my dad's business. At least nothing deserving of a partner title. They want me as a partner about as much as I want to join the firm.

"I love advertising. I love coming up with ads for clients. I've always assumed I'd create ads for Bayou Development." Mr. Landry grows three chins when he looks down to his lap, and Mr. Williams's gargle noises rise above the low hum of the packed restaurant. "But I get the sense that's not what y'all are thinking."

"We have an ad agency for the big projects. I mean, you could manage them. You might want to tackle some of the work yourself. It could save us some money." Mr. Landry tips his head back and forth as he's speaking, as if he's weighing this idea.

"But?" These two are tiptoeing around me, and they absolutely do not need to. I'm joining Bayou Development out of obligation, not because it's my heart's desire. "Just say it."

Both men startle at my words. "We don't believe that's partnership level work. It's not deserving of one-third of the company."

And there you have it. "I agree."

Mr. Williams reaches up and loosens the knot on his tie as he smiles. His ruddy complexion has taken on a redder hue throughout our conversation. I don't think his tea is spiked, but in this town, it's possible. "Todd and I wanted to talk to you, without your dad, because he doesn't see things the way all of us see it. Our sons, they've put in the time. They deserve to be partners."

Bing bang boom. Now I get these two. "But Dad doesn't want Bayou Development to leave our family. His father started the company. I appreciate your asking me to lunch, but you realize Dad's not going to agree? This has been the plan for as long as I can remember."

Seriously, I don't remember a day when it wasn't assumed this is what I would do. Sure, I had the standard childhood dreams of racing horses, being a princess, and flying to the moon. But when it came time to be real, maybe middle school, I understood I'd be stepping into the family business. One way or another.

Mr. Landry reaches up and rubs the top of his scalp, ruffling the few random long strands of gray that remain. Mr. William rotates his iced tea, keeping it in place but turning it in circles.

"What is the succession plan?" Dad's mentioned it a few times, and based on the facial expressions across the table, I'm betting they don't like it.

Mr. Landry clears his throat again, and I push his water glass to him. He doesn't take my hint. "The succession plan isn't particularly thorough. We each own one-third of the business. We would like to buy out your dad's third, but he hasn't wanted to sell."

Mr. Landy adds, "Teddy and Frank Junior are fully capable of taking over. They've been working with us for years. But your dad, he wants you here. He's being a mite stubborn."

I look to the ceiling. "And what does the agreement say? Can you force him out?"

Mr. Williams shakes his head in a slow, drawn-out motion. "Not easily. Not without a courtroom battle royale. But if he doesn't have a successor, yes, we can enact a buyout clause."

"Are you both retiring soon?"

"Not from the board, but we work at the firm about as much as your dad."

Ah. If the last two weeks is an accurate portrayal, that means not much at all. Our lunch arrives, and the conversation segues to holiday plans. These two are good men. They simply want to give the firm over to their eldest sons. And I suppose if I had any interest at all in what they do, I'd be a happy little camper figuring out how I'd carry my third of the business. Mr. Williams has a daughter who handles all the firm's legal transactions. She's at least ten years older than I am, and I don't know her well. She'd be a better third partner than I would. I wonder what she thinks of her dad giving his third of the business to her brother, but I don't care enough to ask.

After I've eaten every bit of my jambalaya, I place my napkin in the bowl to signal to the waitress she can remove it. Then, with crossed legs and my hands placed in a feminine manner on my lap, I lay it out on the table. "Gentlemen, this isn't my decision. As far as I can tell, this is between my dad and both of you. When Dad brought you into the business, the three of you outlined succession plans. I don't see Dad allowing this company to leave our family without putting up a big fight."

TWENTY

Mason

December 11
   To: Mason Herriot
   From: Delilah Daniels

Hey,

   Sorry we keep missing each other. It's great
that Amber is spending so much time with Kara.
She's been posting some great pics on Instagram.
Yes, I follow her, since you don't even have a social
media account. Her posts are a way for me to keep
up with you and Kara. And her band must be

doing pretty well. She has several thousand followers.

I'm happy for you guys. Kara deserves both parents in her life.

Did you know that after varicose vein surgery one has to wear thick stockings for, like, six months? These are the kinds of things one learns in gardening club. Fascinating. And Spanx makes tight leggings that work just as well as the tight stockings, which really are not that attractive, according to Marge. Although, while I'd never admit this to Marge, as it might lead to a lengthy conversation on the subject, I have to agree the nude/natural skin color in thick stocking form should probably never be seen in public.

Kiss Kara for me.

xoxo,

D

The subway rattles through the cavernous tunnels below Manhattan and under the East River. The fluorescent lights blink on one end. The evening rush has subsided. One man stands nearby, holding on to the silver railing overhead as he reads the *New York Post*.

· · ·

I type my response to Delilah.

December 11
     To: Delilah Daniels
     From: Mason Herriot

Hey there, Delilah,

It is good that Amber is back in Kara's life. Although I do worry she will disappear again, and that Kara is old enough that it will hurt more than in the past. But she and I are not together.

Is that why you're avoiding me?

The subway pulls to a stop at Court Street Station. My thumb hovers over the keyboard, and I press delete. When I climb the stairs to reach the street, a dark night sky and the white glow of overhead streetlamps face me. I slip my gloves on, tighten my scarf, and make my way home.

When I arrive, I hover outside my apartment door, shedding my gloves and coat, listening. I want to hear my daughter and her mother. I want to hear laughter or the hum of a conversation. I need to know I am doing the right thing, allowing them to bond. I don't hear anything, so I unlock and push open the door.

"Daddy's home!" Kara squeals.

This right here is my favorite part of the day. I drop to my knees and open my arms, and she runs into them and I crush her to me.

"Daddy, too tight." She pushes away then leans up and lays a wet kiss on my cheek. This little girl is my everything.

My mom walks into the room, and I stand. "Hey. What're you doing here?" She's welcome anytime she wants, but she and Amber don't have the best relationship.

Kara's small fingers wrap around my index finger and squeeze.

"Amber called me to come over this afternoon. She got a call about an audition. She mentioned that she thought Kara would be fine by herself until you got home, but that last time you weren't happy with her when she did that."

I close my eyes and raise my head to the ceiling. *I knew it.* Only a matter of time. After a long, loud, calming exhale, I hang up my coat and scarf, put away my gloves, and address my daughter.

"What have you and Ama been doing?"

The large crayon box sits on the table, and

crayons are scattered all over. Several of her favorite coloring books are stacked to one side.

"We've been coloring." She climbs into a chair, tucks her legs up under her, and resumes work on her masterpiece.

"Thanks for coming over. I wish you would have said something. I wouldn't have stayed at the clinic so long today."

"I was happy to come over and spend time with Kara."

Mom follows me into the kitchen. I open the refrigerator door as I ask, "Have you guys eaten?"

"Yeah. I've been over here since around four. I fixed us a tuna casserole."

I pull out a round glass dish of leftover chili and place it in the microwave. "Did she say if she's planning on picking Kara up from school tomorrow?"

"I think she's gone, honey. You'll have to ask her, but it sounded like the audition is for a band in Chicago. A friend of a friend kind of thing for a band that has a chance to go on tour as an opening act for a well-known band. She talks so fast."

I tap the counter, staring at the dull light of the microwave. "Did she say goodbye to Kara?"

"She hugged her. Said she'd be back to hang out soon."

I lean back onto the edge of the counter. "Mom, I'm getting a lawyer. I'm going to seek full custody. Once the lawyer gives me the go-ahead, I'll call Amber and tell her. It's possible she won't fight me on it."

Mom tenderly squeezes my arm. "I don't expect she'll fight you, honey. You are doing the right thing."

"Did Dad fight you when you sought full custody?"

Mom slides past me to open the refrigerator and pulls out two beers. She carries them over to a drawer and snaps the tops off with a bottle opener.

"I didn't have full custody. We had joint." She pushes an open bottle of beer on the counter to me.

"You didn't? And you didn't make him pay you child support?" We've never discussed specifics, but I know we struggled at times. Mom's brother helped us out more than once.

Ever so slowly, she shakes her head, her lips wrinkled together forlornly.

I take a long swallow of the cold beer.

"Honey, a custody agreement doesn't necessarily mean a parent will or won't be involved. I think what you're doing is the right thing, though. Amber's too self-absorbed. And she's too flighty. I don't trust her. It wouldn't shock me if she showed up when Kara's fourteen and tried to take her to help out at a club she's playing at or if she tried to take her away for weeks to some random city where she has a gig. Maybe tried to talk her into creating a band. She's openly experimental too." Mom jerks her nose up, defensive. "I'm not being judgmental. I experimented some myself back in the day. But she's open about it, and it's been going on for years. At the very least, it's risky. If she becomes an addict, you're much better off having clear legal rights to Kara."

"I'm not necessarily worried about Amber becoming an addict." I say the words slowly. "I am worried about her coming in and out of Kara's life. Going a year or two without a word. How do I prevent that?"

"You can't, honey. You can't control Amber or force her to be an involved parent. But you can talk to her. Beg her to either remain in touch, or to stay away until she's ready to commit to being a more reliable presence in Kara's life."

The microwave beeps, and the hot glass bowl sears my hand as I pull it out, and send it clattering along my tile countertop. "Fuck."

Mom leans against the kitchen wall, sipping her beer. "How's Delilah?"

I take out a fork and stir the chili, letting the steam escape. "Fine, I guess. She's another one who's chosen to walk away."

"Well, she didn't really have a choice. How's her dad doing?"

"Oh, Mom. She has a choice. Her dad's fine. He has MS. It's not a death sentence. She's choosing to stay in New Orleans."

"Have you given her a reason to come back here? A real reason?"

"For what? So she can leave again if he gets sicker?"

"Honey, she can come back here and you two can figure out if what you have is worth making some tough choices for. No parent wants their child to give up their life. From what you've told me, her parents are financially secure and can hire nurses if it comes to that. And you and Kara could move to New Orleans."

"Mom. I'm a part-owner in a veterinary clinic." An almost overextended veterinary clinic with a mountain of debt and too few practicing veterinarians.

"Yes, you are. And if it comes to it, you can sell your share to another vet and buy into a practice in New Orleans. There are always solutions if you open your mind to possibilities."

"She's out of my league. Used to a lifestyle I could never provide."

"Maybe. You'll never know until you talk to her." She pats me on my back and leaves the kitchen.

I eat my chili standing over the counter. In some ways, she's right. The problem is that Delilah and I never got our relationship to the point where we could decide if it was worth making sacrifices. We jumped right in and were hot and heavy in a nanosecond. We were so new when all of this came about. Leaving New York had been something I wasn't willing to consider because of Amber. Now, I suppose that's changing. But selling my share of the business won't make sense until we've built the new locations into thriving practices, and moving for someone I just met would be the definition of insanity. But Delilah doesn't *have* to be in New Orleans right now. She can come back.

Mom's question reverberates in my head. *Have I given her a reason to come back?* The last time I gave someone a reason to stay, she backed out the door. I clean my dish and leave the kitchen to join Mom and Kara in the living room. I hear a soft southern twang, and my heart clinches.

My mom's phone leans against a stack of coloring books, and Delilah's sun-kissed face and bright blue eyes shine through the screen. I stop and stare. Kara beams as she dabs her brush into paint, mixing hues of yellow and red, then holds up her white plastic palette to share the results with Delilah.

"Oh, that's looking good. Maybe add a little white in the mix to lighten it up?"

Mom comes to stand beside me. "Kara asked to speak to her. I hope you don't mind."

"How'd you get Delilah's number?"

"Oh, sweetie. She and I talk almost every day."

"You do?"

She swallows her beer. "Yes. And when I have Kara, we FaceTime. But it hasn't been too much lately. I think she's suspected you and Amber might be rekindling something."

"Why would she think that?"

"Honey. You have been spending a lot of time with her. And have you looked at Amber's Instagram?"

I shake my head as I recall Delilah's email, but before she can say anything else, I step forward and stand behind my daughter.

Within seconds, Delilah's mom's voice rings

through the background. "Delilah, come back outside, dear. Tom came to visit."

It's almost 8:oo p.m. her time. *Who is Tom?*

"I've got to run. Kara, tomorrow afternoon, we'll finish the painting, okay?" Kara and Delilah both kiss their palms and blow kisses off to each other. Delilah doesn't acknowledge me before the screen disconnects.

Mom announces it's time for her to go home. As I hold the door for her to leave, she shoves her phone into my hand.

"Look at the photos she's been posting." Mom has Amber's Instagram open on her phone. Photo after photo of Kara and me, and some selfies of the three of us. I remember her telling us to smile, but it never occurred to me she was posting these. There are also a lot of pictures of my backside with captions like "Nice ass." and "Yum yum." *Unreal.*

After saying goodbye to Mom, I usher Kara to the bath. On the way there, Kara points out the new art she's recently completed with Delilah while on FaceTime. It seems the two of them have a system going, with Delilah as instructor and Kara as pupil. She's still there for Kara but stonewalling me. Once Kara's asleep, I call

Delilah. Of course, her voicemail picks up, so I text her.

Mason: Hey there. I want to be clear. Nothing is going on with Amber and me. Nothing has happened at any point with us romantically. She has been spending more time with Kara, which I encouraged. She was also helping us out by spending time with her when I was at work. I plan to get a lawyer to work on getting sole custody. Can we talk?

TWENTY-ONE

Delilah

I stare at the phone.

Type, "Hey there." Then delete it.

Toy with the home button. Check the weather. Click back to the text. Re-read it. Type, "Hi." Then delete. Repeat typing "Hey" or "Hi" about twenty times, deleting each, then toss the phone on the coffee table and hit the floor for some yoga. I stretch out the muscles in my back in the downward dog pose then flex each leg as I walk the dog, my favorite full body stretch.

It's been two weeks since I've seen him, yet I can't get him out of my mind. The only time I am remotely happy is when I'm stoned sitting in the back yard. Or after dinner when a buzz from my third glass of wine kicks in. I haven't gone to the office yet because I'm waiting for all the men to decide if they want me to. I spend my days working out in the morning, having lunch with my mom, reading, then my afternoon sitting my ass in a chair smoking weed. And, of course, the dinners.

There was Clayton, who showed up on a Tuesday for dinner with a pink bowtie. Matthew, with a bulbous belly that would allow him to play the role of Santa with ease. John, who also went to Tulane and would not drop the name game, even though we weren't at the school at the same time. There was another guy with a thick mustache. The pornstache isn't the way to my heart.

Oh, and Tim. He took the cake with his, "Don't you think you're a little old for a nose ring?"

I pushed my shoulders back so my breasts shifted upward and responded, "You have nose hairs. Don't you think you should get those waxed?"

My mother had not been pleased. I should really try to steal Mom's planner, because she must have gone to rotary club and penciled in every single male deemed eligible between the ages of twenty-five and forty-five on a visiting rotation. If I could nab that book, there's no way she'd remember who she invited over, and she'd be running around the house, flapping her arms in panic mode.

My friends from high school have either moved away or have moved into another stage of life. The happily married with baby stage that means lunch consists of in-depth conversations about what the baby eats, motor development status, and area Kinder Care programs and options. And, in a lot of ways, those high school friends and I grew apart during college. The ties that bound us have loosened and frayed.

I finish stretching and stare at my phone. He's not dating Amber. *Just do it.*

I pick up my phone and press his name. It rings several times, and as my thumb hovers near the red circle, he answers.

"Hello. Delilah?" His deep timbre winds me, and I suck air in through my mouth.

"Hi."

"Did you get my email?"

"Yeah...and yeah, I did think you and Amber might be reconnecting. I didn't want to get in the way of that, you know?"

"She and I are long done, Delilah. I should

have made that clearer to you. Even if she becomes a regular part of Kara's life, she and I have grown apart. I mean, we were never together, together. Not really."

"Well, Kara must be so happy to have her back in her life."

"No. No, actually, she's gone again. Chicago."

"Really? How's Kara taking it?"

"Okay. She's been quiet at random times. Spent a lot of time playing by herself or flipping through her picture books. Last night she asked me if she did something wrong. I hate that she believes any of it's her fault."

"Oh, my goodness. Poor baby girl. Has Amber been in touch since she left?"

"No. I don't expect to hear from her. Not until this gig ends. When she's on the road, I don't usually hear from her."

"What's wrong with her? Doesn't she care about her daughter?"

The sound of a door closing comes through the line. "She's pursuing her dream. She didn't want a daughter. I can't get too angry at her when she wanted to put her up for adoption, and I blocked her."

"You're doing the right thing by seeking sole custody. I hate the idea of Kara hurting. You know, when you first told me about Amber wanting to put the baby up for adoption, I thought she was horrible. But I've thought about it a lot, and what she did was incredibly brave. And full of love."

"Love? That's how you define love?"

"Yeah, it is. Think about it. She was nineteen. Nowhere near ready to be a mom, and she had dreams. I have to believe it was a difficult decision. But she recognized she wouldn't be a good mother. Not at that stage in her life. Not if she resented her daughter. She recognized it and sought out the best option, the best life, for her daughter. I think that qualifies as love."

"I think she was selfish. Only putting herself first."

"Maybe. But I don't think self-love is all bad. We can sit here and debate if she did it for herself or for Kara, but at the end of the day, her choice was the best thing for Kara. Can you imagine what it would've been like if Kara grew to love her mom, and then she popped in and out of her life? She'd be a different kid right now, with a lot of emotional issues. Whether you approve or not, her choice was ultimately the best choice for Kara. I admire her for having the strength to make that decision."

He mumbles something I can't quite catch. Then he asks, "How're things there?"

"Other than feeling like I've been stuffed inside an aquarium, it's fine. We're leaving for Paris tomorrow. Maybe that's what I need. To get away."

"Your dad must really be doing good if he can travel to Paris."

"He's not going. Oh, no. This is Mom's trip. She loves Paris. It's supposedly my welcome home trip, but it's a thinly veiled holiday shopping excursion. It'll be fine. My Aunt Josie's going, and I adore her. She's the coolest."

"I guess your mom isn't so concerned about your dad, then?"

It's my turn to sigh. "She is, but right now things are tense between them. I think they need a break from each other. How're things there?"

"I miss you."

The desperation in his voice shouldn't make me happy, but I smile. "Miss you too. But this is my home now. Sometimes, it's as if I'm living that Shin's song. Trapped in a town I outgrew so long ago. But this has always been the plan."

"Have you started work at your dad's company yet?"

"No. I expect to after this trip. Or maybe after Christmas."

"What happens if your dad needs you, and all of you are in Paris?"

"We'd get a flight home."

"I keep thinking you could stay in New York, if you wanted. You have a good job here. One you love. And if your parents need you, you can fly home."

"It wouldn't be the same. If I'm responsible for a staff and for multiple accounts, it wouldn't be easy to just take off." Folks at our ad agency plan vacations weeks out, and there's also the matter of me only having two weeks of vacation time. "And, anyway, think about Kara. If I moved back to New York, and we got close, and then Dad took a turn for the worse and I needed to move home, I'd be the person disappearing in her life."

"But you'd call. You wouldn't disappear. We'd work it out. And she'd understand."

"No, Mason. You're missing it. I was always supposed to move back home. This whole thing sped the timeline up, that's all."

"We haven't seen each other in weeks. We haven't really given long distance a chance. You don't answer my calls. Let me come visit. Let's spend more time together, talk to your parents together. I have to believe we can find a solution."

My muscles tense. "Wait. It sounds like your solution is to talk to my parents and get them to agree to me moving back to New York. Is that why you asked about talking to my parents?"

"Well, yes. I can't imagine your parents really want you to give up your life in New York. You shouldn't have to sacrifice your life."

"Well, shiitake. You know, I'm not sure how to respond. It sounds like your idea of a solution is for me to change my life." And why does everyone expect me to be the one who gives everything up?

"Change? No, my idea for a solution is for you to not change your life. Not yet, at least."

"No? You want me to come back and stay until it really will break me to uproot. That's what you want? And for what? So we can date? You want me to change my life plans, the plans I have had for years, the agreement I have had in place with my parents for years, so we can date?" By the time I finish my diatribe, I'm shouting into the phone.

"No, no. I don't want to make you give anything up. Dammit. Tell me when I can come visit. Too much time has passed. I need to see you. We need to have this conversation face to face."

Of course he wants to have the conversation face to face. He can touch me, and my brain will go fuzzy. I'll bounce around and be giddy because he's near. And maybe he can pitch his little ol' friends and family investment opportunity to my parents too.

"I'll call you when I'm back from Paris."

"Delilah, we can't keep doing this. You're shutting me out. You go days without responding to emails. Is that what you want? You want to shut me out? End things? Do you want to just be friends? Because I'm not sure we can keep up a friendship with the way things have been going."

Tears stream down my face, and my whole brain goes berserk. The pain I've been so diligently numbing hurts so badly I struggle to breathe. And it's his fault. I've been blissfully numb, and here he goes twirling up all the bloody, fricking emotions. "I've got to go."

TWENTY-TWO

Delilah

My suitcase bounces along the rough brick patio as I wheel it to the main house. When I approach the back porch, angry voices drift outside. Mom and Aunt Josie are at it again, fighting like sisters. They love each other ferociously and have a bond I've always envied.

"You didn't even want two of your four children. I would have wanted all of them." My mother's outrage pours out in her furious tone, her words ringing with resentment and accusation. I leave my bag outside on the patio and creep forward to listen undetected.

"What? I wanted all my children. I love all of my children." Josie's voice breaks as she responds slowly, almost incredulous.

"No! No! You were like 'oops, screwed up my birth control. Pregnant again! La-dee-dah!'" Mom is screeching now, and while I can't see them, I can visualize her using her favorite outlandish dance hands.

"That doesn't mean I didn't want them, Melinda. I just didn't plan each of my pregnancies," my aunt retorts, loud and firm.

"Yeah, well, I planned. I measured. I was poked and prodded. I worked for my one pregnancy. You will never know what that's like!"

"Melinda, I am sorry you couldn't have all of the children you wanted. I am sorry. But it doesn't give you the right to steal Delilah's life."

My mom shrieks, "How dare you! You don't judge me. I didn't do anything any other person in my shoes wouldn't do. She was supposed to come home. I simply stepped in before it became too difficult."

I close my eyes and press my body up against the side of the house. I don't want to hear any more, but I have nowhere to go. Sunlight bounces off the pool and catches my attention. A reflection of the porch settles over the still, clear water. The beams holding up the porch ceiling reflect in the shimmering surface like prison bars.

After a moment of silence, Josie's calm voice responds, "You lied to her."

"I did not! He is sick."

"Yes. But he has many good years left."

"You don't know that. No one knows that. It will be awful when it gets bad. Delilah should be here. Why are you against me?"

"Damnit, Melinda, I'm not against you. I'm for Delilah. Jesus, will you listen to yourself?"

A warm hand grips my arm, and I scream. "Dad? Holy Mylanta, you scared the bejeezus out of me." I place a hand over my pounding heart. Dad is wearing a custom dark suit, ready to head in for a board meeting. His professional outfit commands respect, but his downturned lips and sorrowful gaze are more funereal than business.

"Delilah, is that you?" Mom appears in the doorway. "Hoffman, what are you doing out here? I thought you were on the way to the office."

"I wanted to say goodbye to Delilah. Found her out here." He is somber, and his gaze drops to my mother's feet as she scrutinizes him.

I exhale loudly and reach for my father. "I'll walk you to your car, Dad."

"Are you packed? The driver will be here in ten minutes."

"Yes, Mom. I'm packed."

As we make our way through the house to the garage, I can feel Mom's glare boring into my back. Dad's cane taps the floor, marking our steady progress. Once the side door closes, he envelops me in his comforting arms. "I'm so sorry, baby girl."

I step back and sniffle. "What are *you* sorry for?"

"This whole mess. That your mom brought you home. That we're forcing you to work at Bayou Development."

"Dad, I don't expect Mr. Williams and Mr. Landry are going to go along with your plan. I believe they will go to court before they let me step in."

"I should've never brought them into the blasted company. Your grandfather is probably rolling over in his grave right now." His right hand wobbles on the cane, distracting me. Brown age spots dot the back of his hand. "But whether they like it or not, they don't have the money to buy me out."

"You've been talking to them about it?"

"We've tossed out some numbers. I don't want

you to be forced into the company, but it's too much money to walk away from."

"Dad, I'm not a money gal, but I know they can figure out a way. There are ways. You meet with bankers. Men in suits. They pull out calculators. If they want to buy you out, they figure it out."

"And you'd walk away from it? Live off an art director salary until we passed away and you received your inheritance? Whatever we don't spend?" Ah, yes, that's the heart of it. I can step in as a partner and command a significant salary. Profit dividends. A level of income I wouldn't have as an employee.

I kick my foot against the tire. "So, you're gonna go into the meeting today and tell them to lawyer up?"

The corners of his lips lift slightly, but he doesn't say anything.

I reach out and rest a hand on top of his shaky one. "It's a mistake, you know?"

"How is it a mistake?"

"Forcing me into Bayou. It would be stronger without me as a partner. And it's not what I want."

He scratches his jaw. "If it's not what you want, why are you here? Why are you letting us dictate what you do? Are you that dependent on access to my credit card?"

"No. Jeez, Dad. I'm here because of you."

His brow wrinkles, and it's clear he's not sure he believes me. He considers me for a minute then says, "Honey, I told you I'm okay."

I reach out and squeeze his hand. "I want to be here for you."

"And I love you for it. Here's the thing, baby girl. I could have an aneurysm tomorrow or get hit by lightning on the golf course. We've all got the same ticket out of here, we just don't know our departure time. What we've got to do is live the life we have as best we can. I do wish your mom could be happy with the two of us. I wish she didn't believe her happiness is so completely connected to where you end up living."

"She's not wrong."

"No, sweetheart, she is. She really is."

I grin and shake my head. "No, she's not. You guys were the best parents a girl could ask for. Supported every random dream I had. Hauled my ungrateful ass to all kinds of practices and lessons. Mom spent eighteen years making me her highest priority. It's not too much to ask for me to live nearby and help out as you guys get older." Now, that whole forcing me into the boring as all get-out family business, I have an issue with, but no need to throw darts.

He caresses my chin and angles my head upward. "Sweetheart, that's not how it's supposed to work. Those eighteen years were a gift. A gift to us. Some of the best years of our lives." His grin draws my attention to the hollow, dark circles below his eyes. He's either not sleeping or he's not well.

"You say you're doing good, but look at you. You aren't working full-time now. I never thought I'd see the day. That has to mean something, Daddy."

"Yeah, it means I saw the light. And I'm getting old. Have you ever heard the saying that you can't take your money with you when you go?" That's Dad. Always understated and practical. "Well, your mom and I have plenty. What we may not have plenty of is healthy days. So, if I'm ever gonna improve my golf game so I can finally beat Tom, I've got to get to it. And I'd like to think your mom and I can finally spend time traveling, something she's always wanted to do, but I've been too busy. That is if I can convince her. What did you say to her on the phone that got her so lit up? Did you tell her you were in love with Mason?"

His question surprises me, and I lean back

against his car. I know the exact conversation he's talking about. I must have run my mouth too much, going on about Mason and Kara, and while I didn't say the L word, she knows me well. Mason is probably the first guy I've ever met that I didn't follow up with a "but" statement. But he's a Capricorn. But his socks are weird. But he's way too proud of his alma mater.

The side door opens, and Mom glances back and forth between us, her hand on her hip. "What are you two doing? Delilah, we've got to go."

"I'll be right in." She stands in the doorway, holding the door, her defiant stance telling me she's not about to go inside and give us privacy.

I step to my dad and reach up on my tippy-toes and give him a huge hug, the kind where we toggle back and forth as we hold each other tight. Then I whisper in his ear, "I didn't say it, but she knew. Before I did."

Dad kisses my forehead and squeezes me in his arms. "I love you, baby girl." Then he straightens and stares her down while he speaks to me. "I love you, and I want you to go live your life. Be happy and strong and fall in love." He pinches my cheek and winks.

"What nonsense are you saying to her, Hoffman? The driver is here. We need to go."

"I'm telling her I'm good and you and I are going to be good. We have a lot of traveling and living to do. She needs to go back to her man."

"Hoffman. Don't be ridiculous. She doesn't have a man. Come on, Delilah, let's go. Your bag is already in the car."

Mom sends a death glare Dad's way, the kind that would normally have him cowering, but instead, he stands taller and blows her a kiss. "You ladies have fun in Paris."

I gaze out the window at the clouds on the way to the airport. Mom and Aunt Josie sit in stony silence, each flicking away at their phones. Wispy clouds speckle the light gray-blue December sky. The black limousine slows to a crawl as we approach the departure terminals. One cloud forms into a horse. I've been staring at clouds *a lot* these past couple of weeks, and never have I seen such a complex shape. I tap Mom's knee and point out the window. "Look, it's a horse."

She squints. "I don't see it."

Josie leans across the seat. "I see it. You should look that up. I'm pretty sure it's a sign for something."

Mom rolls her eyes. "You and your signs, Josie. You know what, are you sure you want to come with us? I'm not sure how you can find the willpower to leave those grandbabies behind." There's an unmistakable air of condescension in her tone.

"Keep pushing, Melinda."

Mom's face flushes crimson, and she balls her pale boney hand into a fist. For a minute, she looks like she's going to punch my aunt. The tension breaks when the driver opens the back door of the car to let us out.

The three of us step into the American terminal. I leave the two angry women behind and stand before the departures and arrivals board. Our flight to New York is on time. From New York, we'll take an overnight flight to Paris. I'm fed up with this entire situation. The muscles in my shoulders burn from the tension the entire car ride over here. Josie and Mom stand fighting in the middle of the terminal. I can barely make out the words that have deteriorated into childish squabble.

"Everything always has to be about you."

"Oh. My. God. Everything always has to be about you! Listen to yourself."

"No, you listen. None of this concerns you. You always butt in."

Oh, Mylanta, I can't deal. A whole week listening to this? I can't do it. One of the reasons I'm not an enormous fan of Paris is because of all the stores my mother plans to haul me into. Shopping plus fighting. Yep, it's gonna be fantastic.

The horse cloud flits across my mind, and I stride with purpose to the customer service desk. "Yes, can you tell me if I can change my ticket to London, England?"

The agent's fingers flick away with lightning speed over the keyboard, the click clack of the the keys audible over the hum of airport activity.

"Yes, ma'am. You can. You can remain on this flight to New York, and we can change your ticket to Paris. You are flying in first on the flight to Paris. We also have a first-class seat available to Heathrow. The flight leaves about thirty minutes earlier than the flight to Paris, but you should be able to make it without any difficulty." More clicking sounds. "The change fee will be $3,500." She glances up at me from her keyboard with a stoic expression. This woman couldn't care less if I pay the exorbitant fee, but at this moment, getting away from my mother and the constant bickering and doing something for myself feels monumentally important.

"I'll change my ticket."

"May I have your passport, please?"

My mother comes up next to me as I give the attendant my passport and credit card. "Is there a problem?"

"No. I've decided I don't want to go to Paris. I'm changing my flight to London."

"What? Why?"

"Because I can't handle another minute of the two of you bickering like old ninnies. I grew up wanting a sister because the two of you were best friends. You two figure your shit out. Maybe I'll meet you mid-week. Maybe I won't. But I need space."

I haven't been sleeping. When I do, I dream of Mason. His forest green irises haunt me.

Josie stands to the side of my mother, beside the shiny metal line stanchion, lips upturned as she looks off to the side.

Mom points at Josie, the finger so close to her face she has to jerk her head back to avoid getting nailed. "Did you do this?"

With a smug smile, she shakes her head.

"Mom, I'm doing this. Look, I love you, but this week is supposed to be a gift to me, so I'm taking the gift and going where I want to go. I want the two of you to figure out your shit. And then, Mom, you need to reach out to Dad. You've been treating him like he's the enemy, and that needs to stop."

Her skin color pales, making the pink from her blush strokes stand out more. I expect her to fight me, but all she comes back with is, "Where will you stay?"

I hold up my phone and wiggle it back and forth and bounce a bit on my feet as excitement of my impending solo departure fills me.

"I'll figure it out. We live in the digital age. I'll have a car and hotel confirmed before our flight departs."

"Do you need money?"

Dad's words come to mind as I reply, "No, Mom. I don't need money."

TWENTY-THREE

Mason

When I land at Heathrow, it's 6:03 a.m. GMT. After unloading from the plane like a herd from an overpacked cattle car, I wander through a maze of hallways to arrive at customs. As I weave through the line, my mind spins. Sleep deprivation plays a part, but how quickly I pulled strings to make this trip happen shocks me to some degree. It all started with the phone call last Tuesday.

"Dr. Herriot?"

"Yes." It's unusual to receive personal phone calls during the workday. I wouldn't have answered, but I saw the 504 area code and thought it might be Delilah.

"Hello, this is Delilah's father, Hoffman."

I froze and swear my heart stopped. "Is Delilah okay?"

"Yes, yes, son, she's fine. Do you have a second to chat?"

My 3:30 appointment hadn't checked in yet, and I'd just finished up with my 3:00, so if I ignored the reports I needed to complete... "Yes, sir." My curiosity was enormous. Unless an animal arrived smashed by a car or needing an emergency c-section, I would've talked to him.

"Delilah's talked about you. Now, my daughter, she's a picky one. If she likes you, you must be something else. Her mother parades eligible bachelors through this house like we're casting for a reality TV show, and Delilah spots an issue within five minutes flat with each contestant. But not you. Something about you is different. I'm gonna cut to the chase. How do you feel about my daughter?"

I find a chair and fall into it. "Sir? Feel about—"

"Yes, that's what I said. Back in my day, the father would ask what your intentions are. I won't do that. But I want to know if you love her."

"Sir, Delilah and I haven't known each other that long. We dated briefly before she had to go home, and—"

"I know you haven't known each other long, but I knew the moment I saw her mother that she was the one. Saw her strolling across the street. She was wearing a mini-skirt and had long straight blonde hair that almost touched the curve of her mighty fine ass. One week with her. That's all it took for me. Now, not everyone has a love at first sight kind of experience, but, my daughter, she's a special girl. And I think she loves you. I need to know how strong your feelings are for her."

"Did she tell you that she loves me?"

"Yes, she did."

I close my eyes and let those words sink in. A warmth spreads throughout my chest, and the dull ache I've been carrying with me for weeks lifts.

"Mason?"

"Ah, yes, sir. I do love your daughter. She's an amazing woman, and she's bonded with my daughter in a way I could've never expected or hoped. But I've been searching for solutions. I can't easily move to Louisiana. I'm a part-owner in a vet clinic here, and right now I have joint custody with my daughter's mother."

"Tell you what, son. Her mother would kill

me for saying this, but it has killed me watching Delilah at home these last few weeks. She's been a bird in a cage. A wild bird who's used to flying free in a far bigger jungle. She's outgrown her hometown, and she's lost here. I want my little girl happy. And, I suspect, you make her happy."

"I'm not sure if I make her happy or not. She wants to be there for you. And I get that. I do. But I have legal obligations I need to work through, and I also have a responsibility to my mother. I hoped we could make long distance work, but she hasn't been..." I had to stop, unsure how to put into words the distance she's put between us, a distance far more tenuous than the physical variety.

"Delilah's been trying to be her happy self, and she hasn't been succeeding. Maybe she bought into her mom's point of view that if she put you in the past, all would be okay. But I haven't seen that happen, and now, she's in London. She's taking time to step back and think."

"London? She said she was going to Paris."

"Nope. My girl took the reins into her own hands. She's taking some time away from her mom, taking the supposed gift we gave her and going where she actually wants to go. I'm telling you this, because while she's thinking things through, it might behoove you to make sure she has all the relevant facts at her disposal."

Ashley tapped on the door to tell me my 3:30 had arrived, and I held up my index finger to indicate I'd be a minute. "I appreciate the call. I do. But unless Delilah decides to return to New York, I don't see a solution for us. And what if she returns and..." *What if you get really sick?* It's too difficult to ask, so I don't.

"What if my disease progresses? Well, if it does, I'll be okay. I don't need my daughter to play nursemaid. What I need is for my wife to realize she and I can survive this. I won't say it's going to be easy on her, and, god, I wish she didn't have to go through this with me. But I'm a lucky son of a bitch, and I've done well in real estate investments over the last few decades. She has a wealth of family and friends here. She's gonna be okay. She and I can do this. We're approaching almost thirty-five years together. I can't say it's always been easy. Trying to have kids put us through hell in a handbasket. Adjusting to life without Delilah in the house has been another wringer I haven't been positive we'd survive. And now, my whole health thing. There's a lot of unknowns in life. Hard times. Unknowns. Always unknowns. But when you find the one to dig in through the ups and downs, then that's what you do. You dig in, and you find a way. If you believe Delilah is the one you want by your side when you need to dig in, well, you know where she is right now. And I'm telling you, she's making decisions *right now*."

"Sir?" The person behind me breaks me from my trance. I've reached the end of the line. A sign flashes "1 1 1" in yellow lights by a customs officer on the far left of a long row of officials sitting in cubicles with glass windows. I step over the yellow line and hand the man my passport. He studies it, then me, and asks, "Are you here for business or pleasure?"

As I wait in the taxi line, I pull out my phone, pondering my course of action. You'd think I'd have a plan. I rolled the dice and didn't book a room at a hotel. My hope is Delilah will see me and understand I'm in this. I don't have any intention of letting her slip away. Not without a fight.

I haven't seen her in three weeks, and it's been way too long. My return flight is booked for tomorrow. This is all a touch of insanity, but I couldn't bring myself to plead my case over the phone. If her dad is right, and she's weighing her options now, then I need to make the most impactful and persuasive case I can. A phone call or email won't work. I need to do this in person.

It's 8:03 a.m. when the black cab drops me off at the hotel. A man in a black coat and cummerbund steps out onto the curb for my luggage and to assist me to the lobby desk. I explain that I'm here to see a guest.

"Ms. Daniels didn't answer, sir. You're welcome to wait here in the lobby, or I can leave a message."

I pull up the Find My Friends app and see she's nearby. The orange dot is in a plot of green, indicating she's in a park. "Can I leave my luggage here?"

The woman studies me for a bit. I'm certain she's trying to determine if I might be a danger to the guest staying in her hotel, as there is no note on file to expect my arrival. I must pass muster, because she offers a cordial smile and points me to a gentleman who can store my small carry-on in a closet until I return.

I'm so tired my eyes burn and a rancid taste from being parched fills my throat. I stop and help myself to a glass of cucumber water in the lobby then head out into the sunlight. Well, sunlight might be an exaggeration. The sun cannot be found in the sky. A thick gray cloud cover hovers overhead, portending rain later in the day, but it is bright enough I am forced to squint, though the sky's not bright enough for sunglasses.

Like a stalker, I tap Find My Friends again. I zigzag down sidewalks headed in the general direction of the orange dot. The orange dot isn't moving, and knowing what time it is, my bet is she's gone to the park for her morning yoga routine. I quicken my stride, hoping to catch her before she finishes and before I lose my nerve.

I find the entrance to the park and hold out my phone like a beacon, following the blue dot as I scan the park, searching for a blonde ray of light. Park might be stretching it. It's really a plot of grass surrounded by a black iron fence and a jogging path. The city sidewalk is on the outside of the fence, and joggers and pedestrians pass by at a clipped pace.

My chest clinches and perspiration beads across my forehead when I see her. She's on a yoga mat, hands down, butt in the air, in a downward dog pose. Her hair falls loose and pools around the top of the mat and over her hands. A runner jogs by and almost runs into someone as his head turns to watch her, no doubt admiring her shapely ass. She's a danger to men, and she has no clue. She tilts her right knee forward, then her left, with her ass thrust into the air.

I step onto the grass and wait. City dwellers hustle by, so we are not alone, but no one else has taken up a spot on the small patch of lawn. It's not raining, but the mist is thick.

As if she can sense someone is watching her, she slowly rises and lifts her head to the sun, palms pressed together. Then her neck makes a slow rotation to the side and stops when her wide, light blue irises come to rest on me.

TWENTY-FOUR

Delilah

The crisp morning air bites against my damp skin as I run through my morning yoga routine. My tight muscles release as I shift into downward dog, then walk the dog. My skin tingles from an undercurrent of energy, a sensation so exhilarating that I pull myself out of the pose and search the park perimeter. I stand in tree pose, a solid straight statue, and rotate my head. Joggers pass on the nearby sidewalk. A businessman in a trench overcoat hustles by near the park entrance. A dog walker passes by with four dogs of varying sizes leading the way. I continue to twist, then freeze. I blink and strain to better see the man standing almost directly behind me.

A man with grizzly black stubble, dark hair, and an uncanny resemblance to Mason stands nearby, maybe ten feet away. I rotate slowly to face him. On this dreary early morning, we are the only two sharing the grassy lawn. I rub my eyes, fighting disbelief.

"Mason? What? How?" My mind reels, and my mouth drops open because Mason in London makes absolutely no sense.

He chuckles and raises his eyebrows. "Surprise."

"Holy cannoli. What are you doing here?"

He takes my hands. An electric current churns through me. His long fingers twist through mine, his touch cool. He dips his head, uncertain. "Do you not want me here?"

I blink. This is all like a dream. The last thing I want is for him to suspect I don't want to see him, so I spring up and wrap my arms around his neck, holding him close. He lifts me higher as I tell him, "I'm thrilled you're here. Shocked. Blown away." He squeezes me then lets my feet fall to the ground. We stand there, my arms round his neck, his around my waist.

With a timid smile, he explains. "Your dad called me. Told me where you'd be."

"How did he know I'd be in the park?"

"He told me you'd be in London. Find My Friends led me to you."

I run my fingers over the stubbly growth along his jaw. "I almost didn't recognize you."

"You weren't at the Savoy, so I left my bags there and came searching for you."

"Is everything okay? Is Kara okay?" My pulse quickens as reasons he might show up here in person fly through my mind.

"Yeah. She's fine. She misses you. Your Face-Time sessions mean the world to her." His hold on me tightens. "Have you been avoiding me? Is that why you time your calls when I'm at work?"

"No." He tilts my chin up to meet his questioning gaze. I nod slightly and admit, "Yes. I'm sorry. I've been so confused." And I've needed space because my heart has been crushed, and I need to find a way to be happy back home.

"Well, that's why I'm here. Your dad said you came here to think. He suggested I put all my cards on the table."

"He did? My dad called you?"

"Yeah. He doesn't believe you've been happy

at home. Something about he believes you've outgrown your hometown."

"It's not the same as in high school, that's for sure."

His head dips, and his lips press against mine. Then he pulls back and asks, "Is that the only reason you haven't been happy?"

That's a loaded question if I ever heard one. My ass is parked in London because I'm trying to sift through it all. Weighing what I should do and trying to figure out why doing what I should do is so damn hard. But one thing I'm not confused about at all. "I've missed you. So much."

His lips brush over mine, and I open, a tentative kiss at first, then our connection deepens. When we break apart, my heart races erratically.

He nuzzles my neck. "I've missed you too. Your energy." He toys with my hair and lifts it away from my face. "Your quirky sayings. Your non-stop hand motions. How you make me feel. I've missed you."

"I've missed us making plans each day. Deciding on meals. Cooking together. Spending evenings with you and Kara. Silly, right? We didn't do that for long."

I rest my head against the crook of his neck as the reverberations of his heartbeat penetrates my core. My heart cracks all over again, because there's no way around us being apart. He kisses my forehead and drops to one knee. The world oscillates, a dizzying sensation circling me.

"Delilah Daniels, will you consider spending your life with me? Will you marry me?"

"I. I. I. Can't." He's lost his mind.

He falls forward onto both knees. I remember his story of Amber, and how she backed up, and I leap forward and grasp his shoulders, forcing him to lift his head as I explain.

"It's too soon. Mason, marriage is huge. Ginormous. Marriage is forever. We're still at the getting-to-know-you stage. And things haven't changed. Have they? You can't move to New Orleans, can you?"

A red hue rises across his cheekbones. I reach out for his hand. It's clammy and cold. I drop onto my knees to face him. The uneven ground grinds into my knees, and I shift off of a painful protruding rock. I inch forward until my thighs press against his, punched by the deep hurt I see. I caress his jaw. *He has to see it's too soon.* He presses a soft kiss to my forehead and sits back onto his feet, creating space between us.

Eyes cast downward, dejected, he says, "You're right. Nothing has changed. I'm not any closer to being able to leave New York. With Kara, with my Mom, with the business. I guess I hoped if I put it out there, if I showed you how strong my feelings are for you, and I'm willing to commit, then you would come back. Your dad had me convinced." He stares off over my shoulder, avoiding my gaze. "But why would you? What was I thinking? You're so young and full of life. I have a daughter. You'd be a stepmom. That's not fair to you. That's not what you deserve. You deserve the ideal family. Your children. In New Orleans, like you planned—"

"Stop." My cold fingers wrap around his wrist and tug. "I love Kara. She's not the issue. I mean, at times I feel like a kid myself, so I'm not gonna lie, the whole parenting responsibility thing does freak me out. I'm fairly certain I'd suck at it, but it would be the honor of a lifetime. But you gotta believe me. I honestly want nothing more than to move back to New York to find out where our relationship grows. I've been telling myself there's no way these strong feelings could last. I've never..." I press my lips softly to his. "Ever. But none of this changes my reality. Yes, my mom went about this completely wrong. Ridiculously wrong. But I'm all she has. I get it. And I've tried to explain it, but this has always been the plan."

Then I slap my palm across Mason's chest, and his eyes widen in surprise.

"And marriage? Mason? Really? That's mega huge." He stares off across the park. I tug on his wet coat. "We need time. Time to see if these emotions are fleeting or real. And time is one thing we don't have. I mean, I've already moved. As planned."

His jaw flexes as he swallows. I hate this. But this has always been the plan. I'm simply following the plan. "On the bright side, I'll be a partner, making the big bucks. I can participate in your next friends and family investment round."

He closes his eyes, tilts his head back, and softly chuckles. "God, I have been such a moron."

"Don't say that."

He strokes his thumb across my cheek. His lips fall to mine. Our tongues mingle, and the tender kiss deepens. The pain in my chest throbs and tears flow. We hold each other for a painful moment before he rises. When we stand, dirt stains our lowers legs. We're both soaked and cold.

We don't speak on the walk back to the hotel. He stops at the concierge and collects his suitcase and heads back out onto the curb. I ask him to stay, but he doesn't respond. It's like he no longer sees me. I suppose there are no words left to say.

TWENTY-FIVE

Mason

I push open the door to my apartment late at night, attempting to be as quiet as possible so as not to wake anyone. The blue light from the television screen creates a halo effect on one wall. The golden glow emanating from outside streetlamps offers the only other source of light. My keys scrape the wall when I hang them, a sound that in daylight wouldn't be heard, but somehow in the still of night echoes loudly through the apartment.

My mom's sleepy head rises from the sofa, a dark blot. "You're back. How was your trip?"

"Hell."

"What?"

I circle around and collapse onto the club chair beside the sofa. "It was hell." And it was. As soon as she turned me down, the second woman to say no to my marriage proposal, I wanted to get the hell out of London. The change fee was higher than staying in a crap hotel for one night. What the fuck had I been thinking?

"Tell me about it."

Fuck. I slam my back against the chair, not entirely on purpose, and close my burning eyes. I can't sleep on planes. I barely fit into those cramped, tiny coach seats. "I asked her to marry me. She said no."

A gasp reverberates across the room from the sofa. "You asked her to marry you?"

"Yes." And of course, she said no. Why do I keep thinking someone would want to spend her life with me?

"Honey, I didn't realize you were that close with her. That you were talking marriage."

I can't believe this. "You're the one who told me to go after her!"

"Well, yes. But wait, did you think I meant for you to propose?"

"What did you mean? You were all 'give her a reason to come back.'"

"I meant to tell her you loved her. That you had fallen for her. Tell her you wanted to see where things went."

"Oh. Well, I had already done all that. But no need to worry. We know how she feels now. I put it all out there. Offered her everything, like her dad said. Like you said. She said no." But she did offer to invest in my company. As if it was a consolation. *No, I won't spend the rest of my life with you, but here's a small investment to wish you well on future endeavors.*

"Honey." Her mother voice sounds exactly the same as it did when I was a kid. Back when she kept Toll House chocolate chips on reserve for bad days.

I jump up and stretch my arms to the ceiling. "It's late. Do you want to stay here? Stay in my room, and I'll take the sofa."

She doesn't respond, but I set about gathering a comforter and pillow. All I want is to stretch out and fall asleep. When I return to the sofa with my bedtime goods, she doesn't move. She's going to need to, because I'm ready to crash.

"Honey."

Aw, fuck, she wants to talk. "Mom, I'm tired."

"Hear me out."

Like the good son I am, I sit.

"I love that you put your heart out there. I love that you are so willing to give someone every part of you. But I want you to consider why it is you jump to marriage as a solution. I know you. You always look for solutions, but why do you think marriage is the solution?"

"That's what women want, right? How else are you supposed to...? What did you mean when you told me to give her a reason to come home?"

"I just meant to tell her how you feel. To tell her what you love about her. To tell her that you could see a future. That you are willing to *work* for that future. Had the two of you ever talked about marriage?"

"No." I don't have a lot of experience with relationships, and the fact that my mother is sitting here on my sofa asking these questions highlights that glaring fact.

"What did you do for a ring?"

Now she sounds amused, and that pisses me off.

"I bought one." What does she think I did?

"But if you hadn't been talking about it, how did you know what kind of ring she'd like? Or her ring size?"

"I figured she'd exchange it and get what she wanted. I bought a ring that reminded me of her."

It wasn't a giant rock, but that's not really Delilah. It was a platinum band in what they call a classic Tiffany style. Simple and elegant. A few times, I'd wondered if the ring was the issue. If she expected something grander. Or more unique. But I'm fairly certain she never even looked at the ring. No. She was backing away. Not the first time that's happened to me.

"Mom, I'm exhausted. And Kara's gonna be up early, and then I've got a full day of work."

She leans over and kisses my forehead, like I'm her little boy. At the door, she pulls on her boots. "I'd rather sleep in my bed, so I'm going to head home."

"It's late. Just stay here."

"No. You sleep in your bed. I'll pick Kara up from school. I feel like a cold is coming on, and I'm gonna pick up some echinacea on the way home."

"Are you sure? I can go out and get you something."

She reaches up to caress my cheek then pats it as if I'm a dog. "I live two blocks away. I'm gonna stop at the market on the way home." She leans down and picks up her overnight bag, which I now see she had already packed and left by the door. I won't be able to change her mind.

"Thank you for watching Kara. Thank you for everything, Mom."

"Honey." God, I wish she would quit using that word. There is something about the way she says it that grates my insides. "I love you. But let me share a little something to think about." She holds up her hand as if I'm about to stop her, but I'm not. I'm always respectful to her. Outwardly.

"Marriage isn't the goal. The goal is to find someone who makes you happy, who makes you a better person. Someone you want to spend your extra time with. A partner in life, to share the ups and downs. Someone you want to commit to. Marriage is a document. And before you sign that document, or offer that commitment to anyone, you need to be certain you have all those other things in play. Because it's hard."

I am ready for this conversation to be over. Mom, being Mom, knows this, and continues to pat me to keep my attention.

"Relationships are hard. I liked Delilah, but there's no guarantee she was the one. You guys jumped into things so fast. You needed time. Time with her. Fights with her, over little things and big things. You've got to put in time before you know for sure."

Tell that to Delilah's dad. He certainly has a different spin on it.

Mom reaches for the doorknob, signaling this nightmare of a day is about to end.

"Honey." *Please stop.* "One day, you are going to find the right person. Give it time."

Finally, the door closes behind her. I crash in my bed, and as predicted, at the crack of dawn I'm awoken by a squealing four-year-old with horrible breath jumping up and down on top of me. She lands a knee directly into my abdomen that sends me curling forward. But it's so good to see my little girl, I don't mind at all.

TWENTY-SIX

DELILAH

The blustery wind below the Eiffel Tower has the crowds clutching coats and scarves tightly against themselves. The line wraps around and around, and I stand directly below the Eiffel Tower, straining to read random signs around the perimeter as I attempt to figure out where exactly I'm supposed to freaking go. There's no way my mother stood in this massive line.

Me: I'm here. Where do I go?

Melinda Daniels: I'm sending Louis down to get you.

I read her text as I spot the 58 Tour Eiffel Tower sign.

Oh, Delilah, it's been renovated. Do you have any idea how hard it is to get reservations? Can't you come to Paris for a couple of days? How many times do we ever get to eat in the Eiffel Tower? The Eiffel Tower, Delilah. Her voice rings through my head as I make my way to the sign and a young man in a thick black winter coat and gloves. He has to stand outside all day to greet lost people like me who have no idea how to get up to the restaurant.

I flew in this morning, left my luggage at the hotel, and headed over. I'm a little late, but a part of me stopped giving a damn about the same time Mason refused to come up to my hotel room and instead hailed a taxi to return to the airport. Our final goodbye. Something I'd known was coming but had been trying to postpone. The story of my life.

Mason. Well, I discovered his flaw. He puts his heart out there. Way out there. It's inappropriate.

You don't propose unless you've talked about it. Unless you've each said, yes, I'd love nothing more than to spend my life with you. We were still in the newly dating territory. The yes, I believe I'm dating someone land. Like, if we were one of those nauseating couples who count the weeks that go by, we'd still be celebrating weekly anniversaries.

A young French man pushes past me to insist his name is on the list. A young woman standing behind a desk gathers his information and types away on a keyboard. The young lady with him blushes and stands back as he argues with the woman.

An older gentleman in a washed-out black suit approaches and bends slightly at the waist in greeting. "Ms. Daniels?"

"Yes."

"Right this way, please."

Ah, this must be Louis. The wunderkind tour guide my mother has hired to drive her through Paris on her trip. She's had a lot to say about him, but given I haven't listened closely to much of anything she's said, about all I have gleaned from her lengthy, gushing monologue is she likes this guy and is quite pleased with her decision to hire him.

He directs me to an elevator and speaks in French to the person standing guard. We are ushered past a short line of people. As a child, I was enamored with the Eiffel Tower. I loved the view and the majestic shape and especially the angle of photos taken from a distance that make it appear trees grow right up next to it. Today, I see the throngs of tourists, the endless concrete and ugly metal fences set up all around the perimeter. It's true what they say, perspective comes from within.

The elevator opens onto the second floor of the tower, high in the sky. Louis leads the way through the restaurant doors and past the hostess stand and up a sweeping staircase. My mother stands, exuberant and joyful. Aunt Josie bears a troubled expression I can't fully interpret.

After hugging them both, we sit. Chardonnay has already been poured, and heavy condensation drips down my water glass, and water circles the base, a sign they have been here for a while waiting for me. I should have apologized profusely for making them wait. For disappointing my mother by not meeting her expectations. I should, but I don't. A heaviness presses in on my lungs, and breathing requires effort. No part of me wants to be here right now, so my physical presence will have to be enough.

"How was London?" Mom asks, cheerful and

spry. Her effervescence annoys and chafes every single nerve.

I exhale, shift my shoulders back, and gaze beyond her, out the window at the gray winter sky. There is a chance of snow flurries later, something that would normally have me giddy like a kid anticipating early school release, but instead, the weather forecast does not shift my mood in the slightest.

"Delilah?" she asks in a concerned tone.

I forgot to answer her. I roll my eyes. I shouldn't have come to lunch. I'm so not in the mood to chit and chat.

"Fine." I avoid her judgmental frown and dig into the salad of mixed greens that I do not want. They've already finished their salads, though, so on auto pilot, I eat a few bites so my plate can be taken away without an onslaught of questions regarding how I'm feeling or if I want something different to eat. I have zero appetite.

All I can see is Mason on bended knee. The soft press of his lips on mine before he settled into the back seat of the cab. A kiss to say goodbye. He wiped his face, closed the car door, and didn't look back. And my insides ripped apart, as if a Cat 5 hurricane plowed through.

"Honey, this afternoon we were thinking of

going shopping. I have a private tour of the Louvre scheduled for the three of us tomorrow morning at ten. I know it's early, but the tour will be led by a local historian."

I choose to ignore her and instead people watch. There's a large table of Asians sitting nearby. An entire family. Three generations. All happy and smiling and taking photos of themselves. The waiter comes by and offers to take a picture of them, and several of them get up from their seats and stand behind a few of the others. They shift and adjust so the photo has the best option of the view behind them, which I find to be odd because I doubt, given the lighting inside the restaurant and the light behind them, the picture's going to come out.

"Melinda, look."

"Josie. Shut it."

"You shut it. Stop this."

"Why are you always so mean to me? You hate me."

"I'm sitting in Paris because I love you. I'm giving it to you straight because I love you. Grow up. For once, love your daughter more than yourself."

"She's my only daughter. You don't understand."

"This is ridiculous. Look. Do something."

I stop watching the happy Asian family and shift in my seat. The two sisters glare at each other. Grand. *Fight it out, ladies. Fight. It. Out.*

"I am doing what I need to do," Mom snaps.

"Bullshit. You're doing what you selfishly want to do. Thinking only of you. And you need to stop. It's time for Melinda to care for someone other than Melinda."

"How dare you say that to me? I have spent my life caring about everyone. Everything I do is for others! I'll have you know the therapist said taking care of myself is not an act of selfishness."

"First, I don't think the therapist meant for you to force your daughter home. And second, no, Melinda. No. You don't need her home. You may think you do, but you don't. And she doesn't owe you. Every activity you carted Delilah to was partially about what activities you wanted Delilah to participate in. Every charity you championed has been as much about the people attending and how much you like the galas as actually doing good. Even now, you are making Hoffman's illness about you." My aunt's words are laced with anger.

"It is about me. That may sound wrong to say, but when someone gets sick, it *does* impact their significant other. Don't make me out to sound like

I'm evil. And most people *do* choose a charity that plays up personal preferences."

I stare at the plate in front of me. I notice my full wine glass and pick it up and gulp the liquid down. It stings as it coats my throat.

Out of the corner of my eye, I notice Josie push her water glass away from her. "You are right, Melinda. You're not evil. But for your whole life, our parents have babied you. The baby sister. Plans have always melded around you. And I'm here now, pleading with you. She is heartbroken."

"She is not. And besides, this is her choice. She's doing what she wants to do. This is her decision."

The sky outside hangs like a veil of gray. The clouds are shapeless. The cloud we saw on the way here, the one shaped like a horse, gallops by in my mind. Has this ever been my decision? For as long as I can remember, the plan has been for me to work for Bayou Development. For as long as I can remember, I haven't wanted to. Going to New York was our compromise. And coming back was the plan. But was it my decision? Decision implies I chose it. And doing real estate marketing is not something I personally would ever choose. I've been in limbo, going through the motions, as if facing a guillotine. And that's ridiculous. This is my life. And I should be making the decisions.

The two women argue back and forth until I slam my hand down on the table. "Oh, shut it. Both of you." They close their lipsticked mouths.

"Mom, what you did was wrong. You manipulated me, and I haven't said anything, because that's me. I didn't see the point in saying anything, but you were wrong to do that. You scared me. No, terrified me. I was devastated. I left my company in a lurch. You didn't give me time to wrap anything up." Tears fall as I'm speaking, and this unbearable sadness crushes around me. It's as if saying the words out loud is bringing it all back.

My mother flips the knife on the table back and forth, her lips in a flat line. "You shouldn't feel that way."

A single tear escapes and runs down my cheek. I sit straight. She avoids looking me in the eye by staring at her plate, but I lock my gaze on her.

"No. You don't get to tell me what I should or shouldn't feel. That's not your call. I am telling you how I feel. I should have said something earlier. No, scratch that. It's not a should situation. I am telling you now. You manipulated me. And that hurts. I don't want to be manipulated. I will not allow you to treat me that way."

Her bottom lip sticks out ever so slightly, the only indication she hears me.

"Mom, I'm not going to move back to New Orleans. I'm going to remain in New York. I have an offer for a promotion doing what I love, and if it's still available, I'm going to take it. I'll still be there for Dad, but I'm not going to be his successor. His partners will have to enact the buyout clause." The heavy weight on my chest lightens. There, *now* I've made a decision.

Mom glares me down and sits taller in her seat. "If you return to New York, your father and I will not be supporting you. You will not be able to continue residing in the business apartment." The gauntlet has been thrown down. Am I ready to completely walk away and make it on my own? Yes. Yes, I am. In a way, it's as if my move after college was me testing the waters by dipping my big toe in, while standing with a life preserver around my waist.

"I know. I'll get my own place."

"And you'll have to hand over your Amex. We will not continue paying your credit card."

Oh, for the love of all the berries. She's desperate. "Mom, I love you and Dad. And I will still be there for you and support you. But I'm not moving back home." The meek part of me wants to soften my statement with a "not right now" addendum, but I force my lips closed.

Aunt Josie grins from ear to ear, but she hides it behind her water glass the moment Mom shoots daggers her way.

"Do you love him?" Mom fiddles with her fork. When I don't respond, she lifts her face to me. "Do you love him?"

Tears fill my eyes, obscuring my view. "I do."

She opens her mouth and gasps, like a fish out of water, attempting to catch lifesaving oxygen.

"But, Mom, it's not about *him*. My decision is not about him. This is about me taking charge of my life. If I don't do it now, when will I do it?"

Tears roll down her cheeks, and my chest tightens once again.

"Mom, please don't cry."

She moves the thick white cloth napkin from the table to her nose and blows loudly. Then she sets it down in her lap and asks, "How do you love him?"

"What?" I want to revel in my newfound, kickass strength. My take-charge moment.

"Tell me how you love him. What do you love about him? When did you fall in love?"

I rest my forehead on my palm and close my eyes. When I let Mason into my thoughts, my body resides in this paradoxical state of both pain and numbness. And I'm not stoned.

"Delilah." The mom tone prods me to answer.

"He's not the reason I'm moving back. I'm staying in New York for me. Because I love every single thing about that city. And because I love my job. My career. I love ad agency life. I've only been holding back because it felt temporary. But no more. I'm going back, and I'm gonna be all in."

"Are you still with Mason?"

"Not right now." There's no need to tell her about his half-baked proposal. I stand by that decision. Our relationship is nowhere near ready for that level of commitment. But all signs point to strong possibilities.

Mom stares out the window across the Paris cityscape.

Aunt Josie clinks her wine glass against mine. "Tell us about Mason."

"He's amazing. He has a gift with animals. And with people. He's gentle, compassionate, and understanding. And he looks at his daughter like she's his world and his life. He could've agreed to put her up for adoption, but he didn't. He chose to be a single dad. He's got these strong hands and, when he looks at me, my insides light up and fizz. It sounds cheesy, I know, but I've never had that. With anyone. And he's thoughtful, and... Mom?"

She raises her eyebrows and emits a low "hmmm?"

"I want y'all to meet him one day. And Kara."

"I thought you said you weren't doing this for him?"

"I'm not. I'm really not. And when I get back to New York, there's a possibility he might not want to see me. But if that's the case, I'll do my best to change his mind because I think we're good together. Good for each other."

She's coming around to accepting it; I can see it in her shoulder position. She no longer looks like she's about to go into battle. She's morphed into the softer version of herself, and maybe there's a touch of defeat as well.

"Mom, I haven't known him long. I mean, we could date, and it's possible it won't work out. It's possible the more time we spend together, I'll get on his nerves or we just won't be into each other as time goes by."

"Oh, honey, you could be married to him for decades and it's possible it won't work out." She blows her nose into her napkin. "I was wrong. I just wanted...I want you to be happy. At the end of the day, that is most important. And I want us to be close. And maybe that won't look like what I envisioned. But..." She places a wet kiss on the side of my face and through tears, continues, "I love you, baby girl. Always. And I am so proud of you. But I want you to know, I'm not giving you a dollar. You are officially on your own."

Some part of her may have meant those words as a threat, but that's not how I take them. As she says those words, in my heart, I hear one word. Independence.

TWENTY-SEVEN

DELILAH

The sign outside the clinic reads *Deck the Halls and Whack Off Some Balls*.

Bet's humor makes me laugh. I do love her signs, and I'd be willing to bet most of the other New York City residents lucky enough to pass by do too. Nerves strum through my fingers as I push open the clinic door. I haven't seen or heard from Mason in five days. I spent a day comatose in my hotel room after he left. Then, after my mother's incessant prodding, rode the train to Paris. After lunch with my mom, we went to Shakespeare & Company. Instead of shopping for clothes, we read quotes and discussed books and drank coffee. Eventually, she excused herself to go back to the hotel, claiming exhaustion.

She's disappointed. In me. I never ever wanted to be a disappointment to my parents. I wish for them that they had a son. Or at the very least, a child who would move down the street and happily carry the business on for a third generation. But they ended up with me. And as much as I wish they'd received someone else, it wasn't my call.

I am the person I am. I need to be true to *my*self. It crushes me, knowing I'm not all they want. But maybe by being all that I am, I'll be able to give them more. More of what really matters. Because it doesn't take a tarot card reader to predict that by not being true to myself, I was on a landslide, and in the long run, I'd drag them down into my mental hell.

The next morning, I hopped on the first flight to New York. I returned to the as yet unsold corporate apartment. Then I went into the office today. Met with Margaret in HR to confirm I'm back. Met with my boss. He updated me on work. My promotion was still on the table, and I accepted.

I shouldn't be randomly stopping by to see

Mason, but I want to see him. I need to see him. I have no idea what I'm going to say, nothing planned.

Once I decided to remain in New York, I did consider calling him. But, given how we left things, a phone call felt too weak. I hope he'll still want to date me. Not marry me. That's ludicrous at this stage. We've been together for, like, a nanosecond. But I'd love to be his girlfriend.

Mason and I jumped all in. Maybe that would've been fine, but then all hell broke loose. It's not like I'm an expert at relationships. But common sense says jumping all in so quickly isn't the smartest plan. I'd like for us to find a healthy middle ground, a place somewhere between not seeing each other and marriage. A healthy place that works for Kara.

When I push open the clinic door, I'm expecting Bet's magenta hair, but as I approach the reception window, dark hair greets me. Ashley raises her head from a stack of papers she's scribbling notes on. Her eyebrows angle, creating a deep wrinkle. She slides the window back. "Do you have an appointment?"

"I'm here to see Mason."

"Dr. Herriot isn't here." She reaches to close

the window, and I block it. The waiting room is empty, so I don't have to worry about causing a scene.

"What's your problem, Ashley? You haven't liked me since we first met."

She leans forward with both hands on the edge of the counter. "My problem? You don't know me, but I know you."

I step back, cautious, as if she might bite. "What do you mean?"

She huffs and gives me a look that says she's annoyed she's forced to interact with me. "I'm from New Orleans. I went to school at North New Orleans High. You and your friends would come to the Starbucks where I worked almost every single day after school. It was like I was invisible. Not once did you flash a hint of recognition, even though I saw you almost every day. You and your rich, private school friends in Range Rovers and Louis Vuitton."

"Holy shiitake. I knew you looked familiar. I just couldn't place you. I don't expect to see anyone from my hometown here." There is a hardness to her gaze. I shuffle on my feet. "I'm sorry. In high school, I was a little lost in my own world." It's fair to say I've been a little lost post-college as well, just in a different way. "Ashley, if I did something mean back then, I am sorry."

Her chin juts out, and for the first time I notice a tiny piercing right above her lip. How did I miss her piercing before? She might have been my soul sister back then if I had been paying attention. I sent ripples through my circle of debutante friends when I returned after my freshman year with a nose ring. The expression on her face borders hostile. I'll have to work on developing a friendship with her, now that I plan on staying in New York.

Her scowl softens as I waffle on my feet, uncomfortable. "It was a long time ago. I assumed you hadn't changed."

"I guess I'm like anyone else. In some ways I've changed, and in some I haven't."

She glances at her computer screen, then back to me. "Dr. Herriot had to go pick up his daughter from pre-school today."

"Is everything okay?"

Her rounded nails tap the counter with a slow, rhythmic beat. "His mom's sick, so he had to pick her up from school today. He's a good guy. You're lucky he's into you. You know that, right?"

"I do know. I promise."

She pulls off a neon pink Post-It note. "You know, you may be too late."

"Too late? What do you mean?"

A devious smirk flashes across her face as she scribbles on the note. "I can only imagine how those moms are reacting to a single dad in scrubs." Her tone lifts as she offers the pink square. "Here's the address. Good luck."

I type in the address on my Uber app and escape the uncomfortable waiting room as quickly as possible. My gut tells me if I make an effort with Ashley, she and I could grow a friendship. She's protective of Mason, so she can't be all bad. But it'll take work. And time. And right now, I need to see Mason.

The Brooklyn Heights preschool sits mere blocks from Mason's home. Several women, who I assume are parents, climb the concrete steps into the school. I follow.

The wide hall reminds me of the school buildings from my youth. Classroom doors line both sides of the hall, and the doors and wall space are covered with construction paper cutouts and children's artwork. I stand in the middle of the hall, searching left and right. Toward the end of the hall, to my right, I spot the back of Mason's dark head of hair. I bypass a woman scooping to hug her child as I make my way to the end of the hall.

A teacher stands in the doorway of each classroom. Parents fall in line near their kid's classroom door, and the preschool teacher greets the parent then calls their child to the door. As I approach, I notice a blonde woman standing beside Mason. She's gazing up at him, laughing at something he says, her hand resting on his forearm. The scene before me is a sucker punch of epic proportions. It's been five days since we officially said goodbye. Five. Days. And here he is with a woman on his arm picking up his child.

You may be too late.

If I'm too late after five days, then I'm a crazy fool. It really was all too quick. Everything I've been telling myself about us not having enough time to fall for each other is absolutely correct. The woman's hand glides higher on his arm, and she tosses her head back with another laugh. I spin around and trip right over someone's toddler. The toddler shrieks, forcing me to pause and bend down to make sure the kid I plowed into isn't hurt.

"I'm so sorry. Are you okay?" I gush to both the crying kid and the mom. My heart is pounding. The mom, a woman in black leggings with her hair pulled back in a ponytail, scoops her kid up onto her hip and kisses the plump wet cheek. She turns her back, effectively dismissing me, and I scoot by her, repeating a mumbled apology, when I hear Kara's shrill, "Deelah!"

I pause. Light from outside cascades through the open front entrance doors in the middle of the hallway. A gap in the thinning crowd forms, creating a clear path through the hall.

TWENTY-EIGHT

Mason

The large windows lining the back of my daughter's preschool classroom cast plentiful light over the multi-colored walls. Bean bag chairs crowd one corner for reading, one section of dollhouses, another large table with Legos and building blocks, several empty tables for arts and crafts, and one section of small play kitchens. That's where my daughter is. Mrs. Wordsworth continues to call Kara over as she shows the woman her back, intent on stirring air in a pan on the stove. Julie's mom stands beside me as she also waits for her daughter to be delivered to her. I love this preschool, but I don't know how my mom puts up with this chaos each and every day at pick-up.

Julie's mom tells me about a play date our daughters had. I'm halfway listening but growing increasingly annoyed at Kara ignoring me. I break protocol, and in a you-had-better-listen-to-me-now tone, I raise my voice above the pick-up cacophony, "Kara."

She waves her pudgy fingers at me and gives me a cute smile and all of the frustration melts a little.

Kara puts up her toys in the yellow bin, grabs her coat off the hook, and rambles toward me.

Julie's mom tugs at my coat jacket and asks, "Is Kara available for a play date today?"

"Oh, my mom's sick. I need to take her dinner."

"What's wrong with Cindy?"

"It's just a bad cold."

"I hope it's not the flu. We could still have a play date this afternoon, and I could help you cook—"

Julie's mom's voice gets cut off by Kara shrieking, "Deelah!"

I whip around and scan the chaotic hall. Kara

sprints past me, as a blonde woman runs down the hall and out of the building with Kara in hot pursuit. The woman looks like Delilah, but it can't be her. Kara's wrong; she's just wishing. But she's also out the door onto Brooklyn's city streets, so I charge down the hall, skirting the short minions crowding the hallway. If I knew anyone's name, I could call out for someone to grab her.

As I step outside, heart pounding, I glance left then right, searching for Kara. When I get hold of her, I am going to let her have it. Chasing a stranger? In New York? I grit my teeth, working to control my rising anger and fear when I catch sight of the blonde woman bending on the sidewalk hugging my daughter. I take the steps two at a time then come to a harsh stop.

I blink. It is Delilah.

Her honey-blonde hair cascades around her shoulders and shimmers in the daylight. She's bent down around Kara, hugging her tightly. My chest contracts, making it difficult to breathe. I stand behind them, patiently waiting for Delilah to look up. When she does, her blue eyes glisten.

She slowly rises, and as she does, Kara sidles up to her and wraps her arm around her jeans-clad thigh. Someone bumps me from behind, a reminder we're standing in the middle of a busy sidewalk right after school dismissal. I reach out to guide her out of the way, next to the black iron fence that runs along the front of the preschool. As I move the two of them, a need to protect my daughter fills me, and I reach down and pull her to me, so she stands with me.

"What are you doing here?"

Her expression is tentative, possibly fearful. I don't mean to frighten her, but I've already put my heart on the line. She told me how she feels. She doesn't have any business showing up at my daughter's school.

She rests her hip against the fence and, looking past my shoulder, raises her arm and points. "Are you with that woman?"

"What?" Anger and annoyance surge. "What woman?"

She lifts her arm and points to the school entrance. The mother of Kara's classmate stands with her daughter, watching us near the school entrance. "With her?" I am incredulous.

Delilah smacks her palm across her forehead. "Oh, Mylanta. Of course, you aren't. I just saw..."

I reach out for her wrist and squeeze until those blue irises gaze directly into mine. "I asked you. *To marry me*, and you thought—"

"Ridiculous, right? My head sometimes floats

off, and whatever I'm feeling inside free-flows. I shoulda known. But it's not that crazy because you are you, and like Ashley said, you could basically have anyone."

I touch her shoulder to stop the rambling. "It is crazy. Crazy for you to think that."

She bounces up and down on her heels, her expression a mixture of tentative and hopeful. "Look, I decided to move back to New York. I want to give us a chance. If you want to, that is."

"What about your parents?"

"I decided I want to live in New York. I've accepted the promotion." Her fingers graze the stubble on my jaw, and her blue eyes capture mine. She mouths the words, "I love you, Mason." She glances down to Kara, who is watching both of us. It's clear she's not missing any of this. "Are you...can we try?"

This gorgeous woman who I flew across an ocean for is nervous and unsure of herself. She doesn't need to be. I'm in love with her. Of course I'm going to give this a go. But she didn't say she's back here for me, and it's not like I've forgotten the pain when she turned me down. She and I need to talk.

Her fingers are still against my jaw as she awaits my answer, and I reach for her hand and press a kiss to it. "I think we should consult the 8-Ball."

"What's an 8-Ball, Daddy?" Kara yanks on my shirt to get my attention.

"It's a plastic ball with a dice inside, filled with alcohol and blue dye. There are answers on each side of the dice, instead of numbers, like the dice we play with."

Kara looks at me like she thinks I'm pulling her leg. "You're being silly."

I smirk and pull her up onto my thigh. Yeah, I'm being silly, but I need to buy time to get back to my apartment and have an adult conversation with Delilah.

"If you want to consult the 8-Ball, we can. Or the tarot cards. But I recommend we decide for ourselves. Let the fates decide something else, like whether there will be a white Christmas."

"Why don't we talk about it back at the apartment? How about we go home, and I'll make hot chocolate?"

Kara squeals, "Yes! And, Deelah, you wanna play Candyland? Or color?"

"I'd love to." I take her hand for the short walk back home.

Kara rambles on, telling Delilah about how

she's hung up each and every piece of art she completed with her over FaceTime.

The sun has dropped below the skyline, and the city streets are transitioning to dusk. Holiday lights and decorations line the street and grace almost every store window. Christmas music blares from a store or possibly through an apartment window. Walking with these two, one on my hip, one tucked into my side, feels right. I know it. But when we catch each other's gaze, it's loaded. Loaded with questions. We need to talk.

As soon as we arrive at the apartment, I set Kara up on the sofa with hot chocolate and her favorite cartoon in lightning-fast speed. Today, she's in for a treat. I plan to let her watch several episodes. Delilah moves to sit behind Kara, but I grab her hand and tug her to the kitchen. Once we are in the closed-off room, I pick her up, set her on the kitchen counter, and step between her thighs and press her to me and kiss her the way I've been dying to the whole way home.

When she pulls back, lips red and slightly swollen, I think of other places that are going to be flushed and rubbed raw before morning. I have missed this woman more than I ever thought possible. But we need to talk.

"So, no 8-Ball?"

I shake my head. "But we do need to talk. I need to know you are in this. That you are serious about this." My index finger taps her chest and mine.

"I am. Mason, I promise, I am. I'm in love with you. And it's scary as hell, and I've never been through this, so I don't know what to expect. I don't know how I'll feel a week from now or a month from now. And, logically, I know relationships take work. Right now, it doesn't feel like work. I want to be with you. There's no way it's going to always be easy, but I want to try. I need to try. I don't want to have to wonder about what might've been."

She licks her crimson lips, and I go in for another kiss. She places a palm to my chest and softly pushes back.

"You asked me to marry you."

I nod, ever so slightly. "I did. And you said no."

"Yes."

"Wait, are you saying yes now?"

She smiles big enough to flash her pearly white teeth and shakes her head. "No."

"It's too soon," I agree. It hurt like hell, but that day in the park, she gave the best answer.

"Yes, it's too soon. But..."

I tilt her head up to me and kiss her once again as Kara's fingers tug at my jeans pocket, alerting me to her presence. I lower my hand to touch Kara's shoulder to let her know I see her while I ask Delilah, "But?"

"I'm here. I'm all in. Heart and soul."

EPILOGUE - DELILAH

THREE MONTHS later

"So, moving in together, huh? I never thought I'd see the day." Anna clinks her wine glass with mine with an amused, know-it-all grin.

Yes, it's three months later, and if anything, I'm more in love with Mason than ever. I'd like to say we took it slow, but slow didn't seem to work for us.

We're over at Olivia and Sam's amazeballs apartment. All the women are gathered together in the kitchen, but we can see the men through the glass doors that exit onto his enormous terrace. They're sitting around a firetop table, drinking beer and watching a game on the outdoor television screen. Kara is sitting on her knees, mesmerized by the fire. Mason's beside her, watching, on edge, prepared to snatch her hand away from the fire should she reach into it. She's not a dumbass. At least, I don't think she'll put her hand into the flame, but it's a good thing he's beside her.

"Yeah, kind of crazy, huh?"

"Especially after the grief you gave me." Olivia lifts a bottle and refills our glasses, even though I'm not empty. She's that kind of hostess. The hostess with the mostest. "Hey, I stand by that. It doesn't make sense to jump in so quickly. And we did try to slow things down." We really did. But we found excuses to still see each other after work on most days, and all weekend. And, well, the weeks blurred, and before I knew it, we were together every day. "It's not my fault the corporate apartment sold. And rents are sky-high. It doesn't make sense to be paying for two places."

"That apartment was gorgeous. I can't believe you didn't have us over more." I had them over for a goodbye apartment party a couple of weeks ago. It was an amazing space. No doubt about it. It sold unfurnished, so my parents officially gifted me the furniture. We have more than enough for the apartment we found, and I'll be able to sell some of the furniture we don't need to cover moving expenses. Other than gifting me the furniture, which was technically my college graduation gift anyway, my parents have been true to their word. I am on my own. Cutting up my father's American Express card proved only mildly painful.

As if reading my mind, Anna asks, "How're your parents doing?"

"Oh, good. They've been planning trips. Which is a big step. They went so many years with Dad not taking time off, going from one big project with a stressful deadline to the next one. It's a transition."

"Have they forgiven you for staying here?" She asks the question in a lower voice, as if it's a sensitive topic. It's not.

"Yes. I think it's hard, you know, when a family business leaves the family. And I definitely harbor some guilt for not stepping up." I tap the center of my ribcage to show them where the residual pain resides, the heaviness. "In some ways, it would have been a nice life, but I would've been a drag on the business. A partnership is tricky. They would've resented me, and my mind would have been *boosh*!" I mime an explosion with my hands and mouth. Yes, blown with boredom.

Olivia laughs. "Yeah, I've asked Sam if he's expecting our kids to work at Esprit. He says no way. He wants them to go out on their own. Which, given it's hard to come up with something more boring than backend solutions for financial services companies, I'd have to say it's good he has no expectations on that front."

"Are you guys talking about having kids?"

"One day. Definitely." Olivia sidles up to me. "What I want to know is how's the insta-mom thing going?"

Of course, she's fascinated. I'm the first one of my friends to have a child obligation. I'm not Kara's biological mom, but I am in a parental role in her life. "It's good. She's easy. She's like a mini-me. If he had a son, well, I might not say that. I watch those boys on the playground. They are rough and loud and at times crazy stupid. I'm not sure I'd be so into it if he had a son."

Olivia and Anna laugh, but I'm so not joking. They don't get it. They haven't spent time on a playground. Like, little boys are beasts. "No, I'm serious, ladies. When the time comes, mark my words. It could be worth researching which sexual positions increase the likelihood of daughters."

Chase shuffles through the apartment at that moment, phone to his ear, and throws a wave to us as he heads out to join the men on the patio. Anna angles her glass his way. "I always thought the two of you would make a cute couple."

"Are you insane?" Absolutely no way. "He's always wearing crass t-shirts. And he's such a player. What do you want to bet he's on the phone setting up plans with some innocent girl for after he leaves here?"

Olivia spreads some honey and cheese onto a cracker as she watches Chase through the glass. "But have you noticed he never brings his women around us? He always meets them later. Doesn't that strike you as odd?"

Anna twirls on the stool, a sign she's now on her third glass of wine. "Not true. I've met his girl-friends before. It's been a while, but I'm still friends with one of his exes."

Olivia scoffs. "That was a long-ass time ago, Anna."

At that moment, Jason, Sam's best friend, passes through. He nods with his perma-serious expression and places a bottle of wine and a six-pack of beer on the counter. The dude never smiles. Olivia gives him a hug and thanks him for the offerings.

Once the glass closes behind him, I ask Olivia, "What's his deal?"

She's at the oven, checking on the bubbling casseroles she's made for us. "He's not a talker."

"You don't say."

"According to Sam, he's got a lot going on. He's working through it."

I check the time. It's getting late and, while Kara is most likely full on cheese and crackers, she can be a whiny girl if we don't get her in bed at a decent time. Since no one else here is on a kid schedule, I've got to step up and keep this party moving. It's funny how definitions change, because not too long ago, keeping the party moving would have meant heading to the next bar. "Is anyone else coming?"

Olivia understands what I'm getting at with my question. We hang enough on weekends that they're used to us cutting out early. Sometimes Mason's mom watches Kara, but we keep that to a minimum since she helps out so much during the week.

On cue, the automatic sliding doors open, and Kara enters. Anna and Olivia busy themselves by setting the casseroles out. Kara pulls me over to our cupcakes. She and I spent the afternoon baking Magnolia Bakery blue icing knockoffs, and she's beyond eager to dig in. Not too long ago, I brought wine to these shindigs. Now, we're the designated dessert team. And I wouldn't have it any other way.

Mason sidles up behind me and leans over my shoulder as I set out the cupcakes. Kara eagerly licks a bit of the icing from the side of our carrying case. Mason presses a soft kiss below my ear, and I swipe a touch of icing and let him lick it off my finger. No, I wouldn't have it any other way.

EPILOGUE - MASON

One year later

"Daddy, can we keep her?"

Kara's sitting on the ground, sitting cross-legged with a small, skinny, scared young dog in her lap. I volunteer my time at the ASPCA and treated the animal when it was first rescued, chained to a fence in a lot and abandoned. Bet stands behind Kara with a cat-ate-the-canary smile. The woman loves to find homes for animals, and she knows she's probably got me.

I managed to keep the random strays in the office or at shelters for years, always afraid to bring them home because I could barely manage taking care of myself and my daughter. Upkeep for any animal, even a hamster, would fall on me, and then sometimes my mom.

Now, Kara's animal collection has expanded to include a bunny, a parakeet, and two teddy bear hamsters. I'm going to have to ban Delilah and Kara from visiting the vet clinic or assisting at the ASPCA events, because I don't have the willpower to say no to the two of them, and Kara's playroom is turning into a small animal shelter.

We found a rental near the clinic that Delilah and I could afford together. At her insistence, I kept my apartment and rented it out. She explained to me that while she liked my furniture, we didn't need any of it or have a place for it, and there were others in need who could greatly benefit from it. Yes, my beat-up sofa and La-Z-Boy both went to Goodwill. Without any furniture, the move was quick and easy.

Delilah and Kara had fun decorating her new big girl room, since her bedroom in my place had been her nursery, still painted in baby green, and they explained to me she needed something older now. I still don't completely agree with that assessment. We did pack up her artwork, and Delilah framed a ton of it for her hallways and strung metal lines on Kara's new playroom wall to hang her evolving art.

Under Delilah's direction, she's become a talented artist. She's moved beyond princesses, and now she loves to sketch and paint landscapes. Delilah's urging her to embrace abstracts. The two of them are always doing craft projects.

Delilah's arm wraps around my waist as she steps into my side with a sneaky grin. "Ready for a dog?"

"A cat would be so much easier. We could leave a cat with food when we go out of town on the weekends. A dog means we'll need to either kennel it or have a pet sitter. And it'll have to be walked multiple times a day." I gaze down at her as I consider all the reasons a dog doesn't make sense. Of course, Delilah never worries about money, because she's just not used to doing so, but I know firsthand how expensive dogs can be.

I can't help but weigh all the ramifications of the commitment we are considering. Plus, owning a dog in an apartment bears with it greater time requirements. There's no back door to open and let them run free. And right now, our apartment is close to the clinic, which makes it easier to own a dog, but we've agreed one day we'll buy a place, and it's quite possible we won't be able to afford Manhattan.

She squirms near my side. "I'm more of a dog than a cat person. And look at how happy Kara is. How big do you think the doggy is going to get? Couldn't it fly with us?" We go to New Orleans almost every other month. We would probably go more frequently, but her dad has been keeping his promise to not throw away today worrying about tomorrow and working away on their travel wish list. Right now, they're on a Seaboard cruise somewhere near New Zealand.

I tug on my chin as I consider the odd heap curled up in Kara's lap. It has the ears of a terrier, but the fur isn't curly. It's more of a matted mess. The undernourished dog probably weighs about twenty pounds, and at around a year old, most likely won't get much bigger, only fatter. I'm a fan of mutts, but this one is a less attractive specimen.

As if reading my thoughts, Delilah says, "She's as homely as a mud fence, but that kind of makes her cute, doesn't it? And I bet once we fatten her up and get her groomed, she'll be a total cutie. And she's bonded with Kara." She presses her curvy body against mine.

Kara aims her big, pleading eyes at me. "Please, Daddy. Please."

Delilah's baby blues silently beg, and I'm sunk. The dog will be coming home with us.

I smile, and before a word is out of my mouth, Delilah and Kara are both squealing, and Bet has her hands clasped beneath her chin while she twirls to and fro.

I finish up with some of the vaccinations and answer questions from one couple passing by. Their cat has stopped using the litter box, and we talk about possible reasons that could be as Delilah finishes up all the paperwork required to complete the adoption. Our last responsibility of the day is to help the volunteers load cages to return to the shelter. They set up for the day outside in front of a local PetCo. We all pitch in.

During all the wrap-up activity, Kara remains on the ground with the little mutt snuggled on her lap. I stop and pull out my phone to snap a photo and a short video. Kara's sitting on the ground, chatting up her new love.

"You're gonna love your new home. Daddy's the best vet in the world, so you'll always be healthy. And Delilah, she's gonna be a good mommy. She's not our for real Mommy yet, but she will be. She makes the best mac and cheese."

My breath catches, and I stop the video and step away as she chatters nonstop.

When we get home, Delilah and Kara hurry upstairs to get our new family member situated in Kara's bedroom. I head to our bathroom for a shower. Showering after handling animals all day has become habit.

I'm lifting a shirt hanger from the closet when Delilah presses her body behind mine, the softness of her breasts pushing against my back as her hands roam my bare chest.

"Did you come to shower with me? I would have waited for you." I twist to face her and kiss her soft lips. Her hair is piled on top of her head, and she's wearing a gray crop top sweatshirt with well-worn, faded jeans.

I slip on my t-shirt, and she beams up at me. Her nose ring glints in the light, and I bend down and place a soft kiss above it.

Blue irises peer into mine as she drops to one knee. My chest tightens, and I coach myself to keep it cool. A tentative smile graces her lips, and she inhales deeply enough her chest visibly rises and falls.

"I don't have a ring. I had planned to tie a note to Mary, but I can't get her out of Kara's hands, and she's too skittish to walk up to you, anyway.

You asked me once before, and I wanted to say yes, but I didn't think I could handle it all, be true to you and to the others in my life. You've helped me see I have enough love to find ways to be there for everyone, as long as I'm true to myself first. And I didn't believe I could fall in love so quickly, but I did. Completely. Heart and soul. Will you marry me? Spend the rest of your life with me?"

I drop to my knees and kiss her. My fingers glide along her swept-up hair, and I pull on the hair band until her bun falls out and the golden mass falls down her back.

"Does that mean yes?"

I laugh. "Yes, yes, that means yes. I've been committed to you for life since the day we moved in together. Someone told me marriage was just a piece of paper. I took that to mean that if I want you for forever, I need to commit to forever, but love you as if you could walk away any day."

A small hand taps against my back. Kara sidles up to us, much closer to our height since we're both on our knees, her small mutt clutched in her arms. She's smiling as the dog squirms, clearly not as comfortable in her arms when she's standing as when she's sitting.

She sets Mary down on the ground and

throws her arms around us. "We're getting married."

I kiss the top of her head. "Yes, baby girl, we're getting married."

"That's why I named her Mary."

I hold Delilah close to my side while I ask Kara, "You knew she was going to propose?"

Delilah smiles down at Kara. "I had to ask her permission."

"And I said yes!" Kara squeals with her arms out wide to her side. She's become a regular little Delilah, using her arms and hands to emphasize her words.

I pull Delilah to me and kiss her, a proper kid-in-the-room kiss. Tonight, Kara will be going to bed on time. Maybe even earlier than bedtime.

Out of the corner of my eye, I see Mary sniffing around. "Kara, it looks like we need to walk Mary. You see when she's sniffing around like that?"

"Yes."

"It means she might have to go to the bathroom. We'll have to train her to give us a signal, but for now, we're going to have to watch her, okay? Let's go get our shoes on and take her outside."

It takes a few minutes for Kara to find her missing shoe because, inexplicably, only one sits in the entry hall. Once we all have shoes on our feet, the three of us leave the apartment, heading out to walk our dog.

NOTES & ACKNOWLEDGEMENTS

When I was a teenager, I wanted to be a writer. Aunt Josie encouraged me but made me promise that if I ever became a writer, I would include her in a book, and that I would make her "tall, skinny, and beautiful." Of course, she (my aunt) is beautiful. My father's eldest sister, she has a sharp wit, feistiness, strength, and the well-deserved love of all of those around her.

When I placed out of college freshman English, she told me I absolutely could not skip the class. "It will be the best class you take in college." I am incredibly grateful for her advice. You see, Josie was an English teacher. She knew what she was talking about.

I shared the first few chapters of *Walk the Dog*

with a Gotham writing class. In my first draft, Delilah cussed like a sailor, and the overwhelming feedback was that I needed to curb the enthusiasm. One of my good friends says things like, "Oh, Mylanta" in lieu of naughty words. Her boyfriend sent me a whole list of "Nicole-isms," and I adapted them for Delilah. Someone later asked me if someone would really say these things. The answer is yes. Yes, someone would. A real live person does. Thank you, Nicole Biffle, for providing the inspiration to bring Delilah to life.

On the tennis courts, there are some of us who let it all flow, and there are others who are far more ladylike. A favorite partner of mine, Sharon McAffee, would shout out, "Oh, sugar!" when the ball hit the net. We were quite the pair. While she was sprinkling sweetness, I was dropping f-bombs. A beta reader once asked me if southerners really say, "Oh, sugar." The answer is yes, there are some fine southern ladies out there who do.

Mason is inspired by a sexy veterinarian featured in *People* magazine from years ago. So, yes, these mythical single creatures do exist. Or at least they did. That guy's gotta be snapped up by now. For those who recognized Mason's last name, Herriot, yes, it is a nod to the most infamous veterinarian of all time and his books that I loved.

I'd like to once again thank Lori Whitwam for her editing expertise. She improves the story, and I swear, will one day help me to relearn all those grammatical rules I willingly forgot. Heather Whitehead copy edited this right as COVID-19 wreaked havoc on our lives, and I'd like to thank her for finding a way to focus on this when it felt like the world was falling apart.

Adlina Hamid-Yeow created multiple versions of the cover for Walk the Dog. And when I say multiple versions, I mean she even did an illustrated version. Huge thank you to Adlina for her patience with me and for creating awesome cover(s)!

Walk the Dog has had many beta readers and I'd like to thank them all, even those who only read a few chapters. Allison Miller read the roughest initial draft, and she loved it. Her enthusiasm kept me moving forward through the many, many later drafts, as others criticized there wasn't enough conflict. AmyClaire Mager, serving as a developmental editor, read through it and helped me see where to dig deeper. In the end, I wanted to share Delilah's story, this blonde, energetic chick I envisioned as Anna's colleague, and I can only hope I did her justice and others find her as lovable as I do.

Last but not least, I'd like to thank my husband for his support as I try to find my way into some level of a writing career. I know there are days when he wants to toss my laptop in the lake. His support, and the support of my family and friends, means the world to me.

Sneak Peak into When the Stars Align...
    Jackson and Anna's Story

WHEN THE STARS - SNEAK PEEK

Anna

The snow-white pigeon swoops up and down, flirting with the reflection within the sliding doors. A sign of things to come, Al would say. My Australian labradoodle quivers at my side, ready to charge. She's not one to obey, so her actions amaze me far more than the pristine white bird captivated by its image. The glass door slides open, and the pigeon flies sky high out of sight.

"Chewbacca, my love, how was your Sunday morning walk?" My big curly beast wags her tail so hard her whole body wiggles and weaves. She leaps onto Al, completely oblivious to her human on the other end of the leash. Both paws land right above Al's protruding, bulbous belly. He laughs and gives her a treat. A *treat*.

"Al, you can't give her a treat when she jumps on you." A good dog owner would scold her sixty-five-pound canine and tell her to get down, but these two have a sort of odd love thing going on.

Al ignores me. Normal. "Did you see the pigeon circling the glass?"

"Yes! Have you ever seen a pigeon do that?"

"Nope. Must be a sign. Good things coming."

I smirk. Al and his signs. I'd estimate Al is in his mid-fifties. He's wearing the building doorman uniform of black pants and white button-down shirt. His shirt's never starched. Al and I share an aversion to ironing. We don't share a belief in random signs directing our destiny.

When Al sees Chewie, he always steps out to greet her. He scratches behind her ears, and she licks his chin, making him laugh. Because, yes, she's *still* standing on her hind legs with both paws planted on his chest. Crumbs from the treat she inhaled litter his wrinkled shirt.

"Is someone moving in today? I noticed the curtains are hanging in the elevator." The building hangs quilts to protect the sides of the elevator from gashes during a move. My apartment building, The Wimbledon, features twenty-six floors and four elevator shafts. This one building houses as many people as some suburban neighborhoods. Weekend moves are the norm.

"Yeah, two units. One on your floor, actually."

"Cool," I respond. There are six apartments on my floor, but my neighbors are relative strangers. I have one mean, grumpy neighbor who complains any time Chewie barks. "Any chance Sixteen-C moved out?"

Al grins and in baby talk answers my question to Chewie's bushy face. "No. Mr. Truman's still there, so Chewie here has to be quiet. You have to be quiet, don't you, girl? No barking, right, girl? Gotta be quiet. Yeah, that's a good girl. Such a good girl. Such a good, good girl."

Chewie responds by wagging her tail and licking him from the bottom of his chin up to his nose. He laughs, and she lets her front paws fall to the floor.

"How's the weather out there today? Looks like it's a good one."

"It's gorgeous. You should definitely take your lunch outside. Blue skies. Not a cloud anywhere. The high's gonna be sixty-eight. Couldn't ask for a better September day. Next week, we've got a cold front heading in. But by the end of the week, warm weather will be back."

I nod as he shares the forecast. Al's a walking, talking weather report. "We did the full loop around Central Park today. Some of the leaves have started changing color."

I peer out the glass doors of the lobby at the street and the facing brick building. Cars whiz by, and a faint horn sounds every now and then. You can't see the sky from where I'm standing, but the blue sky and fall-scented air lurk in my mind. A stunning weekend day, yet work calls. It's okay. I have a good view from my home office. "I'm gonna head on up. I'll see you later. You here until six?"

"You know it," Al responds with his signature wink and gunshot finger point.

"See ya later."

Chewie and I only have to wait a minute for the elevator. We walk in, and I hum a bit as I scratch her floppy mass of hair. The elevator door slides to close. A hand shoots through the gap to force the door open. I tighten my grip on Chewie's leash as she attempts to lunge forward to say hello. "Chewie!" I scold.

I grip the leash tightly to keep her at my side. Once I have my shaggy girl under control, I raise my head and see the man standing on the threshold of the elevator. My mouth drops open. My lungs contract.

Hazel eyes I haven't seen in four years stare back at me. The blue-gray suit offsets those chameleon eyes, casting a bluer hue. The short, trimmed beard makes him appear older and more distinguished. The dark, curly, college student hair, now cut in a shorter, controlled, professional style, says business.

My skin tingles. From shock or from being in his presence again, I'm not sure.

Jackson's eyes flick between me and my rambunctious, shaggy brown beast. "Anna?"

"Jackson?" Chewie attempts to jump on him, and I give a quick pull on the leash and command, "Sit." I close my mouth, but I'm still gaping. How could I not be? Jackson lives in Atlanta. I never thought I'd see him again. That door closed.

Through my peripheral vision, I notice Jackson's hands flexing, as if he's stretching his fingers. He blinks his eyes in rapid succession. I imagine he's as shocked as I am. He half shakes his head and exits the elevator. My stomach freefalls. A second later, he wheels in two large black suitcases.

I swallow. My heart's beating a million beats per minute, and I stare at the panel of floor buttons. The door slides closed, and the elevator lurches upward. Proper elevator etiquette reflex compels me to ask, "What floor?"

He doesn't answer but leans over to the panel with his index finger extended. Then he slowly pulls back. "You've already pushed it. Sixteen."

I blink. My heart rate speeds as I scratch Chewie's ears, trying to collect my scattered self. The whole situation feels surreal. I fold an arm against my stomach and breathe as the elevator doors open and we both exit.

The silver door slides closed behind him, leaving us standing in the hall facing each other.

"So, are you visiting someone?" Judging from the two overhead suitcases, either he's the worst packer on the planet or he's staying a while. Or maybe he's not alone?

His Adam's apple shifts as he swallows. His gaze wanders over my entire body, sending chills through my core. This man has intimate knowledge of every part of my body. As his eyes rove up and down, my cheeks burn. I remember. I cross my arms, defensive, and focus on breathing.

His chest heaves, and I hear his exhale. "I'm moving in." He peers down the beige hall lined with dark green painted doors. Dull brass numbers hang on the front of each door. I'm Sixteen-B, and we're standing in front of Sixteen-C.

He points to the end of the hall. "I'm Sixteen-D."

I point in the opposite direction. "Sixteen-B."

Our voices mingle and crash over each other as we speak at the same time.

He squints his eyes. "You go."

"Ah, you're moving here?" My voice comes out squeaky and high-pitched. *Get it together. He's just a guy you used to know.*

He stares ahead at the elevator door. "Good job opportunity."

"What are you doing?"

"Law."

"Are short answers your thing now?" It comes out bitchier than intended.

He huffs and turns his head to me. "I'm at a new firm. M&A. What are you doing these days?" His gruff tone sends a flurry of chills along my spine.

"I'm a creative director. At an agency called Evolve." It's on the tip of my tongue to say more, to tell him I work on the Heineken, Greenpeace, and National Geographic accounts. But I stop myself. His dark gaze radiates an unfriendliness I'm not sure how to respond to. Chewie's picked up on his unusual behavior. She's standing beside me, tail still, watching.

Jackson angles his head in the direction of my apartment door. "Do you live alone?"

"Yes. I had a roommate up until two months ago. She moved to Prague." Again, I could rattle on but don't, forcing myself to stop. My gaze falls to his chest. His hand rests on the handle of one of the suitcases. Beneath his jacket, he's wearing a form-fitting starched shirt. Subtle muscular lines lead to a firm, narrow waist. His clothes fit so well I suspect they are custom. I also imagine he still flaunts a six-pack.

I flush, visualizing his pectoral and ab muscles. The hardness of those muscles beneath my roaming fingers. Over the years, I've thought about him often. Most often when playing with my favorite vibrator. My body temperature rises, and I hope the burning sensation on my cheeks doesn't mean I'm blushing.

We stand there staring at each other. I have so much to ask him, but then again, I don't. Things didn't exactly end well with us. But he's new to the city. *Be kind.* "Do you need help getting unpacked?"

The muscles in his jaw flex as if he's grinding his teeth. "No, thank you. Take care." He heads down the hall, pulling his two suitcases behind him. He stands in front of the door and flips through keys on a ring. I watch. When he looks up from his keys and catches me staring, I unlock my door and rush inside.

I flop down on my futon, a relic from my first post-college days. The stained, beaten-up piece could stand an upgrade, but sofa shopping doesn't interest me.

I pull out my phone and press my best friend's name. She may live in another country, but she's still my BFF. My first call.

She picks up. It's evening, her time. Before she can say a word, I blurt, "You are not going to believe who moved into the building. On our floor!"

ABOUT THE AUTHOR

Isabel Jolie, aka Izzy, lives on a lake, loves dogs of all stripes, and if she's not working, she can be found reading, often with a glass of wine in hand. In prior lives, Izzie worked in marketing and advertising, in a variety of industries, such as financial services, entertainment, and technology. In this life, she loves daydreaming and writing contemporary romances with strong heroines.

Sign-up for Izzy's newsletter at https://isabeljoliebooks.com/#newsletter to keep up-to-date on new releases, promotions and giveaways.

www.ingramcontent.com/pod-product-compliance
Lightning Source LLC
Chambersburg PA
CBHW032201180726
48284CB00001B/132